Sweet Spot

Praise for Kimberly Cooper Griffin

Tides of Love

"This was such a sweet story about coming to terms with change, assessing wants and desires over morals, and putting yourself first…Just a lovely story with lots of heart and sentiment. Great to explore reflecting and resetting everything while being true to yourself."—*LESBIreviewed*

No Experience Required

"*No Experience Required* is full of realistic, multidimensional characters…I liked the honest and straightforward way that bipolar disorder was discussed, and I feel like I understand how those with the disorder feel a little bit more than I had before. I think that so much of this book is relatable to readers in different ways, and can help us all stop and think about others and the bigger picture a bit more. Even if readers do not know anyone with bipolar disorder, or are not in a same sex relationship, the matters at the heart of the story are universal… *No Experience Required* is a well written and engaging book. I thought the issues of dating advice and mental health were very well handled, and I honestly would love to see more from all the characters in the book. I will be reading more from the author."—*Sharon the Librarian*

"The author does a thorough job of explaining Izzy's condition, her internal workings, hopes and fears…This book straddles a space between being a romcom and something more serious (given that the protagonists are dealing with a mental disorder and paternal homophobic physical violence). One of the best things about the book is that at the end we feel that this couple will really be happy together because they seem to have got their shot together and have learnt how to be a couple that communicates and cares for each other."—*Best Lesfic Reviews*

Can't Leave Love

"Sometimes you just need a romance that will melt your heart, bring a tear to your eyes at least once or twice, and leave you with a warm, happy feeling at the end. Add a couple of the cutest dogs, and you have a wonderful story. That is exactly what I found in *Can't Leave Love* by Kimberly Cooper Griffin. Besides being a beautiful love story, this book deals with some serious issues which is where the occasional teary eyes may happen…This is a well-written romance with well-developed characters (both human and canine), set in a lovely small town, with just the right amount of angst to make the story interesting. It is exactly the type of romantic tale that I love to read. In fact, I think I've found a new author to add to my list of favorite romance writers. I will definitely be looking for more from this author."—*Rainbow Reflections*

In the Cards

"Both main characters are very well developed and easy to connect with. The secondary characters are also well-written, especially Marnie, Daria's younger sister who is autistic. As the mother of an autistic son, I can tell you that Marnie is realistically written. The romance is fairly lighthearted and uplifting though the two mains do have several hurdles to overcome. They get a bit of a paranormal/magical push to help them find and fall in love with each other…I truly enjoyed this book."—*Rainbow Reflections*

By the Author

No Experience Required

In the Cards

Can't Leave Love

Sol Cycle

Tides of Love

Sweet Spot

Sweet Spot

by

Kimberly Cooper Griffin

2023

SWEET SPOT

ISBN 13: 978-1-63679-418-1

This Trade Paperback Original Is Published By
Bold Strokes Books, Inc.
P.O. Box 249
Valley Falls, NY 12185

First Edition: September 2023

Credits
Editor: Barbara Ann Wright
Production Design: Stacia Seaman
Cover Design by Jeanine Henning

Acknowledgments

Radclyffe and Sandy Lowe, thank you for giving me and my books a home at Bold Strokes Books.

You know you have a great editor when their voice competes for your mom's voice in your head. You are in very good company, Barbara Ann Wright.

The last year has been a wild one and I haven't been able to spend as much of it with my writing crew. But make no mistake about it, the following people live in the DNA of my writing: Finnian Burnett, Ona Marae, Nicole Disney, Millie Ireland, Avery Brooks, Cindy Rizzo, Jaycie Morrison, and Renee Young.

It seems fitting that I met Michelle Dunkley, the world's best Beta Reader, in the Book Garden. Who would have thought that twenty-two years later we'd still be bound by books?

And always, thank you to my readers. A story is just a dream if there is no one to enjoy it. You make this writer's dreams come true.

Acknowledgments

[illegible]

[illegible]

[illegible]

[illegible]

[illegible]

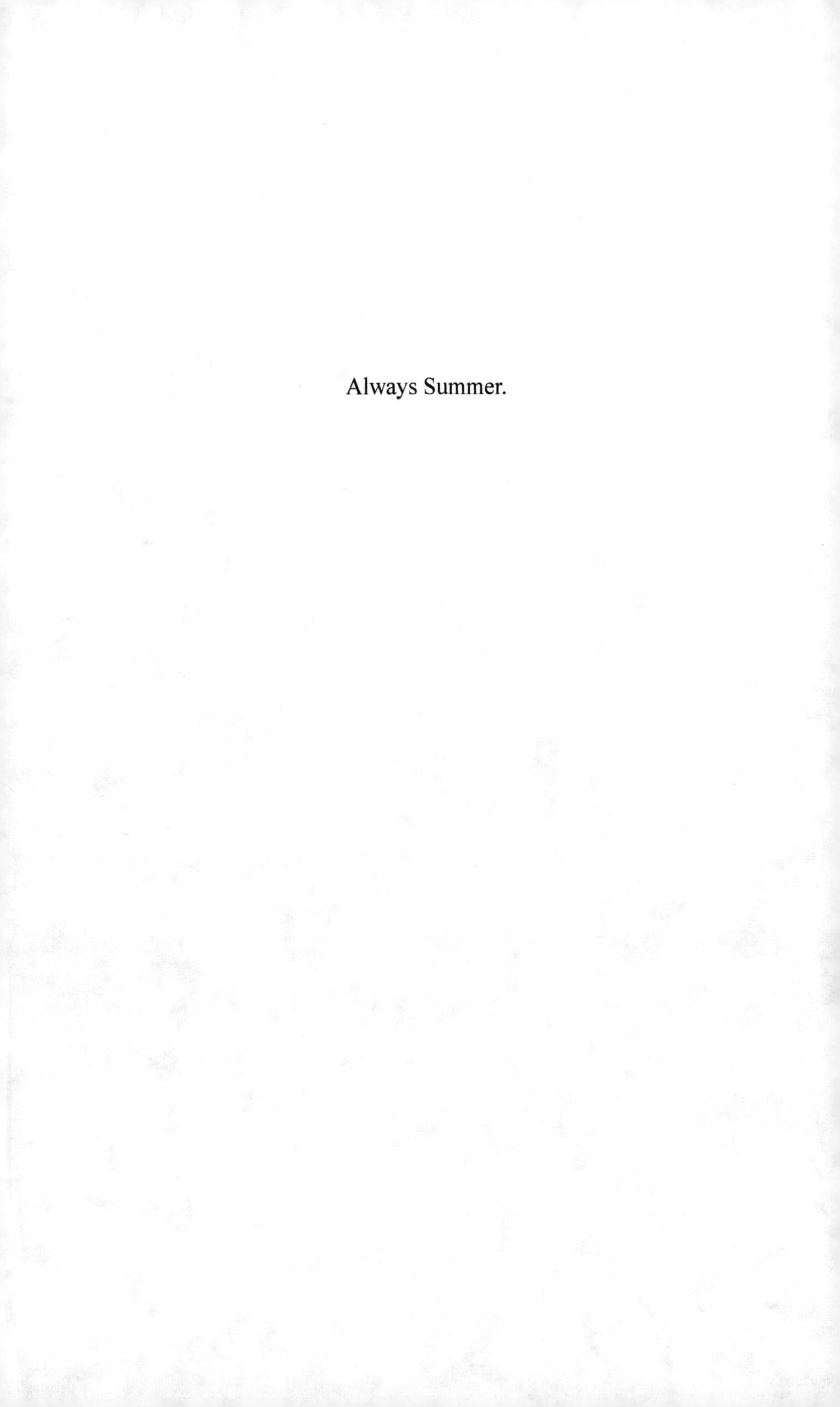

Always Summer.

Chapter One

Shia Turning's surfboard slid through the white water in the receding tide, her forward momentum slowing along with her heart rate and breathing. The wave had been a perfect curl, closing into a barrel, short but solid. She'd pushed out before the collapse, allowing a graceful but visually exciting exit. A high radiated through her after the amazing heat. It was something she only felt when she fell into perfect sync with the power of the ocean. Surfing was her church, the place her spirit soared. Her last ride in the day's surf conditions couldn't get much sweeter than that.

She dropped down into the shallow water when she neared the beach and pulled her board up under her arm as she waved to the crowd and cameras. She couldn't hear the announcers over the roar of the surf, but she knew she'd won round three handily, sealing her position at the top of the leaderboard and with a chance to go against a surfer she'd easily dominated before in the next heat.

Winning this last heat the way she had was a bit of a bummer, though. Lisa Caruthers was a great surfer. Probably better than she was and way more experienced. She'd expected a tough heat. But Lisa had accidentally dropped in on her last ride. Shia had no doubt that Lisa was aware that snaking someone else's wave was one of the bigger rule violations and one of the easiest to avoid. Surfing was about flow and style, not a contact sport at all. No one wanted to see someone getting hit with an out-of-control board in the dangerous and unruly surf, and the five judges had no choice but to shave half the points from one of Lisa's two best rides.

Shia hadn't been feeling the wave anyway, so when she'd kicked out and gone back to the lineup, she wasn't upset. This was a local competition, but it counted in the overall placement in the national competition, and with five sets of judge's eyes, it was hard to get away with anything. Also, she knew Lisa hadn't meant it. Some surfers might try to trick a competitor into jumping priority and accidentally dropping in, but she and Lisa were friends who took the unwritten surfer code seriously and wouldn't dream of harshing the meet.

And having beat Lisa, Shia was among the remaining contestants going into round four of the elimination. She was feeling confident. Round four would be the last of the day with the finals tomorrow. The prize was a decent amount of cash, plus points toward a spot in the US Open of Surfing in August at Huntington Beach.

Shia could use the money and the points, but she didn't expect to make it that far. This was her sixth year at the competition, and she'd never made it past the semifinals. This year she had a manager, though, and with Mikayla's help, she'd built her confidence. Ever since surfing got included in the Olympics in 2020, the sport was getting a lot more attention, and so was Shia, who had recently had a picture in *Sports Illustrated*. A single picture in a larger collage of women athletes, but she'd been paid for it, and it meant she was getting noticed. She was starting to feel like a legit pro surfer and not some aimless foster kid who'd picked an impossible dream.

Wading back to the beach with her board under her arm, she shook her hair out. Tired and a bit waterlogged, she wished she could go home and jump into the hot tub. And she would. Once the horn sounded, signaling the end of the day's surfing after the next heat. Lucky for her, she only had to walk down the beach a few hundred yards to her home in Oceana Mobile Home Park, where a good dinner and a night's sleep would rejuvenate her for the last day of the tournament. Surf conditions were predicted to be the same, but she had backup plans for a number of possible conditions. She had home beach advantage and knew how to surf anything Oceanside Beach had to give her. Of course, every wave was different, so she had to think on her feet to find the sweet spot on each one the moment she popped up and positioned herself on the face.

Movement in her peripheral vision made her glance to the side to see Lisa headed her way in the knee-high water. "Sorry about going all aggro out there," Lisa said, pushing her hand through her wet hair and shaking it out. The unconscious gesture had the same effect on Shia that it always did. A tingle of desire swept along her spine, but she was better at reminding herself of the focus she needed to maintain during competitions. Not to mention that Lisa was straight. And Shia wasn't into stringing her friends along. Lisa's friendship was way more important than a little fun in the sheets. Plus, there was the little issue of Lisa's husband.

"No worries. I'm sorry you drew the penalty."

"I acted like a grommet. Got distracted and thought you were behind me in the takeoff zone. I almost kicked out, but I didn't see a risk, and by then, I was already in." She shook her head.

Shia totally understood the disappointment. "That's what you get for moving down to Baja. When you get used to those heavy sets, these ankle-slappers can be frustrating." She only meant it to lighten Lisa's mood, but it was true. "Are you gonna stick around? Do you want to go back to my place for some solitude? Mikayla has my bag up at the tent if you need the keys."

"I'm gonna stick around to see what you do to get another perfect score."

"Please." Shia laughed. "What have you been smoking?"

Lisa pointed to the board next to the judge's tent, where a couple of scorekeepers were sliding the names of the advancing surfers into the heat four brackets. Above the brackets were digital signs rotating through the scores. Shia scanned them and realized the big one in the middle had "S. Turning 20/20," flashing on it.

A flurry of excitement filled her stomach. She stopped in her tracks at the edge of the water, her mouth hanging open. She'd never seen a perfect score before, although she knew they occurred sometimes. It meant that all five judges had scored her top two waves at ten points each. Most surfers would have been happy to get fifteen out of twenty. This was unbelievable.

"Shit. I wish I had a camera," Lisa said with a laugh. "You look like a kid who got served a ten-foot sundae with all the toppings. I'd feel the same way, though."

Shia closed her mouth. A laugh bubbled out of her. "I can't believe it."

Lisa walked backward toward her own tent. "The protégée has become the teacher. I'll catch you after your next heat and walk home with you. That is, if the stalkerazzi doesn't have you cornered for hours."

"You have me confused with someone who actually matters, my friend."

"Don't sell yourself short, surf goddess."

With a half hour to wait before her heat, Shia slid her board into the rack and made her way to the open-sided tent where Mikayla stood talking to a stunningly attractive woman. Her attention fully caught by the dark-haired beauty, Shia nearly walked directly into a hand mic that had been thrust in her face by a local television station. A chorus of camera shutters clicked around her.

"Shia Turning! Congratulations on cranking out a perfect score. How does it feel?"

"Who taught you the rodeo flip, Shia?"

"Do you think you'll be able to bring that kind of juice into the semifinals?"

"Shia, tell us what happened out there when Lisa Caruthers snaked that wave from you. What was on your mind?"

Although reporters weren't supposed to wander among the tents during the meet, she stopped and smiled. She was getting used to the media. "I'm kind of numb. All my rides felt solid, but no one ever expects a perfect score. I just try to find the sweet spot on the wave and let it tell me what to do. As for Lisa, we all have our bad rides. Other than that, she had an awesome heat." She knew Lisa would have talked her up, too.

The small crowd of reporters had attracted additional people, including some young women from a surf clinic Shia had taught earlier in the day as part of the pre-meet activities. She already taught surfing a couple of days a week to pay her bills, but the clinic was something Mikayla had set up for exposure. Shia liked helping young women get established in the surfing world. She wished she'd had the same kind of support when she'd first started. Their voices added to the ones still coming from the reporters:

"Shia, you were so awesome out there!"

"Shia, will you take a selfie with me?"

"Me too."

"Me too."

A wall of arms went up with cell phones pointed at her. Buzzing with surprise at her accomplishment, she agreeably took a dozen selfies with her fans.

"You're so hot, Shia."

"Do you have a girlfriend?"

A male voice cut into the fracas: "Okay, people." Shia was happy to see the team's assistant coach come up to save her. "Back to the tent. Let's let Shia rest between rounds."

"Thanks, Rick," Mikayla said behind her. When the high school team and others dispersed, Mikayla faced the reporters. "Hey, folks. Shia will come by the media zone after the next round. You can ask all your questions and get your pictures there." Her raised eyebrow and firm tone let the cadre of reporters know they'd overstepped, and they obediently flocked back to their designated area.

Mikayla's stern expression changed to gleeful wonder when she turned, and Shia felt a blush flare across her face. In the last few months, Mikayla had become the mother figure Shia had always wanted. Making her proud was better than winning any tournament. Seeing that amazed smile filled her heart.

"Look at you, Ms. Perfect Score. You've already accumulated quite the following, but that heat was fire," Mikayla said as they walked toward their tent. "I knew it was good when you were out there, but the judges verified it. Could you hear all the clapping and whistling from the beach?"

"I can't hear anything but the surf out there."

"Did it feel as good as it looked? Every wave you took was like you were in a movie."

Shia drank in the praise. Even as a mother figure, Mikayla was still gorgeous and smart. And dating Gem, who was also gorgeous and smart, and Shia couldn't help but have a little bit of a crush on them both, so the gushing felt equally good and embarrassing. "I was in the zone. I'm not sure if it was perfect-score good, but I'm not gonna argue about it." She also hadn't realized she'd performed a rodeo flip. She'd heard about it but had never practiced it. The move she'd done when exiting the last wave had simply come to her, like the ocean had guided her.

"I'm sure you won't argue about the crowd of women swarming around you, either." Mikayla nodded toward the tent the young group had gone back to.

Shia rolled her eyes. "They're kids, Mikayla. I know I look younger than twenty-two but ew."

Mikayla grimaced and looked around. "I absolutely didn't mean it like that. I'm an ass."

Shia rubbed her arm. "You're not an ass. In queer years, you're younger than me. You only came out as bisexual a few months ago. Naturally, you're going to see everything in terms of romance and hot Sapphic sex." Gem and Mikayla had only been a couple for a few months and still had those hot supernova sparks. Shia hoped she'd find someone to have that with someday.

The key word was "someday." For now, she was focused on her surfing career.

"It's still not cool to sexualize women like that."

Shia rolled her eyes. "It's kind of the nature of this sport, at least for women. We're celebrated for our sex appeal as much as we are for our athleticism. I'd be a hypocrite if I didn't say it was the primary reason I was drawn to the sport at first. Surfer women are sexy, and I wanted people to see me like that."

Shia shook her head. "Maybe it was being in the foster system and feeling like no one really wanted me. Anyhow, it wasn't until I caught that first wave that I realized surfing was something you do with your soul as much as your body." She shook her head. "How the hell did we get on this topic? That's a coffee chat next time you drag me to the Seaside Café, not for the middle of a competition."

Mikayla chuckled. "I learn something new about you every day. Under your surfer girl tan and sun-bleached locks, your wisdom runs deep."

"You forgot to mention my sweet ink and killer physique," Shia said, unzipping the top of her shorty wet suit, revealing her only tattoo above her bikini-top-clad left breast: a stick figure drawing of a surfer with long hair standing on a board cresting a wave while posing like a bodybuilder.

Mikayla pinched her cheek. "Better watch out. The entire high school surf league will be back, drooling all over the sexiest surfer on the beach."

"Stop. What if Gem heard you trying to pick up on me?" Shia teased. She draped a towel over her shoulders, laughing at her own joke. She knew Mikayla was only interested in one person.

A hand rested on her shoulder, and a new voice joined their conversation. "Good thing she only has eyes for me." Gem leaned past her and kissed Mikayla as they drew into the shade of the pop-up tent.

Shia smiled and looked away. Mikayla and Gem's quick kiss conveyed a lot more than a simple greeting. She scanned the tent and remembered the dark-haired beauty Mikayla had been talking to minutes ago but waited until Mikayla and Gem moved a few inches apart before asking, "Who were you talking to before the reporters ambushed me?"

Mikayla pulled cheese sticks and fruit from the cooler, along with a bottle of electrolyte-infused water, and handed them to Shia. She always forgot to eat during competitions and was grateful Mikayla was there to remind her. Funny how being in the water all day leached the water right out of a person. She sat in her folding canvas chair and popped a grape into her mouth.

"Hop Callister?" Mikayla asked. "He got all excited about your last score. He'll be back. He said something about getting the mayor to give you the key to the city. I'm not sure if he was joking or serious."

Shia dropped her hand to her lap. Hop coordinated the surfing competitions for most of the San Diego beaches. Over the years, she'd gotten to know him and considered him a friend, but he was also a big deal in the Southern California surfing world. That never really left her mind when she was around him. "Oh jeez. No pressure there," she said sarcastically and blew out a breath. "I haven't even made it to the finals."

Mikayla looked like she regretted saying anything. "That's what I said. I shouldn't have told you. There is absolutely no pressure, Shia. Just do what you do."

She laughed. "Easy to say. But I'm cool. I didn't come here thinking I'd win. I'm chasing the points so I can compete at Huntington." She wasn't exactly cool, and she was a little more confident about possibly winning, but saying it aloud helped with some of the anxiety. Even with the competition on her mind, she was still curious about the woman Mikayla had been talking to. "Anyway, I know who Hop is. I'm talking about the woman in the blue and white sundress with the flower design."

Mikayla lifted her sunglasses so they sat on the top of her head while she appeared to think. "You mean Gem's niece, Rose?"

"That was Gem's niece?"

"You've probably seen her around Oceana. She worked on the landscaping crew for a while," Gem said.

Shia shook her head. "I would have remembered her."

Gem and Mikayla exchanged a look. Shia wondered if she shouldn't have brought it up.

"Do you want her number?" Gem asked, raising an eyebrow.

Shia flapped a hand at her. "Stop it. Is it a crime to be curious?"

Gem chuckled. "If you haven't seen her around yet, you will. She's the new property manager."

"I thought you said landscaping." Either way, she was connected to Oceana and within crossing-paths possibilities. A swirl of anticipation tickled Shia's stomach before she reminded herself she didn't have time for dating as long as she was focused on getting a spot at Huntington Beach. She had to change the subject. "I forgot you were going full-time as a social worker at the hospital. I'll miss having you in the park all the time." Even though she spent more time with Mikayla these days, she had always liked having Gem around when she needed advice. In fact, it had been Gem's suggestion that Shia's dating habits were keeping her from advancing in her career.

Shia had never had trouble finding willing casual sex partners, but she wasn't really a casual kind of person, even when she wanted to be. And casual often turned into not-so-casual, even when she tried not to let it. Women were far more complex once she'd finished college, and she hated hurting anyone's feelings, leading her to spend more time than she had to spare with women who'd caught feelings for her. So she'd stopped dating altogether for almost a year, a decision that sometimes left her lonely.

Gem stepped out from under the canopy. "I'll miss working at Oceana, too, but I'm ready to go back to my real career. About Rose, I'm supposed to meet her at the Canteen bar, so I better get up there. Good luck out there, Shia. Or am I supposed to say break a fin or something?"

Shia might have invited herself to come along and meet Rose, but she had the last round. "Good luck is fine," she said with a grin. Gem's happiness these days was infectious. She and Mikayla's obvious love was something she aspired to, at least in the future. Today was about—

"A perfect score!" Two young women, one with short spiky hair and the other with long straight hair and both sporting nose rings, approached the tent. Shia smiled, recognizing them from the opening huddle of the competition. Neither had advanced beyond the first heat. They didn't seem disappointed. If Shia had to guess, she'd say this was probably one of their first competitions. They were probably vibing on the energy of simply being there.

Despite their exuberant greeting, they carried themselves in the slightly shy way many of the younger surfers did when they were around more experienced competitors. It wasn't like Shia was old. She was almost twenty-three, but that made her one of the older ones.

The young woman held out her hand, introducing herself and her girlfriend. "Great heats out there in the third, Shia. I called the perfect score as soon as you nailed the flying three-sixty."

Shia shook it. "Thanks. I got lucky."

"Lisa's awesome but not as good as you. We were wondering if we can get a picture."

"Absolutely," Shia said, getting up to pose with them while

Mikayla took their picture. She chatted with them for a few more minutes before they thanked her and left. She sat again and finished off a cheese stick.

"You're good with your fans," Mikayla said with an approving look that made Shia grin.

"Well, I want to be a good role model and show people you can achieve your dreams if you work hard." She also felt a commitment to her sponsors to give them a good return for their support. It would kill her if anyone thought she was coasting on their dime.

"You're accumulating quite the fan following. I think most of them have crushes on you."

Shia scoffed. "They don't know me enough to like me as a person, let alone have crushes."

"Those two got a glimpse of you as a person because you didn't blow them off. You interacted with them. I think they left with an even bigger crush than they came with."

Shia looked at her food and shook her head before glancing up. "Should I dial it back? I don't want to lead anyone on."

Mikayla dropped into the chair next to hers. "Not at all. You're being you: kind, honest, and friendly." Mikayla studied her, making Shia shift uncomfortably in her seat. "You're a good person, Shia. The more I get to know you, the more I like and admire you."

Shia's face grew hot. Those words meant a lot to her. "That's a good thing, I think, especially since you're both my agent and manager."

CHAPTER TWO

Almost all the television screens in the Canteen were tuned to the surf competition in progress at Oceanside Harbor Beach. There was a break between heats, so the stations covering it were either doing commentary or showing replays of some of the best rides. Rose Monroe sat at the bar sipping an Arnold Palmer, watching the television over the bartender's head. Shia Turning was talking about the ride that advanced her to the next heat. She was so nice about the interference by the other surfer, saying it could have happened to anyone, even complimenting her opponent.

The empathy was refreshing. Rose didn't know Shia other than what she'd heard or read in the news, which lately had been quite a bit. She also had a couple of radio ads supporting a restaurant in the harbor. Rose had even heard her on a local podcast a week or so earlier, talking about the recreation center. She'd thought Shia was super cute from the first sight of her in an ad on a bus stop bench. She had that all-American surfer girl look that Rose had always been attracted to. But watching her talk about her rival with respect took Rose's crush to a whole new level. A swarm of overcaffeinated butterflies abused her stomach. If she hadn't made plans to meet Gem, she'd have stayed in the tent with Mikayla, hoping for a glimpse of Shia in real life.

"Hey, niece," Gem said, taking the barstool next to her. The sudden greeting startled Rose, but she covered it by jumping up to give Gem a hug. She was Rose's favorite aunt by a long shot. Even so, if the program hadn't gone to commercial, Rose wasn't sure she'd have been able to pry her eyes from Shia.

"It's been too long," Rose said as Gem released her. They'd literally seen each other almost every day for the last month as she'd trained Rose to take over her job.

"Hardy-har-har." Gem peered at Rose's glass. "Whatcha drinking?"

"Arnold Palmer. I'm on call this weekend."

Gem gestured to the bartender that she'd have the same and chuckled. "You're on call all the time. Your boss must be a total dick."

"The biggest." Rose grinned, reseating herself.

Gem raised an eyebrow. "The biggest, huh? I'm not sure how to take that."

"You started it."

"And now I regret it," Gem said. "Especially since the ones I prefer come in boxes."

"And now"—Rose waved a finger at her—"you've crossed the line."

Gem placed a hand on her chest. "Oh no. Not the line. I crossed it?"

"You did. Not by a mere toe, either. You long-jumped over the sucker and cleared the sand pit. The tape isn't even long enough to measure it."

"That sounds like some sort of record. For long jumps as well as big dicks. Which would be me, since I am, in fact, your boss. The big dick."

Rose nodded slowly. "Yep. It certainly is a record. For the length of a bad joke and the bigness of dicks."

"Are we done yet? Have we dragged it out far enough yet?"

"Painfully." Rose tilted her head. She loved her aunt Gem so much. Not only because she was family, but because they had a bond that was stronger than either of them had with siblings or cousins. Of course, Gem would never say it, but she definitely didn't joke around with her sisters the same way. "We've definitely dragged it out longer than it deserves."

"Remember this lighthearted banter," Gem said, waving between them. "You won't feel so carefree and rested in a few months. Or weeks. Maybe days."

The bartender handed Gem her drink. She nodded her thanks. He nodded back and winked at Rose before turning back to his other customers. Jake was new, but Rose liked him already. Some of the other bartenders would have tried to join the joke. This one knew it was only funny because it was the two of them.

She glanced at Gem while sipping her drink. "I know. You already warned me. I'm totally up for it. I'll be the best property manager you ever had." Gem raised another eyebrow. "Besides you and Grandpa, that is."

"Good save. But truly, I would love for you to outshine both of us. I have no doubt you will."

"Good save, yourself," Rose said, giggling. She only ever giggled around Aunt Gem. It was a leftover from when they were kids and Gem would tease her unmercifully. With a six-year age gap, they ended up being more like cousins or siblings than aunt and niece, and Rose had always been proud to be around her cool aunt. She loved their unique relationship. That was why it was so important for her to do a good job as the property manager of Oceana. Not only was she doing it to preserve her grandfather's dream of the park remaining the special place he had made it into and keeping the management of it in the family, but she was doing it for herself.

Being the oldest of all the grandchildren, she'd always enjoyed being a role model. It was a point of pride. She wanted to show them how anything was possible if they put their minds to it. So she'd exceled at team sports, was able to fix anything, aced most academic subjects, and pretty much succeeded at most things she tried.

All that had changed when she'd dropped out of college. It just couldn't keep her interest, was way less social than high school had been, and she didn't know anyone. When it came to student council, she found that she'd previously gotten by on her popularity. As a little fish in a much bigger pond, she didn't know how to run a successful campaign, and with nothing going on at school except academics, she'd grown bored and had barely finished her freshman year.

She'd intended to go back the following fall, but that came and went, and she'd started working at Oceana on the landscaping crew. She'd enjoyed it more than she thought she would. And now with Gem leaving, they'd asked her if she'd like to try out being the property manager. She loved it even more. She got to work mostly outside and interact with people. The first week, she'd fixed the pool pump, installed an air-conditioner in the mail building, retiled the bathroom on the first floor of her grandfather's house, and helped Gem hire two new ground crew workers. She'd gone from feeling like a failure to being a role model again. So who cared about having to be on call? She loved her new job. Best of all, she was good at it.

"I checked out the surf competition a little earlier and saw Mikayla."

Gem took a sip of her drink. "She told me I missed you by like three minutes. I've been studying for a test to keep my license active."

"I don't know how you can stand that school never ends for your career."

"That's one thing I love about it. If I couldn't be a social worker, I think I'd be a professional student."

"No thank you." Rose flapped her hand as if shooing her away. "Anyway, who does Mikayla know at the competition? I wouldn't have pinged her as a surfing fan." Maybe Mikayla could introduce her to the sexy surfer, Shia Turning.

"She manages one of the surfers."

"You're messing with me. My mom said she's independently wealthy. Like, she doesn't have to work. Ever." Like everyone in the family, Rose was intrigued by Gem's new girlfriend. Mostly because Gem hadn't brought many girlfriends to meet the family, but also because Mikayla was so different from anyone she'd met. She was an interesting mix of refined and put together but warm and friendly. It wasn't hard to see why Gem would fall in love with her. It likely had nothing to do with her money. But it probably didn't hurt.

Gem shook her head.

"Is that a 'no, she isn't that rich' shake or a 'you should mind your own business' shake?" Rose asked.

"It's a 'your mom shouldn't be spreading tales' shake. I don't know how much money Mikayla has, and it doesn't matter to me."

"She keeps it secret?" With most people, Rose would have stopped with the questions. But this was Gem, and she'd spent enough time with her to know she wouldn't get offended.

"I've never asked. I'm positive she'd tell me if I did. She doesn't need to work for a living, so you're right about that."

"My mom said she divorced a millionaire and took him for all the money he had before turning into a lesbian." Rose snorted at the look Gem gave her. "Don't worry. I read her the riot act about how there isn't an on-and-off switch."

"It's the curse of the eldest. They think they're always right." Gem pointed a warning finger at her. "You best be aware, my oldest niece."

Rose hated that. Being a firstborn child was one of the few things they didn't have in common. Like it or not, though, Rose was a clone of her mother, also an oldest sibling. It felt like Gem was calling out a flaw. "Tell me the truth, then."

"First of all, Mikayla is bisexual, not a lesbian, although that isn't anybody's business, either. Second, she took her fair share of half of a lot of money, I guess, although I have never asked how much because it's none of my business. She doesn't need to work, at least not right now, but she wants to do something meaningful with her life, and managing things is her forte. Shia needed a manager, so they work together. It seems to be—"

"Hold the phone. Hold the freaking phone." Rose stared, incredulous. "She manages Shia? Shia Turning, surf goddess?"

Gem chuckled and nodded. "Shia would laugh her surf goddess ass off for being called a surf goddess. I can't wait to tell her."

Rose was aware that her eyes were probably bugging out. She didn't care. "You know her, too? How is it possible that I didn't know this?"

"I don't know. Maybe the same way you didn't know the real facts about Mikayla. You've had dinner with her at least three days a week since you started working at Oceana. Some things just don't come up. You and I are always talking about work." Gem got a faraway look in her eyes. "I probably should ask her if I've been too preoccupied with work, actually."

"No, love. You haven't."

Rose turned to see Mikayla approaching to stand behind Gem with her hands on her shoulders after kissing her hello.

"Isn't round four going on right now?" Gem asked.

"They paused the round." Mikayla seemed about to say something else, but turned to the TV that was currently showing people wandering around the beach, the closed-captioning scrolling beneath them.

"Oh, hell no. One of the drone pilots saw a great white breach right outside the lineup where the surfers were waiting for a wave?" Gem's eyes grew ridiculously big. Rose would have laughed if she hadn't looked so terrified.

Mikayla stroked her back. "Don't worry. Everyone is out of the water. They've paused the round to see if it leaves. The drone pilot is watching it."

Gem looked a little calmer but not enough to keep the frightened tone out of her voice. "I thought Shia might have been out there."

Mikayla grimaced. Again, Rose wanted to laugh, but Mikayla shook her head.

"Holy shit. She was out there." The closed-captioning on the TV read that Shia Turning and Stephanie Wang were in the lineup when the shark swam directly beneath them. Event officials on Sea-Doos brought the surfers in.

Mikayla smoothed her hands across Gem's shoulders. "She's fine, love. You can see right there on the screen."

"Did you come up here to make sure I didn't freak out when I saw that?"

Mikayla smiled, all the love they had for each other in that gaze. Rose wanted more than anything to have that with someone. "I waited until Shia was on the beach. I wanted you to know she was safe."

Gem's shoulders relaxed, and Rose remembered how Gem had jumped thirty feet from the pier into the ocean to save Mikayla, who'd accidentally swum into the pier piling. That had been the first Rose had heard about Gem being terrified of sharks, an incongruous fact about the aunt she'd known all her life. Part of her had been a little hurt that Gem hadn't confided in her about it. But she also understood. Some people didn't like to admit they had irrational fears. Sure, sharks were scary. They had been known to hurt, even kill, people but they weren't something Gem faced on a daily basis.

Rose was glad that she didn't have any irrational fears to deal with. If she did, she would tell Gem about them, though. She'd always been an open book as far as her aunt was concerned. "I'm glad she's safe," Rose said when she realized she'd been lost in her own thoughts for a few minutes. A bubble of pride played in her stomach when she noticed the smile her comment brought to Mikayla's face. It was sweet how much she appeared to be protecting Gem from being triggered by the whole event.

Mikayla squeezed Gem's shoulders again. "It was also an excuse to use the restroom. I can't handle those porta potties. Be right back."

Gem looked a little less pale as she remained glued to the unfolding shark situation. The footage showed the shark taking a U-turn and heading south, away from the event. The drone continued to track it down the coast as it made another turn into deeper waters.

All the while, Rose thought about Shia and wondered how she could get Gem and Mikayla to introduce them without coming off as uncool or simply an ordinary fan.

"I got a text from Shia. They're resuming the event," Mikayla said when she came back.

Rose spun to face her. "I can't believe you manage her." So much for maintaining her cool.

"You sound surprised. I thought you knew when you came to the tent," Mikayla said.

"I assumed you were doing the same as me, watching."

"So you don't know her?" Mikayla asked.

Rose shook her head. "Just from local news."

"Why don't you come with me and meet her? I mean, if you two are done."

Rose's stomach filled with butterflies as she glanced at Gem. "We haven't really talked about why she asked me to come."

Gem turned from the television, shuddering, before she focused on them. "Fifteen feet. That's huge. A leviathan." She was obviously distracted. "Sorry. What were you two saying?"

Rose smiled. "What did you want to meet about?"

Gem's eyes returned to their normal, not-scared-of-sharks expression. "I wanted to invite you to move in with me and Grandpa. I figured it might be more convenient, especially for after-hours calls." She paused and sighed. "I'm not gonna pretend that it's not partly about keeping an eye on Grandpa, too. But that's not the main reason. We have more than enough bedrooms. Last I heard, you were living with a roommate at those apartments near the 76 and Oceanside Boulevard."

"I moved back in with Mom and Dad last fall when I went back to school." She rolled her eyes. "After I confirmed my suspicions about Kora cheating on me with her ex." She shook her head. "That one taught me a thing or two about trusting my instincts. I'm focusing on my career from now on."

"Sorry about your breakup."

"That makes one of us." Rose laughed. It had been six months. She was over it.

"Give some thought to moving in with us. The commute down the 78 must be terrible."

"Totally miserable," she said, agreeing but for another reason. "Also, Tyler and Laura moved in a month ago." Tyler was her younger brother, and Laura was his wife. Both were in medical school and had moved home to get help with their twins, two-year-olds, Celeste and Sheldon. God, she loved those kids, but they were a handful. She wanted to be the cool aunt like Gem, then give them back to their mother when she'd had enough. She couldn't do that with them living in the same house. She'd woken up too many mornings covered in pudgy toddler limbs from them sneaking into bed with her. "I don't have to think it over. I'm in."

Gem looked surprised but happy. "Great. Just let us know when."

"Is Monday too soon? I don't have much stuff. I can bring it when I drive into work in the morning."

"Excellent. That's all I wanted to ask."

Mikayla bounced on the balls of her feet. "Perfect. Shia's about to restart the heat." She headed toward the door.

Rose's phone pinged with a notification. Her shoulders slumped. She wished she hadn't looked. "I can't go. Got a toilet issue in unit 352."

Gem snorted. "Told you that you wouldn't be grinning for long."

Rose didn't hold off much when she punched her in the arm. She slid off her stool and waved good-bye to Mikayla, who gave her a sympathetic look.

CHAPTER THREE

The Monday morning sunrise was beautiful. Shia took in the quiet of Harbor Beach. Aside from a couple of joggers running in the damp sand near the water and a half dozen surfers bobbing in the water waiting for a decent wave, she and Mikayla had the beach to themselves. Wordlessly, they dropped their towels onto the sand, slipped out of their flip-flops, and walked toward the water. It was one of those days when neither had much to say beyond their usual good-mornings. It was one of the many things she liked about Mikayla; she didn't feel the need to fill every silence with words.

Shia was still half-asleep, still tired from the weekend competition. And no matter how often she did it, swimming first thing in the morning was a brutal way to start the day. The first steps into the water shocked her awake. It was fine once she submerged herself, but the waves were a violent assault to her senses, even in her wet suit.

Following Mikayla, who was already cutting through the waves to deeper water, Shia had to force herself to dive into a wave, an action that made her body clench from head to toe. As she swam out to the calmer water beyond the breakers, she concentrated on loosening up enough to take deep breaths, knowing from experience that shallow breathing would deprive her muscles of oxygen and tire her out. Soon, she was used to the cold, feeling looser, and she and Mikayla were past the bobbing surfers. They treaded water and fixed their swim goggles over their eyes before angling themselves parallel to the shoreline and for the first of their four laps between the two rock jetties boxing in Harbor Beach.

The sun was higher when they splashed out of the water. The second worst part of morning swims was taking off the wet suit and standing under the outside shower in her bikini top and swim shorts, rinsing the salt and sand away. The water coming out of the public showers was even colder than the ocean. The constant breeze felt like an arctic blast over her wet skin. Before she'd started swimming with Mikayla, her swim regimen was hit-and-miss. She'd lie in bed every morning, talking herself in and out of going, and sometimes—about half the time—her lazy ass won. She'd been her own boss.

With Mikayla as her swim partner and manager, she couldn't make excuses. In fact, she looked forward to it because despite the cold immersion and even colder rinsing off, it started her day in an invigorating way, helping boost her mood and energy.

"How's your shoulder this morning?" Mikayla asked. She rinsed the bottom of her feet and slid them into her flip-flops.

Shia rotated her arm up and around one way and then the other. "It looks worse than it is."

"That bruise looks gnarly. Have you been applying the arnica gel I gave you?"

"Diligently."

"You know, I never thought of surfing as a contact sport."

"I guess it's as much of one as swimming," Shia said, trying to remind Mikayla of the head injury she'd sustained while they were swimming a couple of months ago.

Mikayla rubbed her head. "Right."

Shia had taken a rogue board Sunday morning during surf camp on the last day of the competition. One of the high school surfers had bailed on a collapsing wave and didn't have their leash affixed properly to their ankle. The board had rocketed straight at Shia while she was showing another surfer how to duck dive beneath an oncoming wave. She was lucky it hadn't hit her in the head. She could still see the kid's face when she'd apologized. Shia didn't have the heart to scold her, but she did take the opportunity to remind her and the rest of the class about leash etiquette. Thank goodness the injury hadn't hindered her that day. She'd gone on to place third in the overall competition, the highest she'd ever placed in a qualifying series.

She inspected the softball-sized bruise on her shoulder. "Between the arnica and being in salt water all the time, it'll go away faster."

Mikayla shook out her wet suit before throwing it over her shoulder, and they headed back to the mobile home park. "That saltwater thing is superstition, isn't it?"

"Ocean water, with all the salt and other minerals in it, heals wounds, including bruises, faster. I know mine always disappear quickly."

Mikayla gave her a side-eye. "I'm going to have to look into that."

Invigorated by the swim, they talked all the way back. Before Shia knew it, they were already at the pedestrian entrance next to the front gate of the park where cars were streaming past with many of the residents leaving for work. Shia was grateful that her job didn't include a commute. A few of her friends had argued that surfing wasn't a "real" job, and Shia had been close to believing it before Mikayla had approached her about becoming her manager. Having a manager gave her the sense of credibility she'd struggled with before. Now, everything was changing for the better.

Well, almost everything.

She was feeling lonelier lately. With her next-door neighbor Brandi in London after swapping houses with Mikayla for six months, she didn't have someone to drop in on whenever she wanted company. Gem was all twitterpated with Mikayla, who was all twitterpated with Gem, and that just made Shia lonelier, especially when she was deliberately avoiding romantic entanglements to focus on her career. She had to keep reminding herself that there was always time for romance later. Now was the time to put all her energy into surfing.

"You want to visit the seahorses and talk business for a little bit?" Mikayla asked as if reading her mind.

"You can get me to do anything for those cute fish." Shia held up a hand and shook her head. "That came out wrong. I don't want Gem to kick my ass. So what I mean to say is, I would be delighted to visit the seahorses while you tell me how to be successful at my career."

Mikayla laughed. "I didn't take it any other way. I'm old enough to be your mother."

"You're only thirteen years older than me. Also, that's what you say, but people's girlfriends get all suspicious when a single lesbian hangs out with their girl. They can't seem to believe some of us have other things to focus on, like careers and making something of ourselves."

"Gem isn't like that. And as far as focus goes, I love how passionate you are about surfing and all the other things that come with it. That's what's going to make you stand out, you know."

Shia grew more animated, using her hands to talk. "I want to make a difference. Sure, I want to be good and win, but I also want to help others get into the sport and live their dreams. Surfing was one place I didn't think of myself as some burdensome foster kid trying to fly under the radar and figure out how I was going to support myself when I aged out of the system."

"Is that how you still feel? Like a burden?"

Shia was touched by the look of indignation transforming Mikayla's normally smiling face. "I try not to think about it at all. I like to keep my thoughts moving forward, not back. But sometimes, I'll remember that kid in college who told me I was a freeloader and didn't deserve to have my education paid for when she had to take out loans."

"Someone actually said that to you?"

Maybe it was the way that Mikayla seemed to be ready to go after the bully, but Shia, who usually avoided all discussions about the painful experiences of her past, didn't mind talking to her about them. "All my life. But like I said, I want to focus on the future."

Mikayla sighed but nodded. "Gotcha. Well, your surf camp idea was a roaring success. We had almost all the parents tell us they'd do it again and would recommend it to others. Having pro surfers teach their kids was an experience all of them loved."

"I'm serious about getting the kids from group homes out there. I want to talk to Alice about getting the mission involved with us."

Mikayla looked confused. "Our Alice? The one who lives on the other side of you?"

Shia nodded. "She worked with the mission to get me grants to cover things the state scholarship didn't cover for school and by helping me with my rent. I had no idea where I would live once I aged out of the group home. I'd like to see the mission help other foster kids, too."

"That's a great idea. I had no idea you were involved with the mission."

"That's all Alice. They've never even asked me to join the church. I've never even talked to anyone else from the mission. I guess I should ask when the rent thing will end. With the sponsors, I think I can cover my bills without it now. They could probably use the money to help someone else." Gratitude welled in her for the help she'd gotten when she'd really needed it. She was aware that she was thinking out loud, but she wanted Mikayla to know her mind with regards to her career goals. "You know, things have always worked out when I needed them to. Even you offering to be my manager. I'd started to lose direction, and now my path is clearer than it ever has been. I won't let you down."

Mikayla looked at her with what she could only describe as

affection, something Shia had rarely received from adults in her life. The sting of tears made her look away. She walked over to the aquarium that took up half of Mikayla's living room.

"We make a good team. I can't imagine you ever letting me down," Mikayla said, going into the kitchen.

"Because I won't."

"I believe it." She picked up a large envelope from the counter. "Hop gave me some of the photos from the meet yesterday while we broke down the tent. The event photographers got a lot of great shots of you."

"I went to school with one of them, my lab partner in coding class. I'd go to her house to do homework to get away from the noise at the home. She seemed excited to meet up again."

A mischievous look came over Mikayla's face.

"And, no, I am not interested in her. She has a fiancé." Shia was relieved that Mikayla had the grace to let the subject go.

Instead, she came over and handed Shia a picture. "This is my favorite. It's you taking the selfie with that high school group. Look how they're looking at you. Like you're some kind of *Surf's Up* cover model."

Shia studied the picture. "I usually hate pics of myself, but I like this one. I'll put this one on Insta."

"Wait a few days. Hop gave them to me on the condition we wait to share until they upload them to the website." She pointed to a person in the background of the shot. "Do you know who this is?"

Shia looked closely. "I don't think so. Why?"

"I noticed her in the crowd always smiling and looking at you. I think she might be a bigger fan than these obviously smitten groupies."

Shia shoulder-bumped her. "Stop."

"She looks familiar. I'll bet she's been to the autograph sessions or something. She has a beautiful smile."

"But with the sunglasses and hood, she looks like half the people there. Hell, like both of us now." Shia touched her sweatshirt. "You can hardly see her face."

"It looks like it's not only the school kids who have a thing for you. Soccer moms have the hots, too."

"Stop." Shia laughed again.

Mikayla glanced at her phone. "It looks like we got confirmation from *Sports Illustrated* for their article covering Southern California surfers. You'll be one of fourteen. It'll be the first time they do a multi-gender article. Two of the featured surfers are non-binary, and one's a trans man."

"Sweet. I love the inclusion. I can't believe they're going to interview me. How'd you make this happen?"

"I didn't have anything to do with it. They called Hop and asked for you. You've been making a name for yourself." Mikayla threw an arm over her shoulders and squeezed her, seeming careful of the bruise. "Let's get more arnica on that shoulder."

Shia's throat was too tight to respond. Her dreams were starting to become a reality. Plus, it felt good to have someone watching over her.

CHAPTER FOUR

Standing in the bright morning sunshine in her parents' driveway—and clutching the package of fresh tamales her mother had insisted on sending with her—sent a weird sort of anticipation through Rose as she closed the trunk of her seven-year-old silver Hyundai. The fluttering in her stomach ramped up a notch. It was her last day of commuting from Escondido to Oceanside, a thirty-mile drive requiring traversing three of San Diego's most congested highways. This was the last time she would make the journey, at least for work, and she was ecstatic.

More than that, though, she couldn't put into words how happy she was to get out of her parents' house. As much as she loved her parents and her siblings who still lived at home, she was done with it. She'd miss the family time but not the reminder of how she hadn't gotten her life together yet. At twenty-six, she felt like she should be more established than she was, and as soon as that thought entered her mind, the familiar self-doubt about her ability to follow through with things reared its ugly head and—

No.

She was not going to go down that black hole of self-deprecation and doubt. She'd spent too much time there already. She wanted to coast on the good feels she'd woken up with. This was a new chance. Something about it felt different, like maybe this would be the time she found her own path.

At the last stoplight between her and Oceana, she turned to the small pet carrier on the passenger seat. "Chad, I think you're going to love being at Grandpa's house. It won't be as noisy. We'll even have our own bathroom. I don't know how he and Gem feel about pet rats, but I forgot to tell them about you. We'll keep it on the down-low at first, okay?"

Chad grabbed the door to the cage and watched her, seeming to understand. Who knew? Maybe he did. She gently *booped* his nose as the light changed before she continued toward her new home and her new job.

She wasn't sure what she looked forward to most: living in Oceana or managing it. Both had been dreams of hers since she was a little girl when riding beside her grandfather in his golf cart through Oceana. When she'd joined the landscaping crew, she'd hoped to move to property management. It still didn't feel real that she was now looking after Oceana on her own, but she was well on her way back to being the role model she wanted to be.

When she arrived at the house, a note taped to the kitchen door told her that both her grandfather and Gem had gone out, Gem to her job at the hospital, and her grandfather on his morning walk. Gem had given her a key, though, and after several trips from the car to her room upstairs—the house being the only permanent dwelling in the mobile home community—she was officially moved in, including Chad's five-level rolling cage where he was currently arranging his own things. It fit perfectly in the corner behind the bathroom door when it was open, and while Rose hated that she was tucking her best friend in a corner, she also didn't need to worry about anyone seeing him until she figured out a good way to bring it up. She pushed away a twinge of shame as she unpacked. She was twenty-six, for crying out loud. This was not a good way to start her residence with two of her favorite people.

As if he sensed her thoughts, Chad paused his nest arranging and watched her until she went over and picked him up to deposit him in his favorite place on her shoulder. She vowed to let them know about him as soon as possible. A little less excited, she went back to hanging up clothes, but a few minutes later, she stopped and blew out a breath.

She picked up her phone. "Say cheese, Chad," she said, snapping a selfie with him. His mostly white fur stood in contrast to her black T-shirt and dark brown hair. She sent the picture to Gem and her grandpa, telling them the truth. In all the excitement about the job and moving, she'd forgotten about Chad. She added that she would be happy to rehome him with one of her sisters if it was a problem. Feeling a ton better after sending the text, she was still anxious about their responses. She didn't want to rehome him.

Once all her clothes were put away, she and Chad went downstairs to log on to her laptop at the kitchen table. It being the middle of the month, she printed off a list of residents she needed to talk to about late rent. She'd shadowed Gem on one of her first days as a property manager, so she knew what to expect and wasn't reluctant to take on this uncomfortable task. Gem had been direct but kind, coming to a solution with each resident, and Rose felt confident that she'd work things out with the folks on the list just as comfortably.

She printed off the notices and left the stack on the table as she ran upstairs to change into her work clothes, put Chad in his cage, and get her phone. She sucked in a breath when she saw she already had replies to her text. Her stomach tensed as she opened the message thread.

Can't wait to meet him, Gem had texted back less than a minute after Rose had sent the original text.

She released her breath.

Is that a rabbit? was her grandfather's reply a couple of minutes later. *I hear they are wonderful pets.*

It's a white rat dad, Gem had written along with an emoji of a rat.

Oh. I see that now. Rats are very smart. A minute later, he added, *Hopefully he stays away from my free-range boa constrictor, Godzilla. Otherwise RIP Chad. How do I post a skull and crossbones?*

He doesn't have a snake. Dad, don't scare her.

The last message was a little devil emoji from her grandpa. By then, Rose was laughing, completely relieved. *Thanks. I know you will love Chad. He's very smart and super affectionate. Off to work now.*

With happiness infusing her, she ran downstairs and grabbed the list, heading out to the cart to start her day.

❖

By lunchtime, Rose was down to one house on the list. She'd started at the back of the park and was now on her own street. About half the residents had been home, allowing her to make arrangements to get caught up on their rent. Despite her initial confidence, it wasn't easy to talk to all of them. Some had serious issues affecting their income, and her heartstrings had been pulled. None of them had been unpleasant, however, and Gem's background in social work meant she had a list of resources from which the residents could seek help.

Rose had always known her grandparents were caring people, and Oceana was their dream of giving people who needed help a safe community and a comfortable home. But seeing their life's dream in action showed her how much they really did, from keeping the housing affordable, maintaining a beautiful property, and encouraging the residents to interact with parks throughout the property to a community pool and other recreational equipment. She'd seen all of it while working on the crew, but now, working directly with the residents, she got to see how lucky they were to be living at Oceana. It truly was a special place.

Rose parked the cart in front of a single-wide mobile home two spaces away from Mikayla's place, where she planned to go after she was done with the last resident. She flipped to the notice and was surprised to see the name Shia Turning in the name field. It wasn't a common name, but she still wondered if the resident Shia Turning and the cute-as-hell surfer Shia Turning were one and the same. An excited sense of expectation tickled her stomach.

Summoning an inner chill she didn't feel, she climbed the three steps to the tiny platform in front of the front door and knocked. Although the residence was small, without much adornment, it was neatly maintained. There were no weeds between the flagstones, the landscaping rocks were neatly spread, and the low bushes forming a hedge around the base of the house were freshly trimmed. It looked like the cedar on the platform in front of the door had recently been stained, too. Before she had a chance to ring the bell, the inner door opened. A nondescript someone stood in the shadows behind the closed screen door.

"Hey there," the person said, opening the screen door.

Rose's mind went blank, and her heart beat out of her chest.

Standing before her was cute-as-hell surfer Shia Turning, all sun-bleached hair, tanned skin, and bare feet. To make Rose's blood pressure go even higher, she was wearing a sports bra and board shorts, which showed off quite a bit of her athletic form. Rose could only stare while Shia waited for her to say something. Seemingly patient and holding a book with a finger between the pages, a smile spread across her face as the seconds ticked by. Her big brown eyes with impossibly long lashes gazed back at Rose, who found that her mind wouldn't work.

"You must be the new property manager," Shia said, leaning against the open screen door. "I saw you talking to Mikayla at the tent this weekend. Rose, is it?"

"Um." Rose remained wordless. A sort of weird vertigo hit her. Shia was even more beautiful than the pictures on the internet showed.

Of course she'd googled her. Shia was a local celebrity. A lesbian celebrity. It was required research.

"Gem told me about you. I'm surprised we haven't crossed paths yet." Shia held out a hand. Rose continued to stare. Happiness rushed through every inch of her. Shia dropped her hand with a concerned expression. "Are you okay? Do you need a drink of water or something?" She rested a hand on Rose's arm.

The touch broke her from the weird paralysis that had fallen over her. She shivered, super-aware of the hand on her arm. "Sorry. I'm just surprised to see you."

Shia removed her hand with an amused expression. "Did you expect someone else?"

"No." Rose pried her eyes away and looked at the ground. "I'm sorry. I never act like this. I once met Billie Eilish at a club in LA and kept my cool. God, this is weird. And *I'm* being weird. And I'm making it weird for you." Embarrassment added itself to the other emotions coursing through her, some that didn't even feel like they came from her but some mystical place nearby.

"No one has ever compared me to Billie Eilish before."

Rose put a hand on her forehead and shook her head. "I'm sorry. This is not cool. You're in your home. I've intruded. And now I'm acting weird. Let's try this again." Rose put her hand out. "Hi. I'm Rose Monroe. I recently started as the new property manager at Oceana. How are you?" She looked at the paper in her hand. "Shia Turning?"

Shia laughed. Rose enjoyed the way the sound seemed to flow over her. She was feeling a lot better and more in control. She relaxed a little. "Yes. I'm Shia. I'm doing well, thank you for asking. Is this a social call? Or are you here on official Oceana business?"

Rose remembered why she was there and became extremely embarrassed. Glad that she'd had a dozen chances to practice with people who hadn't made her heart trip over itself, she held out the late notice. "I'm here as a courtesy about the rent."

"Is it going up?" Shia took the paper and scanned it. "Oh, wait. It's late. That's not good."

That morning, people had either known exactly why she was there or were as surprised as Shia appeared to be. Rose tried to be as nonconfrontational as possible to encourage the resident to feel comfortable about arranging payment. "It happens all the time. It's only a few days past the date. Maybe an oversight?"

Shia continued to scan the notice. "My rent is taken care of by someone else, and to be honest, I don't actually know how they pay it, whether they send a monthly check or do some sort of online thing. This has never happened. Do you mind if I talk to Alice about this? She's the one who manages it."

Rose was relieved that it appeared to be a mistake, but an unexpected disappointment hit her when Shia mentioned another woman's name. She had no reason to feel disappointed. She didn't even know who Alice was to Shia. But it reminded her that she had absolutely no connection to Shia and probably never would. She cleared her throat. "Sure. No problem."

"Do you want to come in and sit while I figure this out?" Shia stepped back, holding the screen door open.

When Rose entered the house, she expected to see the Alice that Shia had mentioned. But no one was in the living room. Shia disappeared down the hall. A minute later, Rose heard her talking but couldn't make out any words. She sat on the futon and tried not to be nosey about the conversation going on in the back. She took her hat off and smoothed her hair, which was tied in a simple ponytail similar to the one Shia wore. She looked around the small but cozy living room. A brightly decorated cover was thrown over the futon, and several pillows were strewn across it. A glass of what looked like iced tea was on a coaster on a side table at one end. Rose guessed that Shia had been sitting on the futon reading the book she'd been holding that was now on the dining room table. A small thrill went through her observing Shia on such a personal level. Was she really sitting in Shia Turning's living room?

A couple of minutes passed. When Shia came back into the room with a bemused expression, Rose imagined she could feel the warmth of her gaze etch paths across her skin. "It's fixed. The money will be transferred this afternoon. I guess they pay twelve months at a time, so you won't have to come knocking on my door for a while." She appeared to be thinking about something while she stared out the window over the futon. "It's weird timing, though. I talked to Mikayla about paying my own rent, and Alice made it seem like…" She looked up with a laugh. "Sorry. Why would you be interested in that? I'm going to give Gem a hard time for having you do her dirty work."

Rose stood and shrugged. "It's all part of the job."

"How long have you been working here?"

"About a month. At least as a property manager. But technically, you could say I've worked here my entire life since I used to work on the landscaping crew before that. My grandpa used to pay me to do odd jobs when I was a kid, too. So off and on for twenty-six years."

"That's right. You're Gem's niece or something. How have we never met before now?"

"I'm not sure. I didn't even know you lived here. You would have thought Gem would have mentioned it."

Shia looked puzzled, which made Rose like her even more. She acted like she wasn't a big deal. "Why's that?"

Rose wasn't about to admit that Gem had caught her ogling Shia on the television at the bar a couple of days ago, so she opted for a less embarrassing explanation. "Oh, I asked her why Mikayla was hanging out at the competition last weekend. She mentioned something about her being your manager. I guess that doesn't naturally lead to details about where you live, though." The awkwardness was creeping in again.

"I guess not." Shia seemed okay with the explanation. "Speaking of Gem, you have some pretty big shoes to fill, taking on the management of this place. I'm no expert on what the official job description is, but Gem can pretty much do anything. Also, she knows everyone here. People aren't a name on a list for her. I guess she's not a typical manager."

Rose wondered if Shia was letting her know she wasn't happy with the change in day-to-day management. That sucked. She wanted Shia to like her. "Don't worry, I inherited the handywoman gene. I'm also a people person." She pushed loose strands of hair that had fallen from her ponytail behind her ears before shoving her hands into the pockets of her cargo shorts. "The main thing about me being here is to keep it in the family. It's important to my grandfather. Plus, I love Oceana."

"I'm happy it's staying in the family and that Gem gets to go back to a job she loves. I'm being selfish wishing she was still around as much as she always was." Shia appeared to study her. "I mistook you for Gem at the competition last weekend, actually. But she wouldn't be caught dead in a sundress. With your hands in your pockets and the way you tip your head to listen, it's classic Gem."

Relieved that Shia wasn't disappointed by her taking over the manager job, the tickle of excitement that had been dancing in Rose's stomach since Shia had opened the screen door kicked it up with a vengeance. The swing of her emotions and the powerful way in which they controlled her were scary. But Rose loved hearing that Shia had noticed her, maybe even more than she liked being reminded that she resembled Gem. "Oh yeah?"

"Totally. From a distance, you can easily pass for her. It's super—"

A knock on the screen door made them both turn to see a young man on the porch holding a pizza box. Shia went to the door and took the delivery, exchanged a little banter, and handed him a cash tip. She turned back to Rose with an exaggerated grimace that was devastatingly cute on her. "I'm starving. I need to go grocery shopping but keep putting it off."

Rose recognized the box. "My family used to go to Breakwater Pizza all the time when we still lived in Oceanside." She moved toward the door to leave Shia to her lunch. With no right, she was more than a little disappointed to be leaving. Shia was way more compelling in person than on the internet. "Thanks for working out the rent thing. It was nice meeting you."

Shia touched her arm. "You want to stay for lunch?"

Rose's stomach growled in response to the smell of pizza. She barely noticed it compared to the tingling on her arm where Shia had touched her. At least her ability to speak hadn't fled again. "I couldn't."

"Your stomach says you can." Shia's voice was teasing. However, the playful look in her eyes helped ease some of the awkwardness Rose was feeling.

"Only if you let me pay."

"There's plenty." Shia took the box to the dining table. Rose followed, unable to stop herself from admiring the muscles of Shia's back as she walked. She'd never appreciated the fit of sports bras as much as she did now and didn't realize how close she was following until Shia turned when she got to the table, and her upper arm grazed Rose's chest.

"Oh…sorry." Shia stood inches away while her eyes moved down Rose's body.

Rose automatically stepped back, regretting the space she put between them immediately. "My fault," she managed to say.

The crook of Shia's mouth told her that Shia probably didn't mind or maybe that she'd noticed how Rose's nipples had come to attention from the contact. "Breakwater is one of my sponsors. I get all the free pizza I want. Hope you like mushrooms, olives, and, um, pepperoni."

"My favorite." Even if it hadn't been exactly what she ordered for herself, she would have eaten it just to hang out a little longer.

They sat at the table. Shia motioned for her to take a slice as she handed her a paper towel from a nearby roll. "I mean, why dirty dishes?" she said. Rose had to agree with her.

The pizza was good, but she ate without much thought, her mind still on how her body was now completely tuned into Shia's presence less than a foot away. It took her a few minutes to realize they'd nearly finished their first slices without another word, so she tried to refocus and come up with something to initiate conversation. "So, uh, you were in the middle of saying something when the pizza guy knocked on the door."

"I was?" Shia wore a quizzical look that changed to a sheepish one. "Oh yeah. Probably for the better."

Rose laughed. "I'm even more curious now."

Shia dropped her chin to her chest. "I shouldn't say it."

"Totally not fair." Was she flirting? Oh God. She was out of control.

"Okay. I was going to say it's hot."

"What's hot?" What had merely been an attempt to fill the silence now had Rose invested. She was certain Shia wasn't talking about the pizza.

Shia put down her slice and rubbed her hands together, giving Rose intense eye contact that she felt all through her. This wasn't the distraction she'd imagined. But she couldn't look away. "This can never go outside of these walls," Shia said.

"Okay."

"I used to have a crush on Gem. Your resemblance to her, well, that's hot. That's what I was going to say."

The sensation of knowingly tilting backward off the edge of a cliff passed through Rose…until she realized it was only because she looked like Shia's crush. She tried to hide her disappointment. "Oh, I get it."

"What?" Shia looked confused.

"Don't worry. I won't tell anyone. It's our secret."

"I'm still…" A line appeared between Shia's eyes. "Oh, wait. No. That's not what I meant."

"Now I'm confused."

"I think you might think I meant that I still have a crush on her. I don't. It was only for, like, a couple of months when I first got here. Your aunt is amazing, but I don't see her that way anymore."

Rose laughed. "I'm not sure what we're talking about."

"It's you who's hot." Shia's sun-kissed cheeks turned pink. "She's gorgeous. In an older sister kind of way." She waved her hands dismissively. "Well, that's weird. What I mean is that you two look very much alike, but Gem is off-limits…for a lot of reasons…but you're not, which makes you super hot." Shia's eyes grew large. "God. I'm making this so weird." She closed her eyes with a grimace and opened them again. "I saw you at the beach. You were…are…striking. I don't even know if you're off-limits. Either way, I reacted to how pretty you are. Even from a distance, you caught my eye. And now that I'm talking to you, well…I'm going to shut up now." She smacked her forehead and dragged her hand down her face.

Rose laughed. A bunch of reactions ran through her, the one that rose to the top being the elation of knowing Shia found her attractive. The knowledge gave her a little more confidence. She liked where the conversation was going. "Keep talking. I get the feeling you don't fluster easily. I like that I caused it."

Shia narrowed her eyes. "You're a troublemaker."

"Not the first time I've been accused of it." She was definitely flirting now.

"I'm not surprised." And Shia was flirting back. "Do you want another slice?"

Rose was tempted if only for an excuse to stay a little longer. However, her stomach was too filled with butterflies to eat anymore. She was also fairly certain that she was about to reach her limit for keeping it cool. If she wasn't careful, she was liable to behave recklessly. "I probably should get back to work. The inspector is coming out to look at a couple of remodeled units today. I want to make sure the crew is all set." She stood. "Thanks for lunch."

Shia stood, too, and followed her to the door. Standing close, Rose noticed they were about the same height. It wouldn't have mattered if they weren't, but for some reason, she'd thought Shia was taller. But being the same height meant their lips were on the same level. It would be so easy to…

"Anytime. Don't forget your hat." Shia reached around her for the hat she had left on the end table while Rose focused on other things, like lips. Her standing like a statue and not moving to allow better access to the hat caused Shia to tip slightly off-balance. Without thinking, Rose caught her around the waist. When Shia steadied herself, they were nearly nose to nose, making the lips thing even more compelling.

Rose became aware of so many things all at once: the soft skin of Shia's waist under her hands, Shia's hand that was on her shoulder now, the flush of Shia's cheeks. It was a lot to process. She felt a little dizzy.

She did little more than sway forward and then back under the power of it, but the movement felt like a dance. When she leaned back, Shia's eyes were locked on hers. Before she knew it, Shia's warm mouth pressed against hers.

And what a kiss. Rose forgot where she was and sank into the massive wave of sensations cascading through her, like she was the pool at the bottom of a waterfall catching an untamed surge. She didn't care where she was or that she had just met Shia, it felt right. Her entire body felt the rightness. She was powerless against it, not that she had the slightest inclination to resist. She was a piece of metal. Shia was a powerful magnet. Hands cupped her face, holding her captive; their bodies pressed into one another, and she knew in that moment that she would fight to stay exactly where she was, kissing this woman she hardly knew even though it felt like she'd known her forever. Everywhere her skin touched Shia, an electric current flowed between them. She ran her fingertips along Shia's lower back and up her sides before she slid her arms around her, using her to hold herself up, her head buzzing with all the feelings and sensations rushing through her.

When it seemed she might need to sit or lie down, Shia pressed her against the doorjamb. Desire flashed through Rose at the confident and sexy move, causing her to pour all her focus on the soft lips that had opened and were now exploring her hers, sucking on them, Shia's tongue applying featherlight trails along the edges, tracing the contours, gently nibbling.

Rose leaned against the solid wood behind her and greedily pulled Shia against her, mounting desire spiraling within her. This was the kind of kiss that led to erotic things, like intimate touching, pulsing flesh, cries of passion. This was the kind of kiss that people dreamed of their entire lives. It was the kind of kiss that drove people to do impulsive, reckless things.

Rose was about to do every single one of those impulsive and reckless things, but her phone made a noise, a notification for a work order, but it was enough to jar them both from the spell they'd fallen under. She wished she could fling the offensive thing into the nearby ocean and barely held back a wail of frustration as their lips parted. Their hands stilled. Unfulfilled need pulsed between them.

However, Shia's gaze held her frozen in place. Neither of them moved away. Rose couldn't because her back was against the door, but even if she could, she didn't want to. It might have been embarrassing and awkward looking into Shia's eyes like this after having only known her for maybe a half an hour, but Shia's soft, warm hands cradling her head, her perfectly sculpted body pressed against her, and her firm thigh tucked between Rose's legs distracted her. Instead, she basked in the awareness of how absolutely aroused she was and how, until a mere few seconds earlier, she'd been rocking against that firm leg, a movement she desperately wanted to continue. Her center ached for it. If the heat she felt between Shia's legs against her own was any indication of how hers felt against Shia's, they were both very close to—

"I'm so sorry—" Shia said.

"I don't know how—" Rose said at the same time.

Still, neither of them moved. Rose couldn't help but look at Shia's lips, swollen and dark, glistening from their kiss. When she smiled, Rose forced herself to raise her eyes, seeing the humor in Shia's expression, and they both began to laugh. Shia slowly stepped back, lowering her hands and putting several inches between them. Rose's hands slid away from around her waist. The motion left her with an abject sense of absence and a vivid memory of just how soft and warm the skin on Shia's torso was.

"That was intense," Shia said, touching her own lips.

Rose wished she were the one touching them. "I can honestly say I have never kissed someone within"—Rose glanced at her watch for show more than anything else because she was in no condition to estimate actual time—"thirty minutes of meeting them."

"Me either."

Rose guessed she was lying because no one kissed like that without a whole lot of practice. "I'd feel rude leaving now. After that. Part of me doesn't even want to, but I think I better because…because I don't even know what."

"If it helps, I don't want you to leave, either."

Rose could barely breathe. The look in Shia's eyes told her what would happen if she stayed. The ache between her legs begged her to stay. She squeezed her hands into fists, never wanting anything so badly as she wanted Shia in that moment. "I…I should…" What should she do?

Shia stepped back a few more inches. "I get it."

Rose opened the screen door and stepped out. With one more glance at Shia, she nearly ran out of there, already in the maintenance cart by the time the screen door clicked shut, already punishing herself for letting things get so out of control, even while everything in her wanted to go right back and see where the lightning bolt of lust would have taken them. She didn't even care if it was the right or wrong thing to do. She'd never felt this way before.

Chapter Five

"Holy crap."

Shia let out a long, shaky breath and slowly slid to the floor. If she hadn't been holding on to the open door, she would have collapsed. She'd never experienced anything as intense as that. Never. Something powerful had raced through her at the sight of Rose on the porch. A very physical thing that had caused her to tune out everything else.

Rose. Shia wasn't sure how she'd remained coherent enough to greet her like a normal person, let alone discuss the rent issue. She'd barely kept track of the discussion. Sure, she'd felt so rattled when she'd called Alice, she'd had to leave the room to clear her thoughts. Somehow, she'd gotten through it and was able to relay the information to Rose, who seemed relaxed and unaware of the turbulence of emotion churning inside her.

How she'd gotten the presence of mind to invite Rose to lunch, she had no idea. But eating had helped her to regain her composure, even though she couldn't seem to form words to talk to her gorgeous guest. She was sure she'd come off as a dingbat when Rose had tried to initiate conversation, but she'd even gotten through that and had even started to feel a little more in control of her social skills. But when Rose had looked at her lips and when Rose's hands had landed on her hips, every bit of composure had fled, and Shia had kissed her. In hindsight, she realized she hadn't even asked if it was okay or tried to get more indication that Rose wanted to kiss her, which was absolutely unlike her. Lucky for her, it was very evident Rose wanted the kiss as much as she did. And oh God, it had been explosive. A pulse of fire went through her thinking about it.

A sound on the porch caused her to look up. Rose was standing there. "I forgot my hat." She didn't even ask why Shia was sitting on the floor in the doorway.

Shia rose without a word and opened the door. But the scent of Rose—sunshine and sunblock on clean skin mixed with fabric softener—engulfed her as she stepped by and caused Shia's senses to reel again. She stood there, unable to form a coherent thought as Rose retrieved her hat from the table and began to walk out.

"Do you need it?" Shia managed to ask.

Rose turned, and Shia recognized the dazed look in her eyes as the one she was currently struggling with. "No. I have—"

Shia grabbed the hat before Rose could and held it behind her back. "Pretend you didn't come for it so you have a reason to come back."

Rose looked a little surprised but smiled and backed slowly down the steps, never breaking eye contact. She continued walking backward until she got to her cart. Her amused smile told Shia she would be back.

Shia watched her pull out of the driveway. Once she was out of sight, she plopped the hat on her head and walked over to the table, intending to put away the pizza mess. But instead of gathering it up, she braced her hands on one of the chairs and leaned forward, dropping her head between her shoulders. God. That kiss. Thinking about it revived all the sensations that had crashed through her like a tidal surge against the rocks of the jetties.

Footfalls on the front steps again yanked her from the memory. She turned to see Rose was back, had already opened the screen door, and was walking directly to her. Her expression was determined and dark, and for a second, Shia worried that in the minutes since she'd left, Rose had realized how inappropriate Shia had been. She opened her mouth to apologize, but before a single word was out, Rose had her head in her hands, pushing the hat off, and her mouth was on Shia's in a searing follow-up to a kiss she'd thought she'd never beat.

Shia leaned against the chair behind her, and Rose leaned into her, pressing against her. Shia held on for dear life while her senses were scrambled by the hottest kiss she'd ever experienced. This was a battle of passion they both got to win. When Shia thought her legs would slide out from beneath her, Rose pulled her forward and backed the few steps it took to press Shia against the dining room wall. Her back hit it with a thud, and she spun Rose around so they traded positions. As soon as she did, Rose surrendered, allowing Shia to take the lead.

The switch was so smooth, and somehow, in a move she'd never executed, Shia held Rose's arms over her head, pressed against the wall. Rose let out a sexy sigh, which further inflamed Shia's desire. She held both of Rose's hands with one hand and brought her free hand down to caress Rose's cheek, then her neck, before trailing her fingers down the center of her chest, across her ribs, where she stopped alongside Rose's breast, feeling the heat of her skin through her polo shirt. Her breasts were soft and firm. Shia extended her thumb so she could explore a little more. A pulse of excitement poured through her when her thumb grazed a firm nipple. Her heartbeat doubled when Rose released another sigh. It was deep and breathy and fanned a wave of heat through every inch of Shia's body.

She slid her lips from Rose's mouth, kissing a trail along her jawline, pausing for a moment at her earlobe, and then down her neck to above Rose's collarbone. She kissed and sucked and nibbled at the smooth skin, enjoying Rose rolling her head from side to side against the wall, breathing heavily, causing her breasts to heave and push against Shia, who wanted to explore every inch of Rose at once, even as she wanted to take her time and fully enjoy the parts she'd already touched. As her lips traveled lower toward the unbuttoned vee of Rose's shirt, Shia released her hands and reached to caress Rose's throat.

Rose took Shia's other hand, the one cradling the side of her breast, and placed it against the zipper of her shorts. She cupped Shia's face and lifted her head so they were eye to eye. At first, she only stared deeply into Shia's eyes, her rapid breaths blowing against Shia's chin. "I'd like you to take me to bed now." Her voice was breathy, as if she'd been running. "If you don't make me come soon, I'm going to explode. If you're into it, I'd like to do the same to you."

Shia was into it. So into it, she was having a hard time forming words, a condition only Rose had ever caused in her. She nodded once, and then to make sure Rose knew, she nodded several more times. Rose laughed. But it did nothing to dispel the raw desire in her eyes.

Rose brushed her lips across Shia's. "You need to know, I don't want to go slow. I don't want to be gentle. I'm not into rough stuff. I just want to let go. I'll tell you if something doesn't do it for me, and I hope you'll do the same. But what's happening here…God. It's…I can't even explain it. I don't even know why I'm trying to when I should be showing you."

Shia finally found her voice. "I'm into it so much. I'm a mess, but everything you said. God—"

"Where's your bed?"

Shia kissed her hard, leading her to the bedroom. She didn't need her eyes to find the way. Rose followed without breaking the kiss until the back of her legs met the side of the bed, and she fell backward onto it, landing on her back with her legs dangling over the edge. She sat up and began to unlace her boots, but Shia pushed her hands away and finished the job.

Chapter Six

The sheets were twisted in a pile at the end of the bed, including the fitted one, and Rose gave up trying to extract one to cover herself while Shia used the restroom. She flopped back onto the mattress with a mighty expulsion of breath and covered her eyes with a hand, waiting for her heartbeat to go back to normal. Her arms and legs were still weak from the last orgasm. She didn't care if Shia came back into the room to see her unceremoniously splayed out, half on the bed with her legs draped over the edge. She'd already seen her in far more vulnerable positions.

Rose had shown her the most elemental parts of herself, from every inch of her body to the primal noises Shia had elicited from her as she'd brought her to one shattering orgasm after another. Shia had now seen her as she was without a bit of pretense. A sheet wasn't going to bring back an iota of decorum, and Rose didn't care. Not after the most amazing sex she'd ever experienced.

"Hold still. I want to sear this vision in my brain."

Rose dropped the hand she still held over her eyes and lifted her head. Shia stood nude in the doorway of the bathroom, the light behind her. Rose saw a million shards of dazzling incandescence dancing around her. Her breath left her once again. "You're a goddess in that light, you know."

She couldn't see the expression on Shia's face, although her haloed form shifted in a way that displayed her enjoyment. "I've never been called a goddess unless it was preceded by surf, and I have to say, I like it better as a standalone."

"Well, I've never been called a goddess. I'd take it with any other qualifier."

Shia was standing between her knees in a flash, and as she bent, she placed a hand on either side of Rose so that she was hovering over her, a serious expression quite clear on her face. "I'm absolutely stunned that you've never been called a goddess. You're a goddess of sex. A goddess of delight. A goddess of touch, taste, and total beauty. You're a goddess of many things. The list goes on."

Rose rested her hands on Shia's collarbones. "That's the afterglow talking. We've only known each other about three hours."

Shia's eyes took on a thoughtful expression. "I'm sticking to my story. There are some things you don't need an extended knowledge of to be certain." She lowered herself to nibble on Rose's neck, making her shiver. She squeezed her thighs around Shia's hips and wrapped her legs around her. "Besides, I experienced all that this afternoon. If you'll let me, I'd like a second helping."

Rose couldn't help undulating beneath her, trying to bring Shia's body closer to her throbbing sex. "I was having a hard time standing up after the first helping, which, if I counted correctly, already went into second and even thirds without a pause between."

"Does that mean I don't get dessert?" Shia kissed a trail down Rose's neck and meandered to graze the tip of Rose's left nipple, where she kept the slightest connection, her warm breath providing the lightest of caresses.

"Yes." Rose sucked in a breath as her body clenched in anticipation. "I don't think I'm capable of depriving you of dessert." The words came out in a strangled whisper. "Whatever you want. It's yours."

"This," Shia said, sliding down to her knees at the side of the bed, placing Rose's thighs on her shoulders. Her mouth was on Rose, causing her to arch. Within minutes, Rose was crying out in the unintelligible language Shia brought out of her when she came. This time, though, Rose didn't let the postorgasmic lethargy descend upon her as she languished in the effects of the explosive sensation still vibrating within her. She pulled Shia up from where she was kneeling and pushed her onto the bed, where she guided Shia's hands to the wooden slats of the headboard.

"Hold on, and don't let go," she said, gazing intently into eyes that held a combination of desire and humor.

"Will I be punished if I let go?" Shia asked.

"Not in a good way, if that's what you're thinking."

"How do you know what I consider not good?" Shia asked, but she didn't let go.

Rose, inches away from taking one of Shia's small breasts into her mouth, sat up and made as if to stand. "I guess I could go back to work."

"No. No. No. I'll be a good goddess. I'll keep holding on." Despite the pleading in her voice, Shia was good and did not let go.

"That's what I thought." Rose lay next to her and circled a nipple with the tip of her finger. Empathic sensations teased her own nipples from how Shia responded to her touch. "Now, spread your legs."

Shia bit her lips and did as Rose said.

It was only supposed to be dessert, but one thing led to another, causing Rose to play hooky from work for the entire afternoon. It was well past midnight when Rose reluctantly, and as gently as she could, extracted herself from Shia's sleeping embrace, retrieved her clothes, and tiptoed into the living room where she put them on. Her body was feeling the sexual exertion she'd subjected it to all afternoon and well into the evening, yet she was exhilarated. As she snuck out the front door, she glimpsed her hat still lying on the coffee table. It was sitting in a lone strip of moonlight coming between the closed curtains as if purposefully trying to get her attention. She paused before closing the door behind her. She smiled, remembering Shia's suggestion that it would be an excuse to come back. She probably had other excuses now, but she liked the idea of leaving a part of her behind.

Basking in the cool night air and the scent of wisteria blowing on the breeze, she walked back to the house she now shared with Gem and her grandfather. It wasn't far, only a couple of houses and a small park away. As she passed Mikayla's place, she heard two sets of laughter through an open window, telling her that Gem was staying the night there. It wasn't surprising, but she was relieved that Gem wouldn't be back at the house to possibly witness her returning so late, still dressed in her work clothes. She didn't have to worry about her grandfather. He slept like a dead man, except for the snoring. It wasn't that she thought she'd done anything to be ashamed of; after all, Gem herself was dating a resident. But she wasn't sure what to say if Gem asked where she'd been. Thank goodness she'd walked back to Shia's house that last time instead of riding the cart. Everyone on the street would have known what was going on. At least, they'd have an idea, which was more than what Rose had, now that she was thinking about it.

Had she really just fallen into bed with Shia less than an hour after meeting her?

Rose was about to cross the street to the house when doubt hit her. She veered toward the little park next to Mikayla's place. Neither she nor Shia had talked about what they were doing except for the little bit of teasing and desire-filled requests for certain things they wanted during their sexcapade. They hadn't even talked before they'd both fallen asleep after the last round. Their time together had been purely physical…and mind-blowing.

She took a seat at the picnic table, breathing in the scent of the star jasmine and blooming magnolias. Her good mood amplified the many things she loved about being at Oceana: the sound of the distant surf, the scents of the many flowers and the newly mown grass, the way that the community not only felt safe but welcoming, no matter what time of day or night it was. Rose loved it here, especially now that she was really a part of it. It was home to people she loved, Gem, her grandfather, Shia.

Wait. Not that she loved Shia. What was she thinking? It was the awesome sex that had made her think like that. They'd only known each other for half a day. And most of that time had been in the biblical sense. There was no thinking during that, only feeling and doing, touching and… Her body started to ache for Shia's touch again. A momentary vision of returning to Shia's place and slipping back into bed with her filled her with anticipation and a whole array of erotic sensations. She probably would have done it, too, except she'd locked the door when she'd left. It wouldn't be the same if she had to wake Shia up to be let back in. But if she wanted to…

No. She shook her head. It was a silly thought but a very enticing one nonetheless. She and Shia probably needed to talk a little before she could feel comfortable enough to sneak back into her house in the middle of the night. Talking was the adult thing to do, anyway. They simply needed to have a conversation to determine what they each wanted to happen between them. Hopefully, they would both agree that it would entail more sex. God, they were off the charts with sexual chemistry. She wanted there to be lots and lots more sex. Shia hadn't said anything about next times. Neither had she. Yet Rose was pretty sure there would be. The nuclear fusion that happened when they touched was too amazing for Shia to not want a next time.

But what if it was just sex to Shia? Rose shook her head again. She would have known. She could always tell. It wasn't like this was her first time. She'd had plenty of sex before. In fact, she considered herself a very sex-positive person. Because of her accepting nature around sex, her experience had mostly been good. She owed a lot of that to her mother. As many hang-ups as her mother had, sex wasn't one of them, and even though Rose had hated talking about it with her mom as she'd grown up, her mother had promoted a healthy sense of sexuality in her.

All these thoughts went through her as she tried to decipher what jumping into bed with Shia within minutes of meeting her meant. It wasn't the first time she'd had sex with someone the first time she'd met them, but it was a personal record that it had happened within the first hour.

Maybe she wasn't able to tell with Shia. What if the powerful connection between them was throwing her off? Was this a routine experience for Shia? Rose wasn't judging if it was, but it made things a little harder to figure out between them. If Shia was used to jumping into sex, maybe that was all it was to her, after all. What had she heard it called? A sport fuck. Shia was an athlete. She was super hot. She'd probably had countless offers. So maybe what they'd been doing all afternoon was sport fucking.

A huge sense of disappointment rushed over her. She had nothing against sport fucking, but she didn't want that with Shia. Despite dismissing her slip by calling it love, Rose had to admit that what she felt was more than simply physical attraction. She had feelings for Shia. Major feelings. When Shia had come out of the bathroom with the light behind her, Rose had felt something big stir within her, and by the time they'd fallen asleep, she'd been caught up in an ethereal haze she'd never experienced before, a sensation of their spirits entwined and filled with hope and affection and what she could only explain as a craving for the possibility to be part of Shia for a long time…maybe forever.

Part of it was the perfect way their bodies had reacted to one another, but there was something far more powerful than the physical. Maybe it wasn't love, but it was monumental, and while she had no way of knowing what Shia was feeling, she knew instinctively that it was similar to hers.

Whatever it was, it had happened fast. Was it too fast? Maybe the quickness of it was the thing causing her doubt. With that thought, she decided to give it some time. Forget about love. Enjoy the ride. She'd figure it out one way or the other. In the meantime, she hoped there'd be more mind-blowing sex.

She stood, feeling all the well-used muscles in her body as a delicious reminder of the last twelve hours. Her thoughts had gotten a bit deep as she'd sat in the park, but it didn't stop her from feeling the effervescent aftereffects. She'd only get a few hours of sleep before she had to get up for work in the morning, but she knew she'd have sweet dreams.

Chapter Seven

Shia should have been dragging in the morning after going on six hours of sleep after what had been a physically strenuous twelve hours of pure sex the day before. But she wasn't, especially after the morning swim with Mikayla. In fact, she'd jumped out of bed with more energy than she'd felt in a long time.

There had been a momentary sense of disappointment when she found that Rose had left sometime during the night, but that was followed quickly with a sense of relief. Not entirely because Rose was gone, even though that was part of it, but that they didn't have to do the hesitant dance of checking in and trying to navigate the next steps when they woke with morning breath, and maybe even some questions about what having sex so soon after meeting meant to either of them.

That was what she told herself, anyway. She knew it had more to do with disappointing Rose. When she'd have to say she was a one-and-done kinda person. Only good for a good time. Not someone to hang your hat on. All those trite but completely apt descriptions. Disappointment was not something she liked to serve with a first cup of coffee no matter how many times she'd done it in the past. And she'd done it more times than she liked to admit because of the no-dating rule she'd imposed on herself a little over a year ago when she'd realized how easy it was to blow off practice in favor of the soft skin and sexy smiles offered by the increasing number of pretty fans seeking her out. Her surfing career came first. It had to.

She knew where Rose worked. She'd see her soon anyway, and maybe it wouldn't be so uncomfortable explaining that she wasn't in a place to make someone else a priority these days. Because, against her better judgment, somewhere in the night, Shia had a few thoughts about how nice it would be to make Rose a priority and maybe even be made a priority herself.

That was probably just the orgasm dopamine talking.

"Gem worked late yesterday evening, and I stopped by your place to see if you wanted company out on the water," Mikayla said as they walked back to Oceana, thankfully interrupting Shia's internal monologue. She'd nearly forgotten Mikayla was walking beside her on the way back from their swim.

"Oh yeah? What time? I didn't hear you knock." She wasn't surprised that she hadn't heard the door. She'd been preoccupied with other things, namely Rose and her talented fingers. So much for an interruption getting her away from those thoughts.

"About six, but I didn't knock."

Probably for the best. "Why not?"

"I didn't think you would hear it over all the moaning and whatnot."

Shia felt the rush of heat to her cheeks. "What do you mean?" Oh, she knew. She just didn't want to face it.

Mikayla pushed her shoulder playfully. "I mean, you really should close the inside door when you have a friend over. I didn't even make it up the steps, and I could hear you two going at it."

"I don't know what you're talking about. Maybe I was watching television."

"That's probably it. Were you watching a show called *Oh God, Shia*?"

The impression was embarrassing because not only had Mikayla heard, but it wasn't right hearing her make such sounds. She was like a mother to her.

Unfortunately, Mikayla was on a roll. "Or maybe it was *That's it. Yes. Like th—*"

Shia put a hand over Mikayla's mouth before she knew what she was doing. "Stop," she begged before Mikayla doubled over laughing, shrugging away Shia's hand.

"I'm sorry. I was only teasing," she said, wiping the tears from her eyes. "Your cheeks are so red. I don't think I've ever seen you blush like that."

"What do you expect?"

"I'm kidding. It wasn't that loud. I only heard when I got right up to the door, and I guess you didn't notice that I closed it for you. I don't think anyone else heard."

Shia covered her face with her hands. "I can't even look at you now."

"Come on. It's sex. It's normal. Everyone does it."

"Stop."

"What? Gem and I even—"

"Aah, stop! I mean it."

"Okay. Okay," Mikayla said with more laughter, and they walked quietly for a few minutes while Shia wished the ground would open and swallow her.

When they entered Oceana through the pedestrian gate, Mikayla cleared her throat and put a hand on Shia's shoulder. "Hey. All kidding aside, I'm glad you had a little fun with someone, Shia."

"Why do you say it like that?"

"Like what?"

"Like you're giving me positive reinforcement for doing a good job or something? You know, like, 'Great job making friends at preschool, Mary.' "

"I didn't mean it that way. You've made a point that you've put all extracurricular activities on hold for the sake of your surfing career. It's probably healthy to have more than your career as a priority." Mikayla paused for a few seconds. "Who's the lucky person? Do I know them?"

Shia looked at her out of the corner of her eye and wondered if she knew who she'd been imitating moments ago. "Does it matter? Can we talk about something else?"

"Just curious. I hope I'll get to meet her eventually." Mikayla absently pushed her fingers through her damp hair and shook it out a bit. "I mean, unless it was a one-time thing."

Those comments made her think about things she'd tried not to think about since waking up with the scent of Rose on her sheets and skin. It had happened so unexpectedly, sweeping them away in a fast-moving tsunami. They hadn't had a chance to consider what would happen after the water receded. She wasn't sure she was ready to figure that part out.

"Earth to Shia?"

She realized she'd fallen into thoughts she wanted to save for a later time. "Um, sorry. We didn't talk about anything past last night." Hell. They hadn't even talked about last night.

"Sometimes, it's fun to see where things go on their own."

"Yeah." It seemed as if Mikayla was about to drop the subject, and

Shia was relieved. She needed more time to figure out how to proceed. For all she knew, Rose simply saw it as a one-night thing, which would make things easy. That idea should have eased Shia's mind, but surprisingly, it didn't. Instead, she found herself wondering what Rose was doing right then.

"I really do want to get out on the water with you one of these evenings. I had fun learning how to stand on a surfboard when you were teaching me last week. It might sound wonky, but I've been dreaming about it, and I think I've figured out how to get my feet under me now."

"You figured this out in your dreams?" Thankful for the change of subject, Shia wanted to know how Mikayla's dreams had fixed her trouble with balancing.

"I know. I told you it was wonky, but ever since I moved to Oceana, I've had dreams that have helped me figure things out. Not that the dreams give me explicit advice. I can't explain how it works, but I think my body will be able to feel the right balance, and I'll be able to sense the rhythm of the way the board is on the water and move with it." She laughed. "I told you I can't explain it."

"I get it. Not the dream part but letting the water and the board tell your body how to adjust."

"Right. You get it." Mikayla glanced at her with a smile. "The dream thing, I think, is an Oceana thing. Gem says it's an example of how it is here, and I'm beginning to believe her."

"You're talking about the special energy. I'm glad you can feel it." Shia wondered if what had happened with her and Rose was caused by the special energy of Oceana. That might explain why she was feeling so different about it. Not the conflicted part. That came with the territory. It was everything else.

❖

Shia looked forward to her usual soak in the community hot tub after her swim, and she was glad that Mikayla decided not to join her. Usually, she enjoyed the company, but she wanted to tune out and let the warm water soothe her well-worked muscles, both from the swim and the hours of sex the day before.

She stopped at her house and slid her board into the rack with the others near the rear of the carport, then popped into the house long enough to grab a fresh towel, some dry clothes, and her shower kit. It didn't take long, but she did pause to look at the bed that was still in disarray from the night before. A shiver of pleasure went through her as a few visceral memories played across her mind.

She barely remembered the short walk from her place to the nearby pool, and as much as she'd hoped to tune out, she continued to replay moments from the night that didn't stop as she stood beneath the cold flow of water from the unheated shower. The cold shower, along with the hot memories, made settling into the bubbling water an unexpectedly erotic experience that put her into a fog of remembered pleasure as she soaked. As usual, the pool area was empty so early in the morning on a workday, so she took more time than she usually did, even though she was unable to tune out like normal. If anything, Rose continued to consume her thoughts. When she left the warm tub for the locker room to take another shower, this time with soap and shampoo, she'd even managed to add in a soundtrack effect, like she was in a damn romantic music video. The last thought caused her to laugh aloud, nearly snapping her out of what had become a goofy sexual delirium.

"Who's in there laughing at my singing?" a familiar voice called good-naturedly from the other side of the black-and-white subway-tiled shower wall.

As if the intensity of her thoughts had somehow conjured her, Rose was in the locker room. Or was this more delirium? Shia quickly rinsed the soap from her hair and peered around the wall. Sure enough, Rose crouched next to a grate low on the wall across the room. She held a dingy gray filter in one hand with another clean white one propped against the wall next to her. She was clearly doing her property manager thing. Was it just a coincidence?

"Did you sneak away last night only to follow me into a public shower this morning?" Shia was only half kidding.

Rose stood quickly. "Of course not. I would never…I mean, I can show you my work list. I made it days ago."

"I was teasing." Shia tried to appear nonchalant as guilt about suspecting Rose of subterfuge warred with the bubbles of anticipation flittering in her stomach. Not to mention the fact that she was completely naked. "Um, was that you singing a minute ago?"

Rose had dropped the dirty filter and had taken a few steps toward the showers but stopped abruptly. Shia wondered if she, too, was going for nonchalant. "You mean the singing you were laughing at?"

"I wasn't laughing at you. I was laughing at me. I thought I was imagining…never mind. I wasn't laughing at you. It was nice. What was it?"

"What was what?" She hadn't moved farther toward Shia, who wished she'd come closer. The locker room was dim, and she wanted to see Rose, maybe divine what she was thinking.

Rose walked closer, and Shia's pulse raced. Here she was, peering around a cold tile wall, standing completely naked with her warm shower running a few feet away as soap dripped from her wet skin. Goose bumps rose across her entire body, and she wasn't sure if it was from the cold or the fact that the woman she'd been fantasizing about had magically appeared before her.

"I don't remember what I was singing. Probably some song from the radio."

"It was nice."

Rose seemed to relax a little, and she leaned her shoulder against the wall separating her from most of Shia's body, which appeared not to faze her, much to Shia's disappointment. "Thank you. You still have shampoo in your hair." She touched a strand of Shia's hair and sniffed her fingers. "It smells good. It reminds me of you."

Heat crawled up Shia's neck. "Thanks. Um…" She glanced behind her. "Don't go anywhere. I'll be right back." She backed away from the wall into the stream of water, very aware of the woman in the other room.

"I was hoping to run into you today," Rose said from the other side of the wall. "I mean, not here. This was…I didn't expect it to be here. Seeing you," she said quickly. "I would have called, but I don't have your number."

"Yes, you do. It's on file in the leasing office."

"Oh." Rose paused, and Shia was tempted to peek around the wall again to make sure she was still there. But she wanted to finish her shower as fast as she could because all she really wanted was for Rose to join her, and she wasn't sure that was the right thing to do in the moment.

"Are you still there?" Shia called as she made sure all the conditioner was out of her hair. She'd almost decided against that step, but all the time in the water and sun made her hair brittle if she didn't condition it every day. She ran her fingers through her hair impatiently, rinsing as quickly as she could.

"Yes. Sorry. I'm sort of glitching out over here."

Shia could relate. "We both are." She turned off the water and took her towel from the hook, wrapping it around herself. Suddenly shy, she stepped out of the shower area.

Rose was leaning against the wall but pushed away when Shia drew near. Her eyes kept moving, landing on Shia and then darting away as if she didn't want to be caught staring. Shia wondered what was going on behind those beautiful eyes, and it surprised her that she was hoping Rose was having the same kind of flashbacks she was. It was counterintuitive to her one-and-done rule. But Shia had given up on trying to focus on that rule while the vivid memories of yesterday continued to monopolize her mind and body, and right that moment, she wanted Rose to look at her. She craved the connection they had before.

As if responding to her will, Rose's eyes finally stopped darting about. They lingered, moving down her body, then back up again. Shia felt her gaze like a physical touch. Eventually, Rose's eyes met hers and seemed to click into place. The sustained eye contact was both too much and exactly what Shia wanted. It certainly turned up the heat in the chilly room. The blaze from that stare seemed to penetrate her.

"I'm not sure you know how hard it is to stand here with you wearing a towel," Rose said, her eyes tracing another circuit up Shia's body.

Although the comment stunned her, she found herself stepping forward. "Why is it so hard?"

Rose licked her lips. "A few reasons."

Shia took another step, watching Rose's eyes grow dark with desire, her chest rise faster with every breath, her nipples erect under her shirt. God. What was happening? "Such as?"

"Such as…" Rose bit her lip. "How easy it would be to reach over and simply take it off you."

Shia took another step forward. "And after you took it off?" She noticed Rose swallow and realized how tight her own throat had become. She took another step, leaving only an inch between them. A moment passed while she simply absorbed Rose's closeness, and then she reached to take her hand.

Rose responded by closing the gap between them and backing Shia against the wall, pressing her damp shoulders against the cold hard tile, although Shia was barely aware of that. Rose continued to gaze into her eyes, her lips slightly open as Shia guided her hand through the overlapped edge of the towel, putting it between her legs and guiding her fingers into the warm, soft, and so very wet skin inside.

"Is it something like this?" The last word became a drawn-out hiss of pleasure as Rose pushed her fingers deeper, pressing Shia's own fingers against her clit.

"Yes," Rose breathed out. "Exactly this." She moved her fingers out and back in, making Shia throw her head back. Rose put one hand against the wall beside Shia's head as she responded to her movements.

The towel fell to the tile floor. The chill morning air swept across Shia's naked skin, putting what they were doing into sharp relief, driving her arousal higher. Her core tightened in rhythm with Rose's motions, and her body signaled her impending orgasm. "Press harder on the inside," she said, almost in a whisper as a flare of pleasure pulsed within her. Rose responded perfectly, slowing her thrusts and sliding in a more focused fashion. "Yes, like that. Exactly like that." It wasn't long before wave after wave of pleasure rolled through Shia, and she tried not to be too loud, part of her remembering Mikayla's comments. As it was, the tiled room echoed every sound.

Before the orgasm faded, Rose dropped to her knees and pressed her mouth on Shia's still pulsing flesh, resulting in another powerful orgasm. The move was something she had done to her the previous evening, producing the same results. Shia had never had a second orgasm so soon after another, making the move an immediate favorite.

She returned the pleasure, making Rose come with her hand and then with her mouth before standing and slipping her fingers back into Rose, stroking her slowly as she recovered. It almost felt like a fantasy how her thoughts had preceded their second meeting, and she had to remind herself that what was happening was real, despite the cold tile still against her back and her fingers still inside Rose as her last moan echoed through the room and along Shia's spine. Soon, the only sound she heard was their heavy breathing.

"Jesus, Joseph, and Mary." Rose's voice vibrated along Shia's neck where she rested her head, her face pressed against the skin below Shia's ear.

Shia realized then that she was holding Rose up. "Are you okay?"

Rose blew out a loud warm breath. "Better than okay. I'm just a little tapped out after you attacked me like that."

Shia laughed. "What? I didn't attack you. There was no attacking."

Rose hardly moved. "What do you call what you did with your eyes?"

"My eyes?"

"You know what you did. You fixed those beautiful eyeballs on me, hypnotized me into your clutches, forcing me to become your sex slave. It's your superpower. I have no defense against such evil devices."

Shia slid her lips across Rose's temple. "I did no such thing. I have no powers. No devices."

Rose huffed again, and the warm breath on Shia's skin made her shiver. "Modesty will not work here. You're one hundred percent responsible for my incapacitation."

Shia grinned against Rose's thick dark hair, sliding her hands slowly over the warm skin of her back under her shirt. She wanted nothing more than to lie down with Rose so she could slowly explore every inch of her soft skin. "Incapacitation, huh?"

Rose sighed. "I'll be okay, no thanks to you."

Shia tightened her hold. "I'll be here holding you up until you regain your strength."

"It's the least you can do." Rose was still for a few moments before she started laughing.

"What's so funny?"

"This is a public building. Anyone could walk in on us, me with my shorts around my ankles and my unhooked bra hanging under my shirt. I guess you fit in, on account of this being a shower, which explains your buck nakedness. Me? I have no excuse for my exposed butt."

Shia slid her hands down to Rose's bare backside, and Rose gently pushed away and pulled up her shorts. "Hey. I was protecting your modesty," Shia said. A flush remained on Rose's face, and Shia liked that she'd been the cause of it. She picked up her towel and wrapped it around herself.

"Unfortunately, I need to go back to work." Rose pulled her phone from her pocket and handed it to Shia. "If it's okay, I'd like to have your number."

After far more intimate activities, it was almost surreal that Rose was almost shy about asking. Shia entered her number and handed the phone back.

Rose took it and backed toward the open vent she'd been working on. "Um, I'm going to finish this while you get dressed."

Shia watched her go back to her task while she put on her clothes, wondering how they'd gone from being as intimate as two people could be to awkward strangers in the span of minutes. They both finished what they were doing, gathered their various belongings, and walked out together. At the fork in the sidewalk in front of the building, they turned in opposite directions, each walking backward for a few steps, giving each other a wave, after which they turned and walked away.

Shia was nearly to her house when the unusual mix of emotions running through her became a confusing cacophony. This was all new to her, the raging desire, the humiliating awkwardness, the heart-racing anticipation. And the warning sirens that she didn't have the bandwidth for any of it. There were also a bunch of other feelings she could name if she only had the guts to sit down and really explore them. But she didn't want to. She wanted to continue with her life as an up-and-coming professional surfer, and she wanted to make sure she stayed focused on the things that would keep her climbing the ranks toward the top. That was all she ever wanted.

But, God. She was still tingling. Tingles and pulses and shivers and...she absolutely wanted more.

The thing was, regardless of what the right thing to do for her career was, something about Rose drew her in like a cat to catnip, and when she was near, the effects of their chemistry acted as a drug. She couldn't get enough. Even now, as she opened her front door, she wished Rose was there. It was almost a craving, purely sexual. How could she be this consumed with someone already? They'd known each other less than twenty-four hours.

Maybe that was all it was. A sex thing. The idea gave her some comfort. If it was only sex, they could meet up every once in a while to satisfy their needs, and she'd have all the rest of her time to focus on her career. Casual sex wouldn't get in the way, right? The thought kind of eased her worries. Would Rose be open to casual, though? That was the big question.

As she put away her things, a text from Rose chimed on her phone:

Now you have my number. Had fun. Hope to see you around.

The text was friendly and casual, lowering Shia's apprehensions that much more. Smiling, she considered how to reply. Casual. It had to be casual. She started and stopped a few times before she settled on: *Thanks...for everything.*

Of course, she overthought it as soon as she sent it, but once she hit the button, it was already out there, so she had to live with it. It seemed to give a clear message that she was only interested in casual.

Unless the ellipsis implied she was thinking other things. No. There was no room for that.

She went about her usual morning tasks, occasionally checking her texts to see if Rose responded, but by the time she'd finished her midmorning protein shake, nothing had come in, and she'd started to wonder what Rose had meant by hoping to see her around.

It didn't matter, she reminded herself. She had work to do, including a meeting with Mikayla in a little over a half hour. She decided to get some other work done before the meeting, so she sat on the couch to respond to her email and add more dates to the surf lesson schedule on her website in response to the long wait list that had blown up after the last competition. She plugged in her laptop and kicked off her flip-flops, but before she opened it, she leaned her head against the couch and dragged her hands down her face. She hated computer work, but it needed to be done. When she opened her eyes, the Oceana ball cap Rose had left on the coffee table was directly in her line of sight. She couldn't help remembering the teasing that had ended up with her and Rose tangled in her bedsheets.

Grinning, she took a quick picture of the cap, edited it in a meme generator to put a fake ransom note on it, and sent the picture to Rose. Chuckling to herself, she sat back to begin her work, but instead, she ended up doing a little daydreaming about their shower encounter.

When her phone dinged, taking her out of the detour her thoughts had gone on, a quick look told her that she was late for her meeting with Mikayla. How had she let herself zone out like that? She chided herself about how this was exactly what she was trying to avoid by not letting a relationship distract her from her goals.

She also had to give herself a break, she reminded herself. Like a new toy, the excitement of it would play out. She was about to text Mikayla something about falling asleep, but the sound of someone climbing her front steps saved her from the lie. Good thing. She hated to lie.

"Knock knock."

Shia looked up to see her neighbor Alice and her seemingly perpetual smile. She felt better at once. "Hey, Alice. What's shakin'?"

Alice did a little shimmy. "That would be everything these days. I try to keep it all strapped down, but today's a work-from-home day, with my boss in an off-site meeting all day, so I forwent my daily struggle into foundation garments."

Shia was used to Alice's silly humor, so the words didn't shock her when coming from the normally proper older woman, but she really couldn't tell the difference, other than how much more relaxed Alice looked. And younger. When Shia had discovered that Alice was only in her late forties, she'd been shocked. For as much joking around as Alice did, she was a bit of a prude and always displayed good manners. She also went to bed early and held to her regimen of daily walks. She was a creature of habit. But it was mostly her bulky glasses, her always upswept hair, and more than anything, the way she dressed that gave her the air of someone much older.

Shia had long suspected it was because she was religious and worked at the mission, and that meant she carried around a heavy religious air, and when Shia had finally asked Gem about it, she found she wasn't far off. Because the rumor was that Alice had been a nun at one time, which made sense. Shia had tried several times to get her to talk about it, but although Alice had never said specifically that she didn't want to talk about it, she'd still changed the subject. So they'd never discussed it.

"Let it all hang loose, Alice, my friend."

"Loose as a goose," Alice said, busting out an impressive dance move, even in her comfortable shoes and slacks. She often showed her enthusiasm with a pump of a fist or a little dance, always surprising, given her appearance, but recently, the little dances looked slicker.

"You know, Alice, you've got some pretty fly dance moves. Are they giving lessons up at the church these days?"

"Oh, heavens, no!" Alice put a hand against her cheek. "I'm learning them on TikTok. One of the influencers I follow said it's almost impossible to be sad when you're dancing, and lo and behold, it's true."

"You watch TikTok?" Shia didn't spend much time online, but she'd checked the video site out. For her, it was mostly extreme sports and animal videos.

Alice nodded. "I do. I even have my own channels."

"You make them, too?"

"I do. I posted a couple of videos of the waves hitting the rocks at the end of the jetty, and the ASMR crowd seemed to like them, so I mostly make those. My other channel is where I do TikTok trends. I was in a rut and wanted to find something new and fun to do."

"That's awesome. I'm glad you're having fun with it."

"You should post some videos of you surfing. I bet people would love to watch that."

Shia waved her hand. "People can watch the videos taken by the competition videographers."

"Those are good, too, but people really like authentic content."

"Authentic content?" This was a facet of Alice she'd never expected to see.

Alice nodded. "Overly produced stuff is a turn-off. I took some videos of you at the last competition. Do you mind if I post those?"

"Sure." Shia was cool if Alice's ten followers enjoyed it.

"Thank you. I came over here for another reason. Based on the rent issue yesterday, I talked to the grant manager, and they have decided to make the grant permanent. You won't have to worry about your rent or utilities if you live here."

"That's very generous. But hopefully, I won't need it much longer. I don't even know what the criteria for receiving it is. Who do I inform if I don't need it anymore?" She'd never expected the help, let alone for it to go for longer than a year or so. Four years later, the mission was still helping her, and she'd never had to provide a bit of documentation proving her need. They'd been more than generous, and for a long time, she'd been looking forward to telling them she could pay her own rent. She'd even thought about buying her own unit. Maybe even one of the renovated ones in the back. It never crossed her mind to leave Oceana Place, the little cul-de-sac she currently lived on, but the units on the street were all rentals, except for the owner's house, and if she wanted to own, she'd need to move to a section of the community that let her buy. Either way, she could stay at Oceana. It was her home, her community. She couldn't imagine living anywhere else.

Alice shook her head. "It's permanent. There's no income threshold."

"I don't understand. I won't need it forever."

Alice looked uncomfortable.

Shia felt bad. And she didn't want to appear ungrateful for the generosity of the mission. "I mean, I'm very appreciative of the support, but someone else who needs it should get it. I wouldn't want to take assistance away from someone who needs it worse than me."

"Don't worry. You aren't taking it away from anyone else. Besides, the grant manager has already made the decision."

"I'm grateful, Alice. Is there anyone I can send a thank-you note to, at least?" She already knew the answer because she'd asked several times before.

"Nope. The donor still wants to remain anonymous, and they operate under the idea that—"

"It's Christlike to give without expectation of anything in return," Shia said along with her.

Well, she could respect the donor's wishes, even if she didn't understand the reasons behind them. Besides, not having the pressure of maintaining an income high enough to afford rent and utilities on her own freed her to concentrate on her career. An idea that seemed to be a repeating theme in her life these days.

Chapter Eight

Rose came home from work and was delighted to find her grandfather grilling out back in the garden. It was nice to see him cooking again now that he'd mostly recovered from the strokes that had recently put him in the hospital. Prior to the last major stroke, a series of mini-strokes that no one had been aware of had caused a pretty steep cognitive decline. It was great to see him back at things. He was probably the best cook in the family now that her grandmother was gone. She couldn't wait to see what he was making. It smelled delicious.

When he looked up and saw her, he waved with a pair of tongs.

She waved back. "Hey, Grampa, what's the lowdown?"

He looked down. "Currently, it would be my socks. I seem to have put on the quitters I keep meaning to throw out, but somehow, they always show back up in my sock drawer."

"Seeing as you're wearing sandals, you can take them off and toss them now. The garbage container is right behind you."

"I happened to watch a TikTok this week that deemed socks and sandals were solidly in fashion now."

"True. But I don't think they meant flip-flops. The strap between the toes kind of diminishes the cool factor." She didn't want to hurt his feelings, though, so she hurried to add: "But you do you, Grampa. Fashion should follow you, not the other way around."

"And that's why you're my favorite out of everyone in our family, Rosebud," he said as if he didn't say it to all of them.

"Don't feed his ego, Rose. He's already insufferable."

Rose jumped at the voice from behind her. She hadn't heard Gem's car pull up. When she turned, she saw why. Gem was on her bicycle. "He has every right to be proud of his appearance. He's the most handsome man in Oceana," she said. "Where's your car?"

"Mikayla's borrowing it. Hers is still in the shop, and she had a date with her sister." She looked at her watch. "She should be back any minute now."

Rose's grandfather pulled his phone from his back pocket. "I should probably cancel the call I put into the police about your stolen car. I saw it drive away an hour and a half ago. Since I saw you ride off on your bike this morning, I assumed crime had finally struck our little haven."

Gem frowned. "You called—"

"I'm kidding, Angel," he said using the nickname he'd always called her. "Maybe it's too early to joke about memory issues. I see how your face screws up when I can't find my glasses. I don't need to add to that."

"It's not too soon, Dad. You've always had a great sense of humor, and I missed it for a while there." She stored her bike in its usual place, gave Rose a side hug as she passed, and came up beside him, putting an arm around his waist.

Rose took it all in. Dinnertime had always been a hectic event at her parents' house. She'd loved it because she loved her family, but it was nice to come home to a less chaotic atmosphere. Someday, she hoped to have her own place, but for now, she enjoyed living with her grandfather and aunt. It didn't suck now that she knew Shia lived down the street, either.

Thinking about her brought up memories from that morning, sending a delicious shiver down Rose's back. What had happened in the shower had been on the forefront of her thoughts all day. Damn, the chemistry they had was off the charts. She'd say that it was probably the impulsiveness of their first time and the risk of being caught in the showers, but even before they'd ever touched, she'd felt a fire ignite at their first interaction. The magnetic force that had compelled her to go back, not once but twice, was strong evidence that there was a major force that drew them together.

God. When Shia's towel had fallen to the—

"Rose, have you heard a word we said?"

A surge of heat raced to her face as she worried that Gem and her grandfather knew what she'd been thinking. "Sorry. I was just thinking about…it doesn't matter. What did you say?"

Gem shook her head with a smile. "I was telling you the inspector called today and said she'd be out early next week to look at the remodeled units. She had my cell number, but I gave her yours for future projects."

Rose initially struggled to follow what Gem said as the effects of her thought tangent continued to stream through her. "That's great. Once we get the sign-off, we can list the rentals." There was something else she needed to say. "Oh yeah, I gave all the info to the listing agent. I'll give her the go-ahead to start showing them."

"You're really on top of things, Rose." Gem turned to her father. "I told you, she's one of the best things that ever happened to this place."

"Don't sell yourself short, Angel. Rosebud had a better trainer than you did."

Gem stepped out of his arm around her waist and placed her hands on her hips. "I said one of the best things."

He put his arm around her again. "I was teasing you, daughter. Your niece has big shoes to fill, and they aren't these glorified size-ten shower shoes," he said pointing to his feet. "But from the things my retired ears are hearing, I'm blessed to have such capable progeny looking after the great community of Oceana."

"Good save." Gem still looked miffed until she broke into laughter, and Rose was relieved she'd been faking her anger. She never wanted Gem to have reason to be angry with her. "What's for dinner? I missed lunch and could eat a…" Her eyes darted to the driveway, and she walked that way.

When Rose turned to see what had caught her attention, she saw Mikayla getting out of Gem's car at the end of the driveway, and she was talking to Shia. Part of Rose wanted to join them, but something made her stay where she was, as if her feet were glued to the garden walkway, even when all three started walking up the driveway. Shia carried her surfboard, probably on her way to the beach. Rose swallowed hard. No one had ever looked as hot in a wet suit as Shia. Her muscular legs, sun-kissed skin, and windblown hair would have appeared staged if Rose hadn't already had an up close and personal experience to know that Shia looked like that all the time, in or out of her surfing gear.

She shouldn't have thought about her out of her surfing gear because now that was all she could think about as Shia drew near.

"Hi, Mr. Helmstaad," Shia said but stopped beside Rose, who vibrated in response to the crackling air between them, even though there was still at least a foot between them. Shia stood her board up on its tail and hadn't yet made eye contact with Rose, but when she turned, her gaze was penetrating. "Hey, Rose."

Her stomach was a jumble of butterflies. She stared at Shia's unzipped wet suit and bikini top and couldn't think of anything to say. Her brain and parts of her body had completely short-circuited. No one else seemed to notice that she didn't answer, and after everyone said hello, Gem, Mikayla, and Shia talked to Rose's grandfather about what he was cooking. She lost track of the conversation and watched Shia through her lashes. Memories of that morning came back to her full force. Shia's penetrating glance returned to her often, and Rose couldn't look away. Eventually, Shia didn't look away either. Rose wondered if they were thinking about the same thing. She suspected so because Shia looked like she was undressing Rose with her eyes. Rose's entire body responded to the look with a hungry ache, and she caught her breath.

It wasn't until Shia glanced away with what seemed like a surprised expression that Rose had forgotten they weren't alone. Shia shook her head. "Sorry. I was daydreaming. What was the question?"

"Seems to be going around," teased Gem, glancing at Rose. "I was wondering if you'd like to have dinner with us."

"I was on the way down to the beach to get my afternoon session in." Shia shot what appeared to be a disappointed look at Mikayla.

Mikayla laughed. "Don't look at me with your sad eyes. You're the one who set up your training schedule. Tripp said it won't be ready for another hour and a half, anyway, so you'll be done by then."

Shia smiled, glancing at Rose, who felt it to her bones even after Shia returned her attention to Gem. "I'm totally in. Are you kidding? A real meal that isn't pizza? What are we having? Not that it matters."

Gem shook her head. "Must have been some daydream. My dad's been slow grilling tri-tip all afternoon. There's also rice, butternut squash, and asparagus."

"Rosebud's mother dropped off groceries earlier," Rose's grandfather said with an exaggerated huff. "She's convinced Gem and I will feed Rose nothing but grilled cheese and soup. I'm not going to correct her if it means free grocery delivery. Plus, she brought homemade dulce de leche cake. We'll have that for dessert."

"Yes, I love her cakes," said Gem, pumping a fist. "I don't blame her, though. You actually did eat nothing but grilled cheese and soup for almost a year, Dad. And everyone knows I don't cook."

"Burning popcorn in the microwave is technically cooking," Shia said. “Anyway, I better get down to the water so I can get back sooner rather than later.” Shia ducked to avoid Gem’s teasing punch, and Rose’s chest tightened to see a new facet of her. She looked forward to seeing many more of her facets. There was an entire person to get to know beyond the bedroom…and pool house.

Shia pulled her board under her arm again and smiled at all of them before she left. Rose was sure the intensity of her glance had become a tractor beam when it landed on her because she had to force her body not to lean toward Shia until her eyes moved away.

After that, Rose didn’t know what to do with herself. She tried to help her grandfather with dinner, but he’d already prepared everything. It was just a matter of putting the veggies on the grill for the last half hour. He also insisted on setting the patio table himself, leaving it up to her to figure out what to do until Shia got back. She busied herself with cleaning Chad’s cage and taking a shower. With half an hour to spare, she went back down to the garden with a book and stretched out on a chaise lounge to read, but her thoughts kept returning to Shia. So much so, she had to keep rereading the same paragraph. Finally, she gave up and simply watched the gulls gliding in the wind, people walking on the beach, and the tiny forms of the surfers floating past the breakers. She couldn’t tell which one was Shia from the distance. With the sun sinking behind them, she could only discern their silhouettes against the darkening water and the colors of the sunset starting to stain the horizon.

Her grandfather sat at the foot of her chair. “What thoughts have you so far away, Rosebud?”

She’d been thinking about her reaction to Shia in her wet suit, which had led her to think about that morning, and then, naturally, the events of the previous night captured her imagination. There was no way she was going to tell him any of that. She sat up, putting her book on the small teak table beside her. “The lovely sunset, of course.”

He looked toward the ocean. “Ah. This beauty never ceases to amaze me. After last year, I will never take another sunset for granted. It was one of the things I was grateful to see again when I got out of the hospital.” He turned to her. “Never put off for later the things that stir your soul, Rosebud. Listen to your grandfather. The wisdom that we ancient ones gain through painful lessons is a gift.”

“You sound like Yoda.”

He shook his head with a chuckle. “Yoda would have said, ‘A gift of wisdom is the painful lesson we ancient ones gain,’” he said in a terrible Yoda impersonation and then waved his hand. "Or something to that effect. I'm more of a *Galaxy Quest* or *Spaceballs* guy."

She had no idea what *Galaxy Quest* or *Spaceballs* were, but she suspected they were old movies. She didn't have a chance to ask because Shia, Mikayla, and Gem were back. As nice as it was to see all of them again, it was Shia, freshly showered and wearing short cutoffs and a tank top, who took her breath away. When Shia took a seat at the table next to her, she was elated. And nervous.

"Dinner is finished grilling, the table is set, and all of my favorite Oceana people are with me. Gem, could you turn on the twinkle lights now that it's getting dark? Rosebud, can you get the glasses and both pitchers of sangria from the refrigerator? One is nonalcoholic. Doctor's orders for me, unfortunately. But the other is fully leaded."

"You even made sangria? Dad, have I mentioned how happy I am that you…" Gem rubbed her eyes. "I'm gonna pop into the garage and get those lights turned on."

Rose watched Mikayla follow Gem into the garage, no doubt to make sure she was okay. Gem still had a hard time talking about how she'd almost lost her dad and how difficult the last four years had been while watching his mental health deteriorate. Having him back, almost better than before, was a gift the entire family was grateful for. It was almost overwhelming. Between this and the electric air Shia's presence had brought to the gathering, Rose was at a loss for words. She wondered if her silence was obvious. She turned to get the sangria to hide her teary eyes, blaming her emotions on a lack of sleep.

"Can I help?" Shia might have picked up on it because she walked with Rose into the house without waiting for an answer.

"Thanks. I need both hands for the pitchers," Rose managed to get out, her mind flashing to how Shia's hands had touched her. She wasn't sure if being on the edge of desire was better than being close to tears.

As if reading her mind, Shia shut the door to the kitchen and drew Rose to her, wrapping her arms around Rose's waist. Shia's warm hands beneath her midriff shirt seared their imprint into her skin. The kiss was unexpected and too brief, but the heat it shot throughout Rose's body was unmeasurable. When Shia drew away, she didn't remove her arms. Rose noticed both of their breathing turned slightly ragged.

"I like your idea of help," Rose managed to say when her brain recovered.

"I figured you could use a couple more hands. The lips were an afterthought," Shia said, giving a shaky laugh.

"An afterthought?"

"Could you tell I was dying to do that from the moment I saw you this afternoon?"

"I knew there was something going on behind those intense looks."

"You seem to inspire something primal in me."

The words inflamed Rose's desire. She knew what Shia's primal energy was like in action. "It's definitely a mutual inspiration. I've been having a hard time putting words together when you're near. I'm worried I'll say or do something inappropriate in front of the others."

"I noticed you were a little quiet," Shia said as she nuzzled her neck.

"They'll notice how long we've been gone soon." It came out of her sounding like a question because her voice grew higher along with her need.

"Can you come over after this?"

"I might be free." Rose's breath caught at the unexpected invitation. She wished dinner was already over. "What did you have in mind?"

"That's where the primal thing comes in. My mind has nothing to do with it."

Rose watched Shia's eyes drop to her mouth. She tried to respond, even opened her mouth, but her words left her again. It didn't matter because Shia's mouth connected with hers. After that words weren't necessary. She had no idea how she'd get through dinner, she was so eager to find out what Shia's body was going to tell her when they were alone.

CHAPTER NINE

The crescent moon cast a silver outline over everything, causing Shia to marvel over individual grass, a nearby magnolia blossom, even a garden snail inching its way across the sidewalk. Her senses were dialed all the way up as she waited for Rose to meet her in the little park next to Mikayla's house. It was funny how quickly Brandi's house had become Mikayla's after the two had swapped for the summer. She wondered how long it would take her to go back to calling it Brandi's house when Brandi got back.

Shia missed her. She wished they could sit in the light of the seahorse tank and talk about her mixed feelings about Rose. How seeing Rose erased any resolutions she'd come to about keeping it casual. Even when they weren't alone. Like when she'd seen Rose standing next to her grandfather that afternoon. Then there was all the emotion that had filled her from seeing Rose interact with her family. It had stirred something else entirely in her. She wanted some of that, and with Rose right next to her, she almost had it. The longing had surprised her. She usually felt included with them. But she wanted more than that.

Despite her thoughts, with the scent of the star jasmine on the damp evening air, it was hard to be anything but joyful being outside, especially since she was waiting for a beautiful woman. They'd agreed to meet at the park after Rose's grandfather went to bed. Gem had gone home with Mikayla shortly after dinner, so it wasn't too long after that Shia received the *coast is clear* text. It had been a long time since she had to sneak around to see a woman. Actually, a girl, seeing as she had been with Charlotte when she was still living in the group home. Romances between inmates, as the housemates jokingly called them, had been strictly forbidden. But being forbidden was exactly what had made them so exciting. Shia had only been with Charlotte twice before Charlotte had been released back to her mother, who'd gotten her parental rights back. The whole experience had almost made her glad her mother was dead. Seeing the mix of anticipation and fear Charlotte had about returning to a life that had brought her to the home in the first place was eye-opening.

Why was she thinking about that? Easy. Getting involved with someone always resulted in pain.

"Hey, sexy."

Rose's voice startled her. She hadn't realized she'd fallen into memories she hadn't thought about in years. She didn't spend a lot of time thinking of the past. The future was more interesting.

Rose stood before her, smelling better than the jasmine. Different memories bubbled up with the happy churn in Shia's stomach. Memories featuring the woman before her, who smelled and tasted like the sweetest thing she'd ever experienced.

"What perfume are you wearing?"

Rose grinned, and her perfect teeth almost glowed in the moonlight. In fact, with her dark hair and tanned skin, the white cropped tank top with the white overall shorts stood out under the moon that acted like a black light, emphasizing the lighter colors all around them.

Rose took her hands and pulled her from her perch on the picnic table. "It's coconut vanilla sugar scrub."

Shia threw her head back and gave a little moan as she stood. She wrapped her fingers around the straps of Rose's overalls and smiled. "Thinking about you rubbing coconut vanilla sugar scrub all over yourself is yet another shower fantasy to add to the one you gave me this morning."

Rose wrapped her hands over Shia's and leaned forward. "I thought about what we did in the shower while I rubbed it all over me."

"Did you…" Shia wasn't usually shy with her words, but asking Rose if she'd touched herself seemed too intimate, even after all the things they'd already done.

"I thought about it, but I knew that it wouldn't be the same, so I got out of the shower hoping you'd help me out sometime soon. Abracadabra, here we are."

They started walking toward Shia's house. She had considered asking Rose if she wanted to walk on the beach before going back to her place, but the idea of helping Rose get off set her internal navigation for the nearest private location, and she had to force herself to walk slower. She looked at her through her eyelashes. "Are you still turned on?"

Rose squeezed her hand. "I have been all day."

"Me too. I'm glad Gem asked me to dinner tonight."

They'd reached the steps to Shia's house when Rose stopped walking. "What would you have done if she hadn't?"

Shia pulled Rose toward her by the straps of her overalls. Being one step higher, she looked down and got lost in the dark depths of Rose's expressive eyes. "I'm not sure."

"What do you usually do in the evenings? I mean, on the rare occasions you're alone?"

So Rose thought she was usually busy, probably dating. "I'm almost always alone."

"Liar."

"I don't lie. It's kind of my thing. I try hard to be honest."

Rose examined her. "When was your last date?"

Her stomach tensed. Now was the time for the explanation about why she didn't date. She always worried about how the conversation might go. It needed to happen, though. By now, she should've had a speech prepared.

"You're taking too long. You don't think I'll like the answer." Rose looked apprehensive.

Shia ran her hands up and down the straps of Rose's overalls. "The answer is, I can't remember the last time I dated someone."

Rose's apprehensive expression remained. "I thought you said you don't lie."

"I don't date."

Now, Rose's expression was one of confusion. "What does that mean?"

Shia stared at her hands holding Rose's straps and released them. She was beginning to wonder what it meant, too. "Let's go inside."

"I'm getting a weird vibe here," Rose said before following her. When they entered the house, she remained standing by the door. The only light Shia had left on was a large salt lamp on a table in the corner beside the couch. The soft light bathed Rose in a warm glow but made her eyes look haunted. Shia wasn't sure how the mood had changed so dramatically, let alone how to fix it.

"Do you want something to drink?" It came out hollow, even though she'd tried for light. "It's the sangria. I dehydrate easily, leaving my throat dry. I don't have any alcohol here, but I have tons of soda leftover from the last bonfire."

Rose nodded, although Shia noticed she'd crossed her arms and was holding her shoulders. A very protective stance.

Shia cleared her throat and scanned the contents of her refrigerator. "Caffeine or no caffeine?"

"Just water, please."

Shia got them both a glass of water. They took them to the couch, sitting stiffly as Shia again wished she'd figured out how to explain her reasons for not dating because right now, her usual spiel about commitment to her career was feeling a little weak. In the meantime, Rose still had one arm crossed as she nearly hugged the glass of water to herself. She looked so small tucked up like that, and it hurt Shia's heart knowing she was causing it.

"So…" Shia didn't know what to say next. She knew it was time to draw the line at casual, so why was she finding the words so hard?

"You don't date. Are you married or something?"

Shia laughed. "No."

Rose adjusted her position so that she nearly faced her. "It's weird that you brought that up right now. I mean, after giving me sex eyes all night at dinner and inviting me over. I wouldn't call what we're doing dating, but are you about to tell me we can't continue or something? Cuz it feels kind of like you are."

"Sex eyes?" She was stalling, not at all sure what she wanted anymore. Except she did. She wanted more of Rose. It was simple. But not really. God, she was all over the place in her head right now.

"Don't even pretend not to know. You were watching an X-rated movie every time you looked at me."

"I was not." Rose smirked, forcing Shia to admit it was a lie to say that she hadn't been imagining Rose naked all through dinner. She looked at her hands. "You're right. Kind of. It was hard to be right next to you and not touch you. Exactly like it is right now with you all over on the other side of the couch like that. All huddled and closed off."

Rose put her glass of water on the coffee table. "Sorry. The sudden shift caught me off guard."

"I like you. I like what we're doing. I want to continue, but I felt like I needed to set expectations."

"Expectations? It's been, what? Thirty hours or so since we met? What kind of expectations could either of us have?"

Shia snorted, feeling like she might have been reading way too much into it. "Okay, so here's the thing. I'm an all-in person. There's nothing in the middle. It's either one way or the other. I'm like that with anything I'm passionate about. And for the last six years, it's been all about making it as a surfer. I never really had anything that was just mine. Nothing that made me stand out. Surfing gave that to me. In the foster system, I was a number in a database. After my grandma died, I was placed and…" She paused for a moment as painful memories tried to invade. Now was not the time to deal with them. No time was really a good time to deal with them. She pushed them down and tried to find a way to proceed without getting into the specifics. "Let's just say I know firsthand that some of the stereotypical horror stories of what can happen in the system are true."

She felt a hand on her leg. Feeling vulnerable, she needed the comfort it gave. She let it sink into her.

"Lucky for me, I had a good caseworker who was really on top of things. She always knew when things weren't right. More often than not, she kept them from getting as bad as they might have gotten. Mostly." Interestingly, the worst of it had occurred before she actually entered the system, when she'd been taken in by her uncle. Her mother's brother. Her grandmother's son. There was a reason Shia's grandmother rarely mentioned him, and she couldn't remember ever meeting him before the day she'd arrived at his house with a suitcase, her school backpack, and a deep numbness that had mercifully engulfed her for several months after her grandmother's death. It had made her feel like she'd been floating outside of her own body that somehow continued to breathe and move as if she were actually doing it on purpose.

The numbness had allowed her to remain mercifully unaffected by the things her uncle had done to her. The things she only vaguely understood. She'd simply closed her eyes, and because she hadn't been in her body, the knowledge of it was more like a story she'd heard about some other girl. An awful story, for sure, but it didn't really have anything to do with her if she didn't think about it. So she didn't.

Thankfully, she'd only lived with her uncle for six weeks before her case worker had placed her with other families until an opening came up in a group home. "In the group home, I was one of two dozen kids or so at any given time. So when Lance left me his surfboard when he joined the Marines, it became my prized possession and started me on my current path."

She remembered the sparkle of joy that had overcome her the day her case worker had given her the surfboard. It looked almost brand-new. The fact that Lance had barely acknowledged her while he was still in the home was overshadowed by the overwhelming gratitude she had for his parting gift. "In a way, surfing saved my life. I'm pretty sure my path would have been incredibly different had I remained the way I was, a number in a database. Before then, I'd never thought about life beyond the system."

Now, life in the system seemed like a different lifetime. She shuddered. "Anyway, that's all boring. Hopefully, it explains why surfing is so important to me, why I'm an all-or-nothing person. The thing is, I don't know if I have it in me to have two all-or-nothing focuses in my life. That's where the dating thing comes in. I don't do relationships. It would only end in disappointment because my focus is always on surfing. I won't be a professional surfer forever. But while I am, I want to take it as far as it will take me. I'll have time to put into a relationship later, but I'm in my surfing prime right now. There's little time beyond that for much else." Shia felt a sense of release getting it all out, although some anxiety remained. It mattered to her that Rose didn't take it personally.

Rose looked thoughtful. "How do you know what we're doing is bound for a relationship?"

Shia was a little stunned at the question. "I guess I don't."

"Again, we've known each other about thirty hours. During that time, I've had some of the most amazing sex in my life."

"Me too."

"We have chemistry."

"We absolutely do."

"I won't deny that I like you."

"I like you, too."

Rose scooted closer to her. "I like sex with you."

A bolt of arousal pierced Shia's chest. "Like isn't a strong enough word for how I feel about having sex with you."

The last response elicited a smile from Rose, easing some of Shia's anxiety. The confident and open Rose was back. And those two qualities, when combined, struck a major chord in her. She wasn't proud of herself for it, but insecurity in others usually made her want to run. It wasn't hard to figure out why. She'd seen an enormous amount of trauma-induced insecurity in the group home and how it had brought out the worst in some kids. Most often, it was aimed at the weakest of the bunch. Insecure foster kids became targets. Everyone had their own issues to deal with, so the insecure kids had to toughen up if they wanted to survive. Shia wasn't proud of herself for not always standing up for them, but that was how it was. Because of this, it was interesting that Rose's insecurity didn't make her want to run. Just the opposite. She wanted to protect her.

Rose nodded. "To channel my mother, the emergency room psychiatric nurse, it sounds like we're setting some good boundaries. Do you want to toss aside the good stuff we have on the chance that it will interfere with your career? And speaking about focusing on careers, I'm also trying to establish myself here. As the property manager of Oceana. This is a dream job for me. I can't afford to get sidetracked, either."

"I guess setting aside the good stuff would be kind of stupid." Shia hadn't considered that Rose might have her own reasons for not wanting to pursue a relationship. She also hadn't considered how easily Rose could get her to change her mind.

Rose scrunched up her nose. "That enthusiastic response was an enormous ego boost."

"I mean, hell no! That would be insane." Shia leaned over and scooped Rose toward her. Rose giggled and helped by scooching when the couch cover proved to be a hindrance to smooth sliding.

"Who knows? It could fizzle out in a week, anyway," Rose said when she seemed able to control her giggles.

Shia wanted to say she seriously doubted it but didn't want to examine what would happen if it didn't. For now, she wanted to keep doing what they were doing because Rose's questions had not only reminded her how good they were at sexing each other up but had given her hope that they might be able to keep it casual.

Rose put a hand over Shia's, stopping it from inching its way farther under the bib of her overalls. "Gem is always talking about boundaries. It's a therapist thing. Why don't we agree that if either of us can't deal with something we list now, we agree to walk away?"

It was as if Rose had read her mind. It could work. More importantly, Shia wanted it to work. Having an agreement made her feel better. "Do we have to set them right now?"

"Actually, I have something better in mind right now." A glimmer in Rose's eyes told Shia exactly what it was.

She kissed her, and every bit of her body responded to Rose's soft lips and hungry mouth. She stood, pulling Rose with her, and led her through her dim living room and into the bedroom, slipping the straps of Rose's overalls down her arms, letting the garment slide to her ankles. Rose stepped out of it and her flip-flops at the same time. When they got to her bed, Rose fell back, and Shia couldn't help uttering an appreciative hum at how beautiful Rose looked lying on her white duvet in nothing but a pair of black panties and her cropped tank top.

"Fuck. You are so beautiful," Shia said pulling off her own T-shirt, unclasping her bra, and pulling down her cutoffs and panties, all in one continuous motion before getting on the bed on her hands and knees and hovering over Rose's prone body.

Rose ran her hands along Shia's body, eliciting a barrage of delicious body quakes. Shia wanted her with every cell, some cells more than others. Something had shifted during their conversation. The agreement about boundaries was part of it. Having acknowledged her fear and knowing Rose understood was huge. The shift was bigger than that, though. She felt closer to Rose. She hadn't held back anything sexual with her, but she sensed there was now an emotional closeness that hadn't been there before. Part of her wondered if this was the thing she'd wanted to avoid. The idea came and went as she helped Rose off with her bra and panties, and it was as if she was seeing her in a new way.

Shia kissed Rose and rolled out of bed. "I need some water. Do you want anything?"

"Water would be nice."

She quickly poured the water and went back to the bedroom. When she entered, Rose wasn't there, but a line of light shone under the bathroom door. She got into bed and sat cross-legged, sipping her water, wondering what was next. A glimpse at her phone told her it was after one. She had to get up in less than five hours for work. She was ready to stay up all night if it meant more sex with Rose, though. The more she learned about Rose's body, the more of it she wanted. It was like a drug, only it got better every time. She thought about sleeping with her. Real sleeping. The kind where they could hold each other and wake up in the morning and have breakfast together, and…no. No. No. What was she thinking? That wasn't casual. That was what people in relationships did.

"Hey, there. Whatcha thinking about? You look like you remembered the oven was still on when you were already on the airplane."

"Huh?" Shia looked up to see Rose standing at the foot of the bed.

"You look worried."

Shia smiled but took a sip from her water to take the focus from her eyes because she knew the smile didn't reach them. What was she doing? "It's past my bedtime."

"Yeah. Mine, too. I'm usually in bed by ten and up by six," Rose said.

"Pretty much the same for me."

"We're going to be dragging in the morning. At least it's Friday. I mostly do paperwork."

"I have my morning swim and meet with a couple of sponsors about the competition this weekend."

Rose pushed her hair back with one hand. Shia couldn't believe how beautiful she was. But she could tell Rose was uncomfortable trying to read the situation. She wanted to coax her back into bed, soothe her insecurity, ask her to stay the night, suggest that they start their days a little later than they normally would…no. No. No. She rolled out of bed again and went to her. She ran her hands along her arms, and Rose seemed to relax. Shia kissed her, feeling the passion rise again. It was so easy being with her.

"What do you want to do?" she asked.

"You mean this minute?" Rose flashed a mischievous grin.

"You sounded worried about being tired tomorrow."

Rose took a moment before responding but didn't break eye contact. Shia couldn't help but think she was trying to figure out what the right answer was. But what *was* the right answer? Shia was torn between doubling down on keeping things casual and going with the flow. They hadn't set the boundaries yet, so it was tempting to do what felt good now and do the checking in later. Part of her knew it was trouble to already be negotiating with herself. This was exactly why she needed to keep her mind on her goals and not let her libido chip away at her focus. She'd already missed a meeting with Mikayla because she couldn't resist Rose.

"I suppose I should go home." Rose looked away.

Shia must have taken too long to respond. Or maybe her expression had given away her thoughts. Either way, Rose looked disappointed. Shia was, too, but she couldn't deny there was also some relief that it wasn't her making the decision. It wasn't what Shia wanted, but it was the best choice.

CHAPTER TEN

Between notifications of work orders, various vendor calls, and her mother choosing today to get a head start on her holiday gift list even though the holidays were still months away, Rose's phone wouldn't stop ringing. She absolutely had to get payroll done today, so she silenced it to concentrate. Most of the process was automated, but it was only the second time she'd done it by herself, causing her to double- and triple-check everything before she hit the Submit button. It all checked out, so she said a silent prayer to an entity she wasn't sure she believed in and smashed the Enter button. A silly self-congratulatory chair dance was in order when no alerts or error messages followed, but she barely took a breath before she dove into accounts payable.

Initially, the paperwork aspect of property management had been the last thing she'd looked forward to, but once she got into it, she liked it. She had an aptitude for it, especially accounting; surprising because she'd specifically avoided it in school. There was a sense of accomplishment when she finished, whether it was payroll, prioritizing work orders, or submitting certain files to satisfy all the intricacies of business ownership. If she'd known how interesting it was, she might have gone a different way in school. Maybe she wouldn't have dropped out both times. The thought took a little of the shame away for not having finished her degree.

"Hey there, Rosebud. What has you wrinkling your forehead like that?"

Rose looked up from her laptop to see her grandfather standing in the doorway of the office cleaning his glasses on the tail of his flannel shirt. "Just working on the books, Grampa. Finished payroll and now I'm paying the bills."

"I thought we had an accountant for all that."

Gem had told her that the accounting situation had been one of the first things she'd updated after taking over management of Oceana. It was after her father had instructed her to take all the shoeboxes of receipts and invoices he'd "filed" to his accountant, Swivel Hips Conroy, one of his old military buddies. If the name failed to instill trust in her, the bar-office with its dim lights and dark-paneled walls, heavy with the smell of ancient cigarettes, spilled beer, and another dusky scent that translated to Gem as "old man" definitely did.

Gem had explained that she continued to pay Swivel Hips all his accounting fees to submit the forms to the proper agencies, even after she'd updated the process to mostly digital. Technically, he was still their accountant, but he was under the impression that he was still supporting his old friend.

"We do, Grampa. I just approve the hours and look at where the expenses are going." She pointed at a specific line item, even though she knew he couldn't see it from the doorway. "Like the free Wi-Fi we give to the residents. I'm pretty sure we can get a much better deal and higher speeds with a different carrier, so I'm going to look into it and let you and Gem know what I find." The power bill would be next, along with a few other things she planned to dig into.

His eyes gleamed and crinkled at the edges. "I knew you were going to do a fantastic job here, Rosebud. I'm so proud of you, but I'm especially happy that you seem to have found something you enjoy here at Oceana."

His words settled like a warm hug around her heart. But there was something he wasn't saying. She could feel it. As if he still had reservations. She wasn't sure how she knew, but she did. For now, though, she was happy to be the cause of his pride. She just had to keep proving herself to him. "I have, Grampa. I'm glad to be here."

"Well, don't do what Gem did and let it become your whole life. A job is a job. Always remember, you have a life outside of it."

Strange words from her grandpa, who'd been happiest when he was working. "I'll remember."

He slid his glasses on. "I love you, Rosie."

"I love you, too."

She listened to his footsteps until the front door opened and closed. It was about the time he went on one of his daily walks around Oceana. She expected that he'd bring back a list of things that needed attention. When he'd first given her one of his lists, she'd thought it was his way of saying that she wasn't getting to everything he expected her to get to, but Gem had told her he'd always done it, and she realized it was his way of staying involved. Each day, the lists got shorter as she learned to see Oceana through his eyes.

She mulled over their conversation and glanced at her phone, noticing she'd missed a text from Shia. A confusing tornado of emotions whipped up inside her. The night before had been amazing, up until Shia had gotten out of bed to get a glass of water. They'd spent hours enjoying each other, but when Shia had come back, a wall had gone up, giving Rose a strong sense that Shia had wanted her to leave. To avoid having to be asked, which would have been humiliating, she'd made an excuse about having to get up early that was actually true. She was pretty sure she hadn't displayed any of the disappointment she'd felt, but it was an uncomfortable end to an otherwise mind-blowing evening of sex and connection. Agreeing to be casual had lowered some barriers between them…but, evidently, not all of them.

When she'd left, she experienced an emptiness she couldn't describe. Sure, she'd said that she was good with keeping their… whatever it was, a casual thing, but in reality, it wasn't at all what she wanted, even though she wasn't sure what she wanted. What she did know was that the strength of her feelings was a little scary, so it was probably good to slow her roll. When she'd said she needed to focus on her job, she'd meant it, but she didn't think a real relationship would get in the way. It was only because she cared for Shia that she let her believe they were on the same page. Kind of like the accounting thing. It was what a person did for people they cared about.

Maybe it was the mixed signals: Shia inviting her over after leveling meaningful glances at her all night before declaring she couldn't offer anything but casual. In fact, Rose was pretty sure Shia had been about to tell her they couldn't see each other anymore. The confusing thing was, she was certain that wasn't what Shia wanted. Confusing was actually an understatement. However, agreeing to something in-between had felt like a win. Whatever they had sure as hell didn't feel casual, not since the first time, and even then, something much more than casual had been written in every move, every touch, every orgasm they'd given each other that day. What they had was fucking incredible.

But Rose tried not to read anything into it. They enjoyed each other. They fit together. Everything about them complemented each other. However, Rose couldn't take anything for granted, not that she had been. At least not until she'd come out of the bathroom and found

Shia all closed off. That hadn't felt good. Not at all. And she didn't want to feel that way again.

So with equal amounts of apprehension and anticipation, she opened the text. It was another picture of her hat. This time, it was placed on the salt lamp. *Let me know when you want to visit your hat again. I had fun last night.*

More confusion. She sighed. *It looks good on the lamp. I had fun, too.*

You should see it in person. Maybe even tonight?

Rose leaned back and spotted her grandfather's fedora sitting on the chair next to the desk. She put it on, tipped it to the side, snapped a picture, and sent it to Shia. *I found a new hat.*

It looks phenomenal on you, but I don't think it matches the work shirt.

It is a little too snazzy, isn't it? Rose dropped the hat back.

I have an idea. Do you have time for a coffee break? I'm dragging today. For good reasons of which you are one.

The last part caused desire to swirl within her, but Rose didn't know how to respond. She wanted to see Shia, but she didn't want a repeat of the closed-off Shia. *What did you have in mind?*

Do you know the Seaside Café?

She knew it well, and against her better judgment, Rose agreed. They'd only met two days ago, had spent a large portion of the time since in each other's company, and had had sex on three different occasions. This did not seem like a casual situation. Yet she couldn't find the strength to be the one to apply the brakes.

Shia met her on the street outside of her house, and they began the short walk to the café. Aside from photos online, Rose hadn't seen Shia with her hair down, except in the shower. A shiver rushed through her at the memory. Thick and golden hair down, blowing in the breeze, paired with cutoffs and a white V-neck T-shirt with the sleeves cut off, Shia looked like she'd walked off the page of *Surfer Magazine*, a look that had always appealed to Rose.

"I can feel you staring at me," Shia said without looking at her.

"You're beautiful. I'm sure you get it all the time."

Shia smiled and looked at her feet. "Stop."

"I'm not kidding. Everyone we pass does a double take at you."

Shia gaped at her. "The double takes are for you. Don't even try to act like you don't know it."

"You're delusional. You're the one who needs to stop now."

Shia stopped in her tracks, grabbing her hand. The motion was abrupt, making Rose catch her breath. The serious expression on Shia's face intensified everything she was feeling. "You are the most beautiful person I've ever seen. On the surface and within. You have a presence. Everything about you draws people to you. I felt it the second we met. There's no way you don't know that."

Rose was stunned by the passion in Shia's voice. She appreciated the compliment, but it was as though Shia was trying to convince her because maybe if she didn't, the consequences would be devastating.

Rose knew she was pretty. She had good genes. Her mother looked like Sophia Loren, but she had nothing on Shia. Her allure wasn't solely in her appearance. It was the whole package. Shia embodied everything Rose loved about life. "I was talking about you. I have a hard time not looking at you, sinking into your essence, getting lost in your eyes." She smoothed Shia's hair away from her face. While Shia didn't look away, her cheeks turned pink. Devastatingly cutely pink.

"Thank you."

Rose rested her hand along her cheek. "Thank you right back."

Shia took her hand, gave it a quick kiss, and threaded their fingers together. They started walking again. It had been a long time since Rose had held hands with another adult. It felt good. Before she knew it, they'd arrived at the coffee shop.

"Do you come here often?" Shia asked, holding the door open for Rose after they climbed the front steps of the old Victorian-style house that had been home to many businesses over the years but had most recently been converted into a coffee shop.

Rose smiled at the phrase that had to be the tritest pickup line ever. Shia didn't seem to notice. The familiar scent that wafted out when the door opened was comforting. "You could say so. I worked here off and on for years until less than two months ago, when I took the property manager job at Oceana. I never saw you here. I would have remembered." They joined the line of customers. Rose didn't recognize the two baristas behind the counter.

"I've only been here a few times. Mikayla is an addict and likes to have meetings here." Shia put a hand to the side of her mouth and stage-whispered, "I have a confession. I don't like coffee. I've tried and tried, but I can't make myself like it."

Rose laughed. "Why did you suggest coming here?"

"It's the closest place I could think of."

"I could have gone to your place. Or you could have..." Rose watched Shia raise her eyebrows. "Yeah. Probably not the best idea." She laughed again and noted to herself that they laughed a lot together.

Shia leaned close. "We don't usually keep our clothes on for very long when we're alone."

Rose felt her face flush and saw Shia's neck turn that cute pink again, although her eyes held a roguish sparkle. "True."

When they arrived at the register, Rose ordered a simple drip coffee with cream and sugar, and Shia ordered a lime Italian soda. When their drinks were ready, Rose took her upstairs where it was quieter. Her favorite table by one of the windows that overlooked the beach was free. "Gem told me that you and Mikayla swim the jetties in the morning. Did you go today?"

Shia took a sip and nodded. "I managed to drag myself out of bed. I really thought about telling Mikayla I wasn't up to it, but she'd ask why and, well, you know."

They'd never talked about keeping their…whatever it was…a secret, but she wondered why Shia didn't want to talk about them. It was probably best. Neither of them had indicated that they knew each other at dinner the night before, either, which was mostly true. In some ways, they knew each other intimately, but in most, they didn't know each other at all. "Yeah. It was a little hard getting out of bed. Chad doesn't let me sleep past seven, anyway."

"Chad?"

"My rat."

Shia put her drink down. "You have a pet rat?"

Rose pulled her screen saver up on her phone. "That's Chad. He's cool. Very smart and kind."

"I don't think I've ever known anyone who had one."

"Some people have a problem with them. I sort of did, too, until I met Chad."

"I've just never seen one up close. Harper, my neighbor, has a cat. He's pretty cool, but he's sort of shy so I haven't really held him or anything. I occasionally pet one of the residents' dogs. Oh, and there's Brandi's seahorses. I really love them."

Rose had a hard time processing it. "You've never had a pet?"

"My grandma was allergic, and they don't let you have them in the group home."

Rose couldn't imagine. She'd always had dogs as a kid. Her parents had two labs and two rescue cats now. "I'm sorry. That was insensitive of me."

"Don't be sorry. I'll bet we have a lot of differences between us." Shia shrugged.

The differences didn't seem to get in the way of the blistering hot sex. "Well, now you know I have a rat named Chad."

"And you know I don't like coffee."

Rose pursed her lips. "I have to be honest, I can't help but judge you for that."

Shia laughed. "It seems to be a touchy subject for some. Tell me more things about yourself."

"Me? I'm boring."

Shia leaned forward. "You are far from boring."

The way she held her gaze was intense. Rose wanted to be right back in bed with her, unrestrained, feeling everything without reservation. She didn't know how long they sat there like that, impaling each other with their gazes, but when the moment broke, Rose felt disoriented.

Shia shook her head and blew out a breath, indicating that she felt something similar. She tipped her chin. "Tell me things."

Rose had to force herself to concentrate. "Um, I have two brothers and two sisters, all younger. I'm the oldest of all the grandkids, actually. My mom is Gem's oldest sister, and I'm only six years younger than Gem. What about you? Do you have any siblings?"

"That explains why you and Gem are so tight. I don't think I have any siblings."

Rose felt terrible. "Oh jeez. I did it again. I'm sorry."

"Don't be. You can't miss something you never had. It's a normal question. In a way, I have a bunch of siblings if you count the ones at the group home. Did I fantasize about brothers and sisters? I guess. Sometimes. But honestly? Most of the time, I was glad I didn't have any. I would have worried and felt responsible for them. It's better this way."

Shia told her not to feel bad, but Rose did. "Do you have any family?"

"Not that I know of. My mom and I lived with my Grandma Turning until my mom went to prison when I was three. Then my grandma adopted me. I was twelve when she died. After that, I lived with my mom's brother for six weeks until I was removed to the group home run by the mission. I don't remember my mom, so my grandma was the only real family I ever knew, besides my uncle, who doesn't count. He's in prison or maybe dead. I never knew my dad. Not even his name. It's not on my birth certificate. My grandma told me that my mom died in prison. I don't like to think about that, but when I do, I imagine the worst. She was only nineteen when she went in."

Rose's stomach churned. Shia had recited everything almost woodenly, making Rose wish she hadn't asked, hadn't forced Shia to relive it again. No child should have lived like she had. It wasn't fair.

An almost physical awareness crept over her, telling her that Shia had managed her emotions and damage from her childhood by tucking it away so that it didn't affect her day-to-day life. Rose didn't know how she knew, but she did. She also knew Shia was unaware of the pain that leaked out sometimes, affecting her in subtle ways, both good and bad. It was one of the reasons Shia had a kind and compassionate nature, with an exceptional awareness of how she affected others. Beauty from pain was how it felt. Rose didn't know whether to smile or cry.

"Can I ask you something?" she asked.

"Sure."

"Do you think surfing is important to you because of what you've gone through? Like, it gives you a sense of control you didn't otherwise have? Or it took you out of your group home situation or set you apart in a way that, I don't know, proves you have…" She tried to think of the right word. "Overcome is the word that comes to mind, but defeat might be better." Shia took a moment to answer, looking at her as if she might have said something uncomfortable. Rose's heart dropped. "I'm sorry if I overstepped. I—"

Shia's soft hand covered hers. "I've never had anyone understand it like you do. Surfing was the only thing I had that was mine. One of the older guys in the home surfed. And all of us were envious of his board and wet suit. Other kids had things like bicycles, skateboards, laptops, and phones. I had a laptop and a phone. But the surfboard meant that he was allowed to go to the beach. It was a privilege. It was freedom. When Lance left for the military and gave me his board…it changed me. It was before I turned sixteen, and I wasn't allowed to go anywhere on my own until then. Those days of waiting were torture. I couldn't wait to go to the beach. The day I turned sixteen, I took the bus. I didn't have a wet suit, but I went out in that cold water and took wave after wave, teaching myself how to stand up, wiping out, trying again. When I was surfing, I didn't think of anything else. I was free."

Her unfocused eyes gleamed. Rose imagined that she was right back in that moment of escape. Even though it was Shia's personal moment, Rose felt like she was there, almost as if she was part of her.

It was a sensation like nothing she'd ever experienced, as if receiving hope after being deprived of it all her life. And because she didn't know she'd not had it, there were no other emotions like resentment, bitterness, or even antipathy to weigh it down. It was bliss. Pure bliss.

Where was this coming from? Was this awareness of Shia's deepest emotions a form of empathy made poignant by their intense physical connection? Rose wasn't like her grandfather with his gift of seeing people's essences. But maybe she'd picked up on it a little.

Shia squeezing her hand reminded her where she was. "Hey. I'm sorry. I kind of fell away there for a moment. Did I make you sad?"

"I'm not sad at all."

"Why are you crying, then?"

Rose touched her cheek. It was wet. "Oh, I didn't realize, um…" She smiled, shaking her head. "The way you described how you felt when you surfed for the first time was beautiful. I like how you said you could think beyond. Like it removed a barrier for you."

Everything fell away when Shia stared into her eyes. Rose had a dawning sensation of complete acceptance between them. Without any words, anything that had constrained them or held them apart was gone. Some sort of pathway had opened between them. She could see in Shia's unveiled eyes that she felt it, too.

"I…" Shia rested her hand on her chest. "What were we talking about?"

"How surfing opened up something inside you." There was so much more to it than that, but Rose wasn't equipped to go there.

"It gave me a sense of purpose. Surviving wasn't enough anymore. It got me to go to college, my path out of the group home. Before that, I couldn't imagine what was going to happen. The college surf team gave me a sense of belonging and a support system I'd never really had. Having goals kept me from languishing."

"So surfing is pretty much everything to you."

Shia nodded. "I feel like you can see exactly what it means to me."

Rose wanted so much to explain the connection she'd recognized between them, but part of her was worried that Shia might see it for what it was: anything but casual. "You're being true to yourself. I guess I vibe with that," she said, as close to the reality as she wanted to go.

Shia shifted in her seat but kept hold of Rose's hand, as if it was important to keep a physical connection. "When I talk about focusing and not being able to be more than casual, not allowing distractions, that's where it's coming from. It has nothing to do with how much I'd like to be distracted, especially by you. It doesn't mean that I want to push you away, either."

The statement sent tingles of hope throughout Rose's body. "So last night wasn't a mistake?"

Shia looked shocked. "What? No. Being with you hasn't been a mistake." She leaned forward as if to emphasize her words. "It's how I feel after that complicates things. If we were successful at casual, I could be that way with you and do my normal things without wondering what you were doing, without wondering when I would get to see you again. But it's not casual when I'm with you. I feel intense things. I don't want you to go. I feel like I'd rather wake up with you than train. And I do think about you all the time. It's almost obsessive."

Those words set off a war of emotions in Rose. Hope. Anticipation. Fear. Even desperation. They had to get this right, but it was a tightrope. "So what do we do? Will you be able to keep it casual?" She wasn't sure she could even do it herself.

"I don't know," Shia said. "But I want to try. I don't want to not see you. I crave time with you. But we need rules."

"The boundaries we talked about. Maybe not staying up too late? Like, figure out how much time we'll spend together before things start to happen where we might lose track of time? That sort of thing?"

"Yeah." Shia sounded excited. "I was trying to figure out how to avoid the part about losing track of time, but I think that's a great idea. Like being together now. I have a meeting at two, but I'm open until then. We could spend that time together if you're open. What about work?"

"I think I see." Rose was excited, too. Maybe they could do this. "The thing about work is, I'm always working. It's mostly an on-call sort of thing, meaning I get to make my own schedule. Like today, I need about an hour to finish my review of the books, and I have a thousand work orders I need to go through, but I could do that after two."

Shia smiled. "I like this. That gives us three hours to enjoy our time together before we have to go back to real life."

Being up-front was exciting. And some parts of Rose were more excited than others. Way more excited. "Do you have any ideas? You know, about how we could spend this time together today?"

Shia gave her a look that should have scalded her. It forced her to look away. "I have lots of ideas. But I kind of like what we're doing now, getting to know each other. I mean, my first impulse is to drag you to my place, but how do you feel about getting a sandwich from here and taking it down to the beach for a picnic?"

Rose's body was primed for Shia's first impulse, but she also liked getting to know her better. This would be a good opportunity to exercise restraint. There was a different kind of excitement in delayed gratification, right?

Chapter Eleven

The conversation about how they should conduct their illicit affair went so much easier than Shia had dared hope when she'd suggested they go for coffee. She'd felt like a real jackass after Rose had left the night before. She knew she'd run Rose out with her insecurity. She hated having made Rose feel anything less than completely wanted and desired, which Shia absolutely did feel for her, but her disappointment in herself over saying one thing and doing another had crept in. Now they were walking along the beach, back to being at ease in each other's company.

There was something between them, and damn, she felt it hard. When Rose had agreed to coffee, she was ready to set some boundaries so they could get back to where they'd been. But when Rose had called her beautiful, a door inside her had opened, bringing her a different kind of ease, one she never expected to have.

Always, when someone had told Shia she was beautiful, it had made her feel powerless. Depending on who said it, sometimes even fearful. It came with the implication that her looks were the only thing she had of value and that she could get things if she used her appearance to manipulate people. As a foster kid, that was a huge thing. When she had nothing and no one, the temptation to use whatever she had to get what she needed, let alone extras, was enormous. Before surfing had given her an identity beyond her looks, her appearance was a liability that attracted unwanted and sometimes terrifying attention. It was the source of her darkest memories, those she intentionally never brought into the light. When Rose had called her beautiful, it was the first time she didn't expect a painful demand to follow. It was the first time she remembered being happy about being pretty.

For the first time, she was comfortable in her own skin.

Even more, when she expressed how surfing had given her a purpose in life, not only had Rose seemed to know exactly what she was talking about, she'd also related to it like they were linked in a way. At first, she'd thought she was simply reacting to a shared emotion, feeling a special connection, but it didn't fade as the moment changed. She still felt it. It was more than a connection, something more powerful than that.

She'd once seen a movie where a person described two people who were meant to be together as twin flames joining. As cheesy as she'd thought the analogy at the time, she wondered now if that was what this was with Rose. That she'd found her twin flame.

She handed one of the sandwiches to Rose as she studied the water, unsure how to verbalize what she was thinking and feeling before she decided she couldn't. At least not now. "The surf is a little bigger than forecasted. I hope this lasts through the weekend."

Rose opened the panini and rearranged her caprese sandwich. When Shia gave her a questioning look, she rolled her eyes. "There has to be the right ratio of tomato, mozzarella, and basil in each bite. I was only getting mozzarella, and my tastebuds were lonely for the others."

"You're weird."

Rose shoulder-bumped her. "Yeah, but you like it."

Shia smiled at the bubbly feeling the exchange gave her. "Guilty."

Rose closed her sandwich and took a bite. "Now my tastebuds are happy. Do you train on the weekends, too?"

"I usually take the weekends off, but I still surf for fun most days. I hope the surf stays on the bigger side because there's a competition this weekend. An oil spill down in Baja had the organizers move it up here. It's not for points, but there's decent prize money."

"What are the points for?"

"We collect points through the season to qualify for the US Open of Surfing. This is the first year that I'm in the running."

"That's great. So you'll be doing the surfing thing all weekend?"

"Yeah. There's a lot going on besides the competition, what with meeting with sponsors and the media. And on Sunday, there's a party at the Canteen after the competition. I also teach a surf camp each day before the meet."

"Sounds like you'll be busy all weekend," Rose said. Was that disappointment in her voice? "Do you mind if I drop by your tent during the meet?"

The question chased away her own disappointment about being

too busy to see Rose all weekend. "Not at all. Mikayla would probably like the company when I'm out on the water. We both do a lot of sitting between heats. You can pick up some sweet swag, too."

"What do your days look like during a normal week?" Rose asked, taking another bite.

Shia grinned to see that her pinkies stuck out as she held the sandwich. It struck her that she didn't know Rose well enough to tease her about having tea with the queen, but she knew exactly how she sounded when… Nope. They both had work to do that afternoon. If she started thinking about that kind of thing, she'd miss her meeting. This boundaries thing was going to be hard.

"Hello?"

Shia almost choked on her lunch. She'd forgotten that Rose had asked her a question. "Sorry. My mind wandered to the meeting I have this afternoon." It wasn't a total lie. "What was the question?"

Rose gave her side-eye, like she knew what Shia had been thinking. "I asked what you usually do during the week. I know you swim with Mikayla in the morning and surf in the evening."

"I've been trying to get into a consistent schedule since I finished college, but now that I have Mikayla as my manager, I feel like I need to really crack down."

"You mentioned being on the surf team. I didn't even know there was such a thing."

Shia nodded as she swallowed a bite of her egg salad sandwich. "I went to UCSM for marine biology."

Grinning, Rose made a claw with her hand. "Go, Cougars. I went to UCSM, too. Never graduated, though."

"You seem to be doing well without the degree. I have no idea what I'll do with a degree in marine biology. Seemed fun when I selected it."

"Well, Ms. Smarty-pants, have you settled into a schedule?"

"I'm still getting used to it. In addition to training at the beach in the mornings and evenings, I also go to the gym at Oceana for an hour and a half two or three times a week, usually in the morning right after my swim. Let's see, it depends on the season, but I run surf camps twice a week in the summer, guest instructor at a few of the high school surf clubs in the spring and fall, give private classes when someone hires me, work with Mikayla on booking contests, setting up sponsorships, and that kind of thing. Then there's the occasional appearance at various events, photo shoots, and interviews." She tried to think of anything else. "Oh yeah, I volunteer at the group home at the mission. For fun, I also go out on day trips sometimes with some of the research biologists I know from the Scripps Institute. That's how I know Rick, the biologist who helps Brandi with the seahorse breeding program."

"You mentioned her before. You mean the Brandi who Mikayla swapped houses with? She breeds seahorses?"

"You haven't seen them yet? Barging in on Brandi, and now Mikayla, to watch them is one of my favorite things to do. I'll take you."

"Yes, please," Rose said. "You sound busy. Do you ever hang out with friends?"

"I'm not that busy. Different things happen at different times of the year. Summer is the busiest time, especially with the surf camps, but it sort of spreads itself out. As for friends, I hang out with a few people from my old surf team, and up until recently, some friends from the units on the other side of the park to play cards. Oh, and that reminds me. Once in a while, everyone on our little street gets together for a bonfire behind Mikayla's place. Alice and I usually coordinate them." Shia rested a hand on Rose's shoulder. A little zap of something passed between them. She was starting to get used to it. "We'll do one soon so you can meet everyone."

Rose covered Shia's hand. "It sounds fun. Right now, I'm going to get my feet wet. I need to cool down, and it's not just the sun making me hot. That shirt on you is really sexy, especially when the sleeveless part opens up and I get little peeks of…mmm." Rose purred with a glint in her eye.

Shia enjoyed how Rose leaned on her while she took off her shoes.

Rose waded out to where the water was halfway up to her knees when the tide came in. Something about watching her stand in the water looking out over the ocean made a bubble of happiness explode in Shia's stomach. She stepped out of her flip-flops next to Rose's boots and secured the wrappers from their lunch underneath so the wind wouldn't scatter them across the beach, and followed Rose into the water. When she reached her, she slid her hands around her waist from behind and rested her chin on her shoulder. It felt like the most natural thing to do, but the sheer ordinariness of it rushed through her, causing a sense of pending…something. She didn't know what it was, whether it was good or bad, but the closeness she felt to Rose in that moment was either the safest or the most dangerous feeling she'd ever experienced.

"What's the matter?" Rose asked, rotating to face her.

"Nothing. Why?" Shia said. She honestly didn't know if it was a lie.

Rose's expression was a mix of concern and confusion. "I'm not sure. Something felt…I don't know how to explain it. Kind of, like, suspended? No, that's not it. More like that feeling you get when you do something that could end up being spectacularly awful or horrendously wonderful. Like, it could go either way. You have no control over it."

"Like a tidal wave. All that raw, beautiful power. I think every surfer has had the dream of being on a massive wave and getting the ride of a lifetime but knowing that kicking out of it will probably kill you."

"Why would you have to kick out? Why not keep riding it? It's a dream, right?"

"All waves crash when they hit the shore."

Rose looked at the water around their legs. When she looked up, she had a mischievous look on her face. "I'm wet."

Shia couldn't look away. "Me too. We have an hour or so before my meeting. Do you want to do something about it?"

Rose didn't even answer. She took Shia's hand, picked up their stuff, and led her up the beach toward Oceana.

CHAPTER TWELVE

There was only an hour left of the surf competition on Saturday. Frustrated at having missed almost all of it, Rose made her way down to the beach. One of the units off Poinsettia Court had sprung a leak in the water heater. Thankfully, it was one of the older units, and the tank was next to an outer wall, so the water didn't flood the home, and access was easy. She and DJ, the head of maintenance, had it replaced in less than half a day. It would have been even faster if they hadn't had to replace a few pipes that had corrosion due to the salt air.

Sometime between installing the tank and getting out of the shower, when she didn't have the emergency to distract her, Rose started getting self-conscious about whether she should even go to the competition.

What had started off as a quickie after their walk the day before had turned into an entire afternoon when Mikayla had texted that she had to cancel their meeting, and DJ had texted Rose that he had taken care of all of the work orders she had been planning to tackle that afternoon. The fortuitous coincidence left them both with wide-open afternoons that drifted into evening, and then, exhausted, they'd fallen asleep until Shia's alarm had startled them awake. While Shia had gotten her things ready, Rose had hurriedly scrambled a few eggs and a protein shake to make sure Shia had enough fuel to compete. That was when she'd received the emergency work order for the water heater. She'd been moving ever since with no time to reflect, no time to question, no time to let other thoughts invade her mind. She'd simply gone through the motions of her job and let herself bask in the afterglow of the best fucking sex she'd ever experienced.

But it wasn't just sex.

It had been a hell of a lot more.

At the time, she'd simply gone with it because everything had been perfectly spontaneous, perfectly hot, and perfectly uncomplicated. From the moment Shia had waded into the water after her; to the run back to Shia's house, laughing all the way; to the moment Shia had kissed the shit out of her against the front door as they'd gotten inside; to when Shia had thrown her onto the bed, then all through the night as Shia had held her as they slept.

Perfectly perfect.

No distractions, no lingering doubts, no insecurities. It had been the two of them, already familiar with each other's bodies and nothing to diminish the pleasure. All of it seemed to line up, allowing something enormous to pass between them. It was like the wave Shia had described, terrifying but exhilarating all at once. Her entire body and psyche had reacted to the possible calamitous impact of an epic wipeout, even while the possibility of being on the precipice of having everything she'd ever wanted was right in front of her. But the most amazing thing was that she was precisely aware that she and Shia were as connected as they had ever been or maybe even could be. That significant thing had stayed with them the entire time they were together, and she was still feeling the effects of it hours after they'd moved on with their separate days.

She shouldn't have been surprised when the doubts rolled in. The fading sensation of Shia's touch had allowed room for distractions, doubts, and insecurities. Questions such as what it meant and how much was it going to hurt if things didn't work out. Was it possible Shia was feeling the same way? Would she be withdrawn again when Rose went to the beach to see her?

While in the shower, she started wondering if Shia had been being polite when Rose had asked if she could come to the tent. And then, sometime between getting dressed and walking out the door, she'd started wondering if Shia had surfing friends she'd rather be hanging out with rather than having to entertain a woman she was "casually having sex with."

Rose went back into the house, dove onto her bed, and screamed into her pillow because she knew she was overthinking it. She spent the next hour continuing to overthink it until it was midafternoon and she was paralyzed between blowing off the competition or going simply because she'd told Shia she would be there. Ultimately, having told her she'd be there was the thing that made her go.

She scanned the tents, spotting Mikayla talking to a man with the word EVENT on the back of his shirt. A few feet away, Shia relaxed in a chair while looking amazing. Raw desire flamed through Rose, stopping her in her tracks.

The desire didn't surprise her. It only got stronger the more time she spent with Shia. But as she watched, a woman with an event bib identifying her as another surfer knelt by Shia's chair, initiating another feeling. One that did surprise her. Maybe it was her fear of Shia having her pick of women demonstrating itself right in front of her. Or maybe it was the hand the woman casually placed on Shia's shoulder and the way Shia reached up to touch it. Whatever it was, it caused a flare of jealousy to shoot through Rose. Even worse, it was followed by the sting of tears.

She told herself she didn't have any right to feel that way. Casual was the opposite of any sort of commitment, making jealousy unjustified, adding embarrassment to the already painful situation of deluding herself into thinking casual with Shia was even possible. Part of her wanted to walk away, but another part, the masochistic part, wanted to keep watching, to see how familiar the two might get. It didn't make sense to punish herself that way, but nothing made sense regarding how this thing with Shia was going, how she'd fallen in love with a person she barely knew who deliberately wanted to keep an emotional distance between them while also having the best sex Rose had ever had in her life.

Wait.

Love? Was she really in love with Shia? This was the second time the idea had manifested out of nowhere. The first time had been easy to dismiss as mere confusion. They hadn't even known each other for two days then. But this was different. There was a connection beyond sex. Granted, they still had known each other less than a week, but they'd spent more time together than apart.

If it wasn't love, what was it? Lust? No, it was more tender than that. Affection? No, it was fierier than that. But, but, but…it couldn't be love. They'd said they would keep it casual. Well, Shia had said it, but Rose had agreed. So even if it was love, Rose couldn't let Shia know.

"Rose?"

She about jumped out of her skin.

Gem stepped back and laughed. "Didn't mean to sneak up on you. I thought you heard me call your name."

Rose laughed a little harder than she meant to. "I was trying to remember if I'd closed out a work order this morning." She could be forgiven a white lie to cover the turmoil within her.

"Are you just getting here? Me too. I had a half day at the office."

Rose trailed her, wishing she had left when she thought to. Now she was headed to the last place she wanted to be: to watch Shia be all touchy-feely with another woman. And she had to accept it. Because she'd said she would. What an idiot she was. When they arrived at the tent, Rose stopped at the edge of the canopy, not wanting to interrupt Shia's conversation with the woman who was irritatingly attractive up close. Her heart sank. Shia's back was to her, but she turned, and Rose looked away so Shia wouldn't catch her staring with an aching heart.

"Rose." Shia stood and walked toward her. "I've been looking for you."

"The emergency call took longer to take care of than I thought." As conflicted as she was, Rose couldn't help but smile. Shia looked happy to see her. More than happy, actually, taking her hands, standing close. The electricity that surged between them crackled.

"I'm glad you're here."

The genuine tone seeped into Rose's chest. "How's the meet going?" She hoped she sounded normal with all of the emotions warring inside her.

"One more heat to go today. So far, I'm doing pretty well."

"Pretty well? You're smoking your heats." The woman Shia had been talking to held out her hand with a warm smile. "You must be Rose. I'm Lisa."

Shia slipped an arm around Rose's waist. "Lisa is probably who I'll go up against if I make it into the semifinals tomorrow." Shia pointed to a tent a few spaces over. "That's her family over there. Those two littles are hers and Tom's."

Rose took Lisa's hand, letting the information sink in. She felt bad for having hated her for a few minutes.

Lisa let go and rested a hand on Shia's shoulder again. This time, Rose saw it for what it was, just a friendly gesture. Shia interacting with a friend. "Speaking of which, I probably need to get back. I'm done for the day. Tom probably wants to get out of here after wrangling the kids all day. Good luck with your heat. Nice meeting you, Rose. See you tomorrow."

Shia waved. "Kiss those munchkins for me," she said, her eyes still on Rose. "Is the emergency taken care of?"

"Emergency?"

"The emergency call."

"Oh, yeah. It was a water heater leak. Water was all over the place, running down the street. We replaced it. It's fine now."

"You know how to replace a water heater? That's impressive. And hot." Shia's half grin and narrowed eyes sent a shiver of excitement through her.

"They're easy, just heavy, and building code requires a plumbing permit to get it inspected, which drags it out a bit. DJ tried to talk me out of the permit by saying no one would know, but I don't bend those kinds of rules, especially since the application's online. But," she said when she realized she was rambling, "you didn't need to know all of that. Sorry."

"It's interesting." Shia tightened the arm around her waist.

Gem stepped closer. "Sorry, I heard you say DJ tried to talk you out of the permit. Good job not listening to him. We get periodic inspections. He knows better. They don't normally check individual units, but they could. If you want me to talk to him, I will."

"I think he got the message, but thanks." Rose couldn't help but be proud of herself for standing up for herself. Having Gem's endorsement made her feel even better about it.

An airhorn sounded. Both Shia's and Mikayla's heads swiveled toward the judge's station. "What's that for?" Rose asked.

"The end of the last heat, which means the next one is in ten minutes," Shia said, dropping the arm from Rose's waist so she could pull on the rest of the wet suit she'd draped down between heats. The image of the yellow bikini top on her smooth, tanned skin was already etched in Rose's mind, though. When she struggled to grab the string attached to the zipper in the back, Rose helped her zip it closed, dragging her fingers along Shia's warm skin as she did. Shia's response of leaning back into her eradicated the last of the dark feelings she'd arrived with. "Will you be here when the heat's over? It's only twenty-five minutes long. I'll be done for the day."

"Sure. I'll be here."

Shia turned and smiled. "Great. See you in a bit."

"Good luck."

Shia walked down the beach toward the quivers where her board was stored.

"You two seem to have hit it off," Gem said. Rose had forgotten she was there. "Am I reading into it, or is there something developing between you?"

"We've been hanging out a little." It was the best way to describe what was happening between them, even though things were definitely developing on her end.

"Shia's a very sweet person."

"I agree," Rose said.

"It's none of my business, but do you want to be more than friends?"

The question hit Rose almost physically. "Why do you ask?"

"I sense something between you. You know, a little zip of something. Well, actually, a big zip."

Rose wasn't surprised that Gem had picked up on her feelings. She didn't understand the gift Gem and her father had, but she didn't doubt it existed. She'd seen them use it too many times to not believe it, although she'd seen her grandfather use it more often. Gem didn't talk about it a lot.

"I don't know. She's really focused on her career. She can't afford distractions."

Gem paused while seeming to search her eyes. Rose wondered if she was scanning her to pick up more vibes or whatever it was she did to read people. If it had been anyone other than Gem, she would have hated it. But Gem being her favorite person made it okay. "Gotcha. You're pretty much doing the same thing at Oceana, too, right? Focusing. I know it's important to you that Grampa is happy with your work. Well, he is. Me too. You're kicking ass, Rose. We're so glad you're here."

Rose hoped the tears clouding her eyes wouldn't fall even as a couple escaped. Embarrassed, she wiped them away quickly. "That means a lot to me. Thank you."

"You're welcome. And if you ever want to talk about the other thing, let me know. Love is a tricky minefield."

Rose gave her a thumbs-up because her throat was too tight to reply without risk of revealing all the emotions welling up within her. She wasn't surprised that Gem had zeroed right in on it. Gem had always been able to read her like a book. But she didn't feel right talking to Gem about something if she couldn't talk to Shia about it, and she definitely couldn't talk to Shia about her feelings if she wasn't supposed to have them.

CHAPTER THIRTEEN

Shia came out of the water high on endorphins. She'd won the heat easily, not because her opponent was bad, but because she'd had a few incredible runs. The waves were perfect. They weren't overly large, but they had great form, making it easy for her to hit the sweet spot without even trying. Now that the heat was over, she was excited to see Rose near the water's edge as if her thoughts had summoned her. She waded out of the ankle-deep surf and headed right to her.

"You were amazing out there," Rose said as they fell into step walking back to the tent.

Before Shia could respond, the press descended upon her, asking her all the usual questions. She tried to give them the sound bites they needed, still well aware of Rose, who stood quietly beyond the small crowd of reporters until they moved on to the next surfer.

"Sorry about that," Shia said as she rejoined her.

"Don't be. It's obvious they love you. You make surfing look so easy."

She shrugged. "I let the ocean do its thing and follow its lead."

"It's easier to see when you're watching from a zoomed-in camera on TV. But in person, it's incredible how your confidence really shines. And that jump or whatever you call it at the top and the swoop back down onto the wave? Damn. The announcer went nuts."

"Oh yeah? I can't hear them out there at all. Mikayla and I usually watch the replays to see what got people excited."

"She doesn't really hit me as a surfing coach."

"She isn't. She's my manager. I don't have a coach. I have a few surfing buddies who give me pointers if we're out on the water together, but mostly, except for when I was on the surf team in school, I've been figuring things out on my own. I don't think I'd be able to do it if someone was telling me exactly how. Every wave is different. I have to feel the power guiding my board. I'm not sure how to explain it."

Rose shoulder-bumped her. "I think you just did. You talk about the power of the ocean with a kind of reverence, like it's your religion."

"To me, it is." It occurred to Shia that Rose understood her connection to the ocean in a way no one else had ever seemed to. There was an acceptance that told her she didn't need to explain how her spirit seemed to flow with the water. Sometimes, it felt a lot like that when she was with Rose, like they were fully in sync with one another.

Mikayla met them as they approached the tent. "Hey, surf star. If you keep it up, you'll have a direct ticket to Huntington."

"There are no points for this one." Shia leaned her board against one of the tent posts. No matter what, she was in the money now, even if the contest didn't contribute to her points for the season.

Mikayla flapped her hand. "I'm talking about the next meets. You beat the third-place winner from last year at Huntington today. That's pretty big. You get better every time you compete. Your confidence totally shows. That's what I'm talking about."

Shia had to agree. She did feel a lot more confident.

"What's Huntington?" Rose asked.

"It's the US Open of Surfing," Mikayla said. "Shia is in seventeenth place in points this season so far. Only the top fifty-five women surfers get invited to Huntington."

"Is that good?" Rose asked.

Shia smiled because the placement system was difficult to understand. "There's a lot to keep track of, but the main thing is that each season there are ten qualifying competitions to get to Huntington. It's still early in the season, though. Most serious surfers will try to hit as many competitions as they can to collect points."

"Is Huntington the very top?"

"It is for the US. There are several surf tours throughout the world."

"When you win in Huntington, will you move on to other competitions?"

Shia looked at Mikayla. "She said 'when,' not 'if.' Did you hear that?"

"She's a smart one," Mikayla said with a wink.

"Right now, I'm focusing on Huntington. I'll look beyond that when it's over," Shia said. "In the meantime, I'll compete in all the qualifiers for it." This was the first year she could say that thanks to the sponsors Mikayla had helped her pick up. Travel and registration fees added up quite a bit, not to mention maintaining her equipment, all of which her sponsors covered in one way or another.

"I'm a little starstruck right now. I mean, I knew you were a pro surfer when I met you, but I really didn't know what that meant. You're playing in the big leagues. That's super impressive."

A couple of emotions went through Shia. The first was simple pride because she cared about Rose's opinion. Usually, she tried not to think about what people thought of her. Her childhood had taught her that if she gave too much weight to other people's opinions, she'd always be let down. It sort of blew her away how easily Rose had grown important to her in such a short period of time. The other emotion was brand-new. Unexpected. Rose's questions told her that, as far as Rose had known, Shia had been nothing more than a glorified beach bum, with nothing more than competing in local competitions on her mind. While Shia had been insisting on putting her career first, Rose respected her dreams without question, not knowing that Shia really had a chance at the big time. Rose had agreed because it was important to Shia, nothing more. No strings. Shia was not used to no strings.

All of this caused another emotion to settle into her heart, and this one was too scary to think about.

❖

"Thanks for sticking around at the post-competition party," Shia said after finishing her second street taco. They were sitting at her dining room table, and she was starving. She picked up the stray pieces that had fallen onto the table around the cardboard to-go box and dropped them onto the lid. If Rose hadn't been there, she would have popped them into her mouth. She loved tacos, but they were so messy. Her last sat waiting for her to eat, but she didn't want to look like an animal wolfing down her meal in front of Rose, who was still finishing her first.

"These are so good," Rose said, licking her fingers. "I'm so glad Gem thought to bring us dinner."

Shia watched Rose's lips wrap around her fingers. All thoughts of food left her mind when fast, hot desire hit her square in the most sensitive parts of her body. "Someone needs to tell Hop that chips and salsa are not enough food for a party."

"Not with the amount of beer and liquor being consumed," Rose said.

"I don't know how the other surfers do it after all weekend in the sun and water. All I could think about was a huge, ice-cold Arnold Palmer."

"They were all probably trying to drown their disappointment that they didn't win."

Shia lifted the medal hanging from the ribbon around her neck and kissed it. The trophy was sitting in the center of the table. "I can't say I blame them. I've attended my share of post-competition parties down at the Canteen, wishing it was me sitting at Hop's table with the trophy and fat check."

"Did you stay long at last night's gathering?"

Shia shook her head. "I left a few minutes after you left to go to your parents' house for dinner. I was tired. Did you have fun at your mom's birthday party?"

"We always have fun when all my aunts are there. The way they whip the banter back and forth keeps everyone laughing."

"Gem's told me a lot about her sisters and their families. I don't know how I didn't know you were one of them."

Rose nodded. "I wouldn't give it up for the world." Her eyes were warm and bright but suddenly grew round. She lowered the second taco as she was about to take the first bite. "I'm sorry. That was insensitive of me."

Shia waved a hand dismissively before picking up her last taco. "Don't be sorry for loving your family. It makes me happy to know there are people in this world who really do have the dream family. It gives me hope for my future."

"I wouldn't say our family is a dream, but it's perfect for me. Maybe…uh, never mind."

"What?

"I was going to say maybe I can invite you over, but that might be a little too not-casual."

Shia finished off her last taco. Without saying anything Rose transferred her last taco to Shia's to-go box. "You're a saint. Thanks." Shia poured hot sauce over it and took a big bite. As she chewed and swallowed, she thought about Rose's comment. "I don't know if meeting your family is in the realm of not-casual. I've met the parents of lots of my friends."

Rose wiped her mouth and hands. "We're in a gray area of not being in a relationship or just friends. Maybe this is where we need to identify the boundary as far as meeting family and friends go and how we behave in public. When you came out of the water after winning your last heat of the day, I didn't know if I should hug you. And at the party. At one point, you put your arm around my waist while we were talking to some of the other surfers. I wasn't sure what to do."

Shia remembered all of that vividly, having the same thoughts. The times she'd put her arm around Rose's waist had felt natural and good, but she'd wondered if Rose was comfortable. "Yeah. I guess we should figure out what we should do in public. For the record, I enjoy standing close to you. We fit together pretty well, don't you think?"

Rose blushed, reminding Shia that she was the cutest thing ever. "We do."

"So the arm around the waist thing is cool?"

Rose seemed to consider it before nodding. "I'd put that in the cool category."

"Probably full-on making out is off the table?" Shia said, wiping her mouth so Rose wouldn't see her smirk.

"Definitely. I don't do that in public as a rule. You know, decorum."

"True. Plus, when our lips get to work, it's only a matter of microseconds before I want to rip your clothes off." Rose blushed even harder, and that also got her thinking about clothes coming off.

"What about…" Rose shook her head. "Never mind."

"What about what?" Shia reached across the table and took her hand.

"Okay. Yesterday, when I got to the tent, I saw you with Lisa. And before you introduced us, I thought, well, I wondered if she was someone…other than a friend. Like maybe she was like me. In the gray area. I wondered if I should leave."

Shia had to let that marinate a moment before she answered. "First, I'm glad you didn't leave before you found out that Lisa is a friend. A very good friend but still a very good, straight, and married friend. Who sometimes stays with me when she comes down here for competitions without her family in tow. Second, I'm curious. Did it bother you?" Shia's heart rate spiked as she wondered what would be worse: Rose being bothered or not.

Rose dropped her gaze. "Well, shocked, I guess." She looked back up. "Disappointed. But mostly, I say mostly, I felt hurt." She looked away again. "I know I shouldn't—"

"Hey, it's okay. I don't think I would, I mean, I know I wouldn't like it if I found out you were seeing other people that way. Something like that needs to be discussed. For a lot of reasons, but mostly because there is no reason we should keep something like that from one another. It can only lead to bad surprises." Shia squeezed Rose's hand while Rose continued to look down. "Right?"

Rose looked up. "Right."

Shia cleared her throat. "But there's something you should know about me. I'm kind of a one-person person. I can't imagine being intimate with more than one person at a time. Well, except for one time that was too weird to ever do again." She laughed and was glad to see Rose crack a smile. "I don't have the ability to share that kind of energy with multiple people. Not that I have anything against those who can. In fact, good for them. But even if I wasn't already trying to limit that kind of energy so I can focus on my career, I wouldn't have the ability to connect in that way with more than one person."

It was only at that moment before she realized maybe Rose *was* that kind of person, that maybe she was asking about it to get it on the table so she could see other people while she was in this…arrangement with Shia. "But if you want to see other people, we can certainly talk about it."

Rose did a couple slow blinks and shook her head. "I don't want to be intimate with anyone else as long as we're in this *arrangement*. If it comes up, I'll have to decide on you or the other person. That is, if you haven't kicked me to the curb already." Rose laughed, allowing relief to flood through Shia. "And I need to hear about the one weird time."

"The one weird time was a joke." Shia laughed, enjoying the lightness of being with Rose. "That was an unexpected detour in our dinnertime talk." Shia got up and collected their empty to-go boxes. She licked her lips. "By the way, did your tacos have as many onions on them as mine did?" She stuffed the boxes in the garbage can and made sure the lid was securely seated. "I might have to take this out before bed. Delicious but pungent. I think I need to brush my—"

When she turned around, Rose was right there. Actually, her lips were right there, but the rest of Rose followed, and then she was kissing her. All thoughts of onions left her mind because the kiss did taste of tacos, but it also tasted of Rose and felt like nothing Shia had ever experienced except in Rose's arms. And as much as her desire spiraled upward as the sensations of Rose's mouth and hands fanned her flames, she settled into the peaceful home that Rose had created in her heart.

Chapter Fourteen

Rose slipped her foot into a work boot and began to lace it up. While she tied it, she glanced around for the other one and spied the toe sticking out from under the bed next to her bra. At the same time, Shia wrapped her arms and legs around her from behind. Exquisitely soft skin pressed against Rose's back. She left the boot and bra where they were and leaned back into the sensuous hug, aware of how Shia's breasts slid against her and how Shia knew exactly how much pressure to use when she rolled Rose's nipples with her lithe fingers, fingers that had been driving her over the ledge of orgasm mere minutes ago. Her sex clenched with the memory and from the hands on her breasts as Shia kissed the side of her face, then her neck.

"I could definitely get used to these kinds of lunch breaks," Shia whispered in her ear.

"If you keep enticing me over for lunch with pizza and sandwiches, I could get used to them, too," Rose said, her voice breaking as shivers ran up and down her body.

"Is that all you come over for? The food?" Shia slid her hands lower and slipped her fingers into Rose's unzipped shorts. Shia hissed with pleasure when her warm fingers brushed along either side of Rose's clit, which was still very sensitive from having Shia's lips wrapped around it minutes earlier.

"God. You know I come here for this. I'd skip lunch every day to have your hands on me. Keep doing that." Rose's eyes were closed as she focused on what Shia did to her, one hand slipping lower, teasing her folds, then sliding deep inside her while the other hand worked her clit with such expertise, Rose knew she'd come in a few more strokes.

Shia whispered encouragement between kisses, her warm breath tickling the side of Rose's face. "That's right. Let it go, Rose. I feel how ready you are."

Rose rolled her hips, cradled against Shia's body, completely immersed in experiencing every touch, every breath, every sound. When she came, it was as if her body flew apart and reassembled, leaving her to feel every sensation with each individual molecule of her being. It took a while for her to regain her senses enough to know she was lying on her back atop Shia, who was still stroking her, humming softly in her ear.

"I can't move," Rose said, not even trying to.

"I'd tell you that you don't need to, but you said you have to go meet someone."

"Oh, jeez." Rose tried to sit up with Shia laughing under her, trying to help. "I was already cutting it close before you beguiled me with your magic hands and perfect body." She stood, grabbing her boot and bra from under the bed and her shirt, which was draped over the oversized check for ten thousand dollars Shia had received as the prize for winning the contest on Sunday. As she pulled on her shirt, she felt a breeze on her butt; strange because she was still wearing her shorts. Reaching to touch it, she realized the fabric of the crotch and butt of her shorts was wet. "Oh no. I can't go there like this. They're going to think I peed myself."

Shia covered her mouth, laughing. "Tell them the truth. You squirted while having a nooner with one of the residents." Shia laughed so hard that tears filled her eyes.

Rose picked up a pillow that had fallen to the floor and whacked her with it. "I'm meeting with potential renters, you perv. They might get the wrong idea." Rose contorted herself to see how obvious the wet stain was. To her chagrin, it was very obvious. Maybe she could tell them she spilled water when she hit a bump in the cart.

"I've got a pair of cargos almost exactly like those. Let me see if I can find them." Shia got up and rummaged through a couple of drawers before she lifted a pair of shorts in victory and handed them to Rose, who slid out of her damp shorts and panties, struggling a bit when she tried to get them over the one boot she still had on. She breathed out a sigh of relief when they fit.

"I knew I still had them," Shia said, pulling on the T-shirt Rose had removed from her an hour ago. "You didn't eat your sandwich. Take it with you."

Rose pulled on her other boot and quickly laced it up. "I'm starving, too."

"Multiple orgasms will do that to you."

"Stop it," Rose said with a chuckle, pulling her hair back into a tie. "My hair's a mess. Do you have my hat?"

Shia looked around. "It's around here somewhere."

"I don't have time to look. Is my hair okay?"

Shia cupped her face with both hands and kissed her. "It's perfect. Like you."

"Thanks for the sandwich," Rose said accepting the wrapped sub Shia handed to her, hoping Shia didn't see the way her words had laid open her heart.

Scattered, still feeling the aftereffects of her last orgasm and floating on Shia's sweet words, she arrived at the units. No one was there. She'd opened them earlier to make sure they were in showing condition, so she distractedly checked all ten before she thought to check her phone and realized the appointments weren't until the next day. Slapping her forehead, she realized she'd entered it wrong in her calendar. Crisis averted. All she had to do was rearrange a couple of things she had penciled in for tomorrow. Thankfully, they were both tasks she could do anytime, so it was easy.

Still coasting on the amazing sex, she locked up all the units and got into the cart to go back to the office, thinking she'd get ahead of some of the work she had scheduled for later in the week, but before she took off, she rested her chin on the steering wheel to take a minute to breathe. She closed her eyes, and the first thing she saw was Shia's face wearing the expression she'd had before Rose left, an expression that seemed to show more than amusement, more than affection, definitely more than casual. If she had to name it, she…wouldn't because it was supposed to be casual. And more than slightly ironic, casual was supposed to be avoiding situations like today.

Was she going to point that out to Shia? No. She wasn't about to give up the sex, and she wasn't going to put a stop to expressions on Shia's face that made the rule about keeping it casual bearable.

She set the cart in motion, feeling like she'd been on the run all day, and she had, even though some of it had been on her back. She laughed out loud at the thought, and her stomach growled. She reached over for the sandwich Shia had given her, wondering what the next lunch enticement would be.

CHAPTER FIFTEEN

Shia rarely went to bars, but here she was at the Canteen for the second time in three days. The first time was the after-competition party Hop had thrown Sunday evening, and here she was, two days later with Mikayla, sitting at the bar, waiting for Hop to show up. She sipped a cranberry and 7-Up and flipped through pictures on Mikayla's laptop. There were a lot of incredible pictures from the competition, many featuring her. Even for being the winner, her face dominated the collection.

She paused on a picture of her talking to Lisa and Rose in the tent. It was a nice candid photo of them laughing about something, but there was a sense of closeness coming from them that made her happy. Lisa was resting one hand on her shoulder and was holding Rose's in her other, while she had one hand resting on Lisa's lower back and the other around Rose's waist. She was pretty sure it was when she'd introduced Lisa and Rose. The picture had some weight to it after Rose had told her that she'd thought that Lisa might have been more than a friend, so she examined it closely. All of their expressions were friendly, open, and warm, as if everyone was happy to see each other. Even Rose, who had admitted to feeling hurt and disappointed before finding that Lisa was just a friend. None of that showed on her face. It made Shia wonder if Rose was hiding any other emotions.

Something else stood out to her. She was used to seeing herself in pictures, but mostly, she was the only one in them. Surfing was a solo sport, so it made sense. She hardly ever saw herself interacting with others unless it was with fans, and she was always "on" for those moments. Seeing herself in a moment, unposed, with all facades removed, the picture of the three of them made her look like she belonged. When she flipped through the next few, all shots of the same scene, the impression of closeness only got stronger. She wanted a copy of every one.

"Stop there for a sec." Mikayla tapped the screen.

"This one?" Shia asked.

"Do you know this person?" Mikayla asked pointing to a woman standing several feet away from the tent, appearing to watch them. She had sunglasses on and the hood of her light jacket up, with her long blond hair draped forward and down her chest. Nothing about her particularly stood out. She was dressed in shorts and flip-flops like most of the spectators and contestants, blocking the sun and trying to keep warm in the constant beach breeze.

Shia zoomed in on her. "I don't think so. I usually recognize people by their eyes. Except for her long nails, she could be me for as much I can see. Or half the women in San Diego."

"She was there all day." Mikayla continued to stare at the photo.

"So were we."

Mikayla rolled her eyes. "She was obviously not with any of the participants or the organization. Also, she hung around the tent but never approached."

"Were you casing her?"

"The better question is, was she casing you?"

Shia squinted at her. "Stop. You seriously think that?"

"You're a hot-shit celebrity surfer. Why wouldn't she want to case you?" Shia blew out a sound of disbelief. "Did you guffaw at me?"

"I don't even know what a guffaw is."

"Well, you just did it."

Shia typed guffaw into a new tab. "I didn't chuckle, chortle, or horselaugh at you. It could have been considered a sound of mirth but definitely not a guffaw."

Mikayla waved a finger. "Technicalities. But seriously, you need to get used to having a following."

"I think I do okay with people. Don't you?"

"With people you know. But how will it be when more people start to recognize you?"

Shia flapped her hand. "Not likely to be a huge issue for me."

"You might change your mind after we talk with Hop."

"Did I hear my name?" Hop stood behind their chairs. He didn't even need to order. The bartender handed him a glass of whiskey. "Thanks, Lincoln. Can you bring a bottle of Cristal with three glasses to the booth, please? Ladies, please follow me."

Mikayla collected her bag and computer while Shia picked up their drinks, and they followed Hop to a round booth in the back corner with a Reserved placard on it. The owner's table.

Shia was impressed with the invitation, even though she'd known Hop for four years while competing in the local surf events. He was known as a father figure among the locals and had once been a well-known longboard surfer, thus his interest in the sport and the tournaments. She'd only been invited to the booth once before, and that had been two days ago, after she'd won the competition.

"I've watched the video of your heats, Shia, and there's one I keep going back to. It's that rodeo flip you do. First—and I apologize in advance for generalizing—but few women attempt it, let alone ever get it down. I've never seen it successfully completed in a women's competition. But you busted it out there in the last two competitions. No one ever mentioned it was in your wheelhouse."

"I did it for the first time at the competition before last weekend."

"Without practicing it?"

"I've played around, mostly wiping out. I hit the sweet spot during both competitions, though. The waves were almost pristine, and I went for it. It felt good, but I didn't even know I'd done anything spectacular until I saw the scores."

Hop shook his head and nodded at the bartender as he brought the champagne and poured three glasses. "Thanks, Lincoln." He held up his glass. "Here's to doing things because they feel right."

It wasn't the time to tell him that she didn't drink, so Shia tapped her glass to his and Mikayla's and simply held it as he downed half his. She'd done the same Sunday night when he'd brought her a glass of whiskey from his personal stash and toasted her win.

Unlike Sunday, when he was preoccupied with the crowd, he nodded at the glass. "You don't like champagne?"

"I'm not much of a drinker." She used to say it like it was an apology, but she'd stopped doing that.

"Jeez. I stuck my foot in it. I should know better since I'm in the business, and now I'm making it weird. Sorry about that." He got Lincoln's attention and pointed to her empty cranberry and 7-Up, signaling for another.

"No worries," she said, sliding the champagne flute over when Mikayla crooked her finger for it.

"I won't let this yummy champagne go to waste, but no more

for me after this," Mikayla said. She had a knack for making every situation as easy as she did now, taking the focus off Shia.

After Lincoln delivered Shia's drink, Hop held up his glass again. "To Shia."

She tapped her glass to theirs and took a sip. "Thanks."

He settled into his seat and looked at her. Studied her, really, as if she was under a microscope. "You're making quite a name for yourself. I'm going to cut right to the chase here. You've got a way about you. You're California. You're becoming a surfing star. People like you. I like you. I'd like to propose a partnership."

Shia schooled her expression. "A partnership?" She glanced at Mikayla, who appeared interested but not surprised. Hop had obviously talked with her in advance. If they were here talking, it must have meant that Mikayla was interested in what he was proposing. "With me?"

"You say that like you're surprised."

"I am. There are a ton of better surfers to partner with."

"I think you're underestimating your talent."

"I know I'm good, but I still have a lot to learn. I mean, look at Lisa. She's been dominating surf contests up and down the coast for a while now."

"She's a hell of a surfer, you're right. But she plateaued a couple of years ago. She's getting ready to retire."

"Yeah, she mentioned it this weekend."

"You're still rising. I can't wait to see what you'll be doing in the coming years." He leaned forward. "But it's not limited to your surfing abilities, Shia. You're the whole package. You embody the image of what people think of when they think of a California surfer. It's what people see when they think of Southern California."

"How does this work into a partnership between us?"

"I want to give you more exposure. I want to connect surfing with North County. San Diego proper gets the lion's share of tourism. Bars like mine get our share of the locals, but it's the tourist money we need to go after, too. We need to entice them up this way. When we have surf contests, we see a huge surge in revenue. When I only owned the bar, that worked well, but I've always wanted to get more contests into the area. I've wanted to make surfing more accessible to more people. You're already doing that with your surf camps."

"I do it because I want to give more to kids in the foster system."

"Which is awesome. I'd love to expand on it." He shifted in his seat. "You've heard I bought the old water park in South Oceanside by the lagoon, right? I want to turn that into a sort of surfer's amusement park, with a wave pond and everything."

Shia was intrigued but didn't know how she factored into this. She didn't have the kind of money to become a partner in something so big. "I didn't know you bought it, but I've seen some of the work going on there. I thought it was being torn down to expand the bird sanctuary."

Hop shook his head. "That was the plan, but I've made friends with the environmentalists. I'm working on a way to support conservation efforts while helping people recreate something closer to nature. Since it's next to the bird sanctuary, the county has strict protections in place, and I've been working with them to make sure we not only meet the requirements but do better."

Mikayla leaned forward. "You have a steep battle ahead of you if you want to build anything in that area. Everyone's protective of the birds and the views. Locals are not going to be happy about bringing more tourists up here. Most of them hate the traffic and crowds they bring already. The beaches are so full during tourist season that the locals don't even want to go anymore."

Hop nodded. "You're talking to one of them. I grew up here. I think the park will bring people off the beaches. Our design focuses on blending into the environment."

Shia liked his ideas. Most entrepreneurs tried to get around environmental regulations. Hop seemed to want to go beyond them. Her respect for him grew. "I can get behind that. How do I factor into this?"

"I'd like you to be our spokesperson. The project will take a few years to come together. In the meantime, we can start aligning you with the image. We'd have to be careful to not individually connect you with the contests because that would be a conflict for you as a participant, but as you keep kicking ass while shredding the waves, you'll still be attracting sports media to the area."

"How would this affect my sponsorships?" She hated having to ask, but sponsorships were her primary income.

"For now, it doesn't, except to possibly bring you more, but sometime in the future, we'll probably want to talk exclusivity. By then, we hope it will be so lucrative, you won't think twice." He poured himself another glass of champagne. "What do you think? I'm not asking you to commit to anything yet. I want to know if you're interested in the idea and maybe get your creativity flowing so we can hit the water paddling when we get busy making it happen."

Shia looked to Mikayla, who had stayed quiet during most of the exchange. There was a glimmer in her green eyes that said she was excited about the idea. The little bubble of anticipation Shia had started the meeting with had grown to a much larger bubble that bobbed around in her stomach. Surfing had always been her happy place. When she'd decided to take it up as her career, she'd hoped that she'd be able to make it something she could do in and out of the water. The surf classes she gave to local youth had been the beginning of that. Now it appeared as if she'd have an opportunity to expand on it.

The thing that astounded her the most was that moving in that direction seemed almost effortless. She'd trusted in her ability to make it happen, but others had helped her along. The same thing had happened when the mission had helped her make ends meet when she'd moved out of the group home. It had happened again when her first sponsor had offered her an unlimited supply of free fish and chips and a pop-up tent if she would let them display their name on the tent. Then Mikayla had offered to become her manager, and now Hop was interested in making her his spokeswoman.

It seemed the universe was helping her all over the place. Somehow, she'd found the sweet spot. She couldn't wait to tell Rose.

CHAPTER SIXTEEN

The kitchen door handle rattled, rousing Rose from her intense study of the water usage report she'd pulled for the last six months. She was impressed with the detail it provided. It gave information about the usage of the entire park, all the way down to specific units. She could even see rates all the way down to the hour. When she got up with a hitch in her step from stiff legs, she realized she'd been sitting there for close to two hours. She pulled the door open, causing Gem to almost fall through, but Rose steadied her.

"Whoa! You've got your hands full. Let me take some of that," Rose said, relieving Gem of the two boxes she was balancing under a plastic dish and a small stack of files.

"Thanks. I'm surprised you're here," Gem said, placing the dish and files on the kitchen table.

"Why's that?"

"You've been spending a lot of time with Shia lately."

"Not really. Does it seem like I do?"

"I wouldn't have said it if I didn't mean it."

"Oh." She should have anticipated Gem's curiosity increasing after the chat they'd had last weekend. But she didn't have a definition for what she and Shia were doing. It sounded cheap if she said they were just sleeping together. Whatever the in-between place they were in, she didn't know how to describe it. And honestly, she really didn't want to. Because if she did, she'd upset their balance.

"Do I sense a romance blossoming?"

The question ripped her from her thoughts. "It's not like that."

"The Ring camera seems to indicate otherwise. I get a notification when cars go down the cul-de-sac. I've been meaning to adjust the sensor so it doesn't pick up the road traffic, but I haven't, and I see you driving the cart past the house. You seem to be spending a lot of time on her end of the street."

Rose felt like she'd been called to the principal's office, but she shrugged and hoped it looked casual. God. She was starting to hate that word. "We're friends."

"Who might, perchance, be a little more than friends?" Gem winked.

She slid her hands down her face, not wanting to talk about it. Actually, she did want to talk about this casual thing that her heart didn't think was casual at all. "It's complicated. Yes, we're friends who are more than friends. We're keeping it casual."

"Complicated but casual?" Gem said. "I don't know how that works."

Rose wanted to say she was trying to figure it out, too, but as much as she wanted to talk about it, she didn't know how. "It works for us. We're both busy. It's easier this way." She tapped the boxes she'd put on the table to redirect the conversation. "What's in all these?"

"I stopped by Scripps this morning for Mikayla. Rich, the guy who helps maintain her seahorse tank, brought the wrong shrimp for the seahorses yesterday. I took them back and got the right ones before work since her car is still in the shop." Gem laughed. "Funny story. Everyone at work got excited that there was shrimp in the freezer, thinking I'd brought some in for the office potluck. They were disappointed when I told them it was frozen brine shrimp meant for seahorses."

"What did you bring for the potluck?"

"I forgot all about it. Mikayla's gonna give me grief. I slipped out and picked up a veggie plate." She pointed at the plastic dish. "I brought most of it home. Everyone was into the hot wings."

"Aren't we supposed to call veggie plates crudité these days?"

"That's what Mikayla calls it. Only, she sounds sophisticated when she says it. I feel like I'm putting on airs. I'm telling you, I've lost all flow when it comes to working in an office again. Birthdays, potlucks, thirsty Thursdays. I can't keep up."

"Are you regretting going back?"

A grin spread across Gem's face. "Not one bit. The social work part of my flow came back as soon as Margo gave me the first case."

"You seem a lot happier these days. Like everything has clicked for you. It's like you feel clear when before, you felt fuzzy." Rose shook her head, not knowing if what she'd described made sense. It was something she felt rather than saw. That was how it had always been between them, they knew each other so well.

"That's a pretty good observation. I do feel clearer. You're getting clearer yourself."

"You mean, you're seeing something with your telepathy? What?"

"What makes you think I have telepathy?" Gem's demeanor switched from light banter to serious, throwing Rose off.

"Everyone knows you and Grampa have it."

"What do you mean?"

"Grampa talks about his ability to see people's true essence all the time. He says it's a big part of what makes Oceana special because he can tell who should live here and who should not."

Gem squinted at her. "What did he tell you about me?"

Rose shrugged. "That it ran in the family. Why are you acting weird? You lorded it over me when we were kids. If I had it, I'd be stoked. It would save a lot of time knowing who to spend time with and who to avoid."

"I was messing with you back then. I didn't even know I had it. Besides, it's not telepathy. I can't read minds. I feel weird about being able to sense people's true natures, what they're feeling, their intent, that kind of thing, what Grampa calls their essences. He does it so naturally. I feel like I'm being intrusive." She seemed embarrassed.

"Why? I think it's awesome. It's like a shortcut to knowing them. It would make it easier to, I don't know, get along with them. You've always seen right through me."

"But it's not that easy. Therapists, at least good ones, have to be careful about not leading their clients but guiding them to create their own paths. People don't know who they are themselves half the time. In fact, they often act the opposite. It causes conflict in them. It confuses me when I sense something they haven't figured out, then I might respond in a way they don't expect. It's hard to explain."

"Is it like you're constantly thinking they'll go one way, but they go another, but you're already prepared for the way you thought they'd go, so you have to scramble to catch up to them?" Rose asked as something started to click for her.

Gem studied her. "It's not that simple, but yes. I've always thought about it as being like when you try to get by someone in a narrow path. You both move in the same direction, getting in each other's way a couple of times like you're dancing before one of you stays in place, letting the other pass."

"Yeah, and sometimes. you both laugh about it, and other times, somebody gets pissed." Rose thought of her and Shia and the whole keeping it casual thing when it really wasn't casual at all. For either of them. And she was almost positive it wasn't for Shia, despite her saying otherwise. In fact, she had the strong feeling that Shia needed to believe they were casual, not only for her career, but like her life actually depended on it. It occurred to her in that moment that Shia didn't trust that they could make whatever it was they had work. She wasn't sure why she felt so strongly that this was the case. She just did. And she also knew that while Shia told herself they wouldn't work out, there was a deeper, stronger desire to make it work. Sometimes, she wished she had the gift her grandfather and Gem had. It seemed like it would make things easier.

Gem looked at her funny. "Sounds like you might have the..."

"The gift? Me? No. I've always been a pretty good judge of people. You know, in the normal way. Not that you're not normal. I mean, like other people do." She blew out an exasperated breath, knowing she was trying to justify something Gem already knew. "You know what I mean."

"I get it. Not many people are perceptive. You might have a little bit of the gift. I didn't know I had it until I was almost your age."

Rose had always thought it was cool that her grandfather had this special ability to read people. When he'd told her Gem had it, she'd imagined what it would be like. It would be cool to share this with them. But she doubted she had it. She'd actually tried to use it in the past, but the harder she tried, the more convinced she was that she didn't have it. Not more than most perceptive people did, anyway. She couldn't really tell if someone was good or evil or anything like that. Well, not really. She sometimes got creeped out by people, but it wasn't like she was able to tell that a person was a murderer or anything. She could usually tell when a person was good, though, in the same way others could. "I don't know. It seems like I would know it if I did."

Gem looked at her intently. "The thing is, you don't know until you do. It's like seeing something out of the corner of your eye. It's not there if you look directly at it. One day, it's there, and you realize it's been there for a while. It took me a long time to realize, but once I did, it was obvious."

"So it's just normal now?"

Gem laughed. "Normal is a subjective word."

"You know what I mean."

"It's a part of me. It always has been. I didn't feel different after I knew what it was. I guess I found a way to see it more clearly. It's hard to explain. You know when you know."

"So you can tell me if—"

"Are you going to ask me about Shia? Like, is she a match for you? Please don't. I can tell you yes or no. But I can't tell you if it will work out. People screw things up because they have a hard time seeing their true selves. They stay with people who aren't a good match, and they push away people they're perfect for, and there are different levels of matches in between. Knowing one way or another doesn't guarantee anything. It can even get in the way of a natural connection."

"Sounds complicated."

"Only until you learn to see things out of the corner of your eye." Gem squeezed her shoulder as she moved past. "Are you on your way to her house?"

"I have dinner at my 'rents tonight. You wanna go with?"

"Sounds fun, but I have to get the shrimp over to Mikayla before the seahorses run out. She's making Cajun salmon for us. Next time?"

"Sure thing."

"You should take Grampa. He's out back thinning out the calla lilies."

It was a good idea. Rose went out to ask him. It helped take her mind off how much she wanted to go to Shia's instead of her parents' house. And now she had this gift thing to worry about.

Chapter Seventeen

Shia was wiped out from her evening surf. She looked forward to going out, especially in good weather, and it was perfect that night. It wasn't like the morning swim that she often dreaded or the weight training that stressed her patience. On her surfboard, it was as if she was free. Her body was moving, her mind was focused, and she knew how to find the perfect spot on the wave to get the most satisfying ride. There was no better feeling than when she dropped into the sweet spot. That evening, she'd surfed her ass off because it was like she couldn't miss it if she'd tried.

Maybe it was excitement about the prospect of teaming up with Hop on the surf park concept, but it felt like every wave had a perfect ride in it, giving her the inspiration to try a few moves she'd been watching on the internet. She'd taught herself how to surf by watching videos. Even more by talking to other surfers. But her real learning came from tuning into what each wave was telling her. If the wave was breaking smoothly, she could predict a landing on an aerial move and how much time she had to stick it. If the undertow was stronger, she could get an extra kick if she shifted her weight and accelerated along the face, pulling some snaps to produce impressive splash wakes that were always a good visual move for points.

Even the direction and strength of the wind gave her information about what speed she could get out of her board. She had to take in all this information and a whole lot more to set up her ride and figure out if she could attempt a certain move. And tonight, the waves had given her a lot to work with, including a bunch of aerial moves that had stretched her capabilities. She'd found herself dropped into the soup more times than she could count. Her muscles ached from the workout. It felt good.

As she walked past Rose's house, she wondered what it would be like to casually stop in. If someone had been outside, she probably would have. But Rose had told her in an earlier text that she was going to her parents' house that night and probably wouldn't be home until late. She'd text her later to connect. She missed her, having not seen her in two days.

A small shiver went through her as she remembered Rose letting go so completely. She'd never experienced anything like it, but she let out a laugh at the thought of the moments immediately after, when Rose had discovered her wet shorts.

Low voices pulled her from her thoughts: Mikayla and Gem sitting on Mikayla's porch watching the sunset. Tiny glints from their wineglasses told her they were probably relaxing after dinner. She adjusted her trajectory to pass more closely so she could say hello but not encroach on their private time. It would be rude to pass without saying anything.

"Hey, you two," she said with a wave.

"Hey, Shia," they said in unison.

"How were the waves?" Gem asked.

Shia slowed down but didn't stop. "Pretty epic. Got a lot of play. I didn't want to come in, but I'm wiped out."

"Sweet," Gem said.

Shia waved. "Enjoy the sunset."

"Um, Shia?" Mikayla said standing up. "Do you have a minute? I know you like to go for a soak in the hot tub, but I wanted to talk to you."

Something in her voice set Shia on edge. She didn't know why. She walked up the pathway to the bottom of the porch steps and leaned her board against the deck. "Sure, what's up? Why am I getting an ominous vibe?"

"Sorry. Nothing's ominous. Maybe surprising. And maybe a little…you know what? I'll let you decide. Do you want to go inside? You might be cold." She stood and waved her up.

"I'm okay. It's warm. I have my hoodie." She flipped the hood over her damp hair. "You sound, I don't know. Serious? Is something wrong?"

"I came across some information today that I think you should know. I feel sort of weird dropping it on you, but I can't think of a good time for something like this." Mikayla glanced at Gem, who nodded, and that drove up Shia's apprehension.

The hair on the back of her neck stood up. "Are you okay? Are you sick?"

"It's nothing like that. I'm fine. Everyone's fine." Mikayla pointed to the wide steps. "Let's sit."

"Okay. Whatever you say, there's definitely a vibe, though." Shia sat on the top step next to her. Gem sat on the other side. Shia hugged her knees and rested her chin on them, dreading whatever she had to say.

"Before I begin, I want you to know that I'm only bringing this up now because I don't want you to find out any other way. I didn't want you blindsided."

"*Okay.*" At this point, she wanted Mikayla to get it over with.

"When we talked to Hop the other night about his plans for the surf park, he mentioned the environmental impact group he was working with, right?"

"I remember." God. She hated the gurgling this was causing in her stomach.

"Well, I've been involved with environmental groups up and down the coast as a volunteer or supporter, so I know most of them, and I know quite a bit about the ones that oversee the bird sanctuaries because Grandma James was a birder and we..." She flapped her hand. "Never mind. That's not important. The thing is, those groups are super protective. That's why I support them. We need them. So when Hop said he'd already started talks, I was both happy but also wary because I know how those groups work. They pull you in being all nice, gather as much information as they can, then use it against you to make sure the places they're protecting stay protected. They've been burned over and over, and that's made them that much more paranoid and stringent. With all that in mind, I contacted the organization responsible for our lagoon. I wanted to get a feel for how the project was sitting with them. Because if they don't like it, it's already dead in the water. I wasn't sure if Hop understood this or not, and ultimately, I didn't want you to get excited about something that wasn't likely to happen. I know Hop has deep connections in our community, but he's no match for environmental groups."

Shia started to get a feeling about where this was going. It had seemed a little too good to be true. "I get it. They don't make deals over a bottle of expensive whiskey."

"Right? Well, I met with the woman who heads the group. The good news is, Hop wasn't being overly optimistic. He's had lots of talks with them. They're eagerly working with him. There are a few things they still need to work out, but they believe he's as concerned about protecting the land and the wildlife as they are, so they're working through it."

"What is it, then? You have my curiosity dialed up to a thousand out of ten."

"Well, when I walked in, the woman I was meeting with smiled, and I got the strongest impression that I had met her before."

"Had you?"

"No. But the feeling kept nagging at me. It wasn't until I left that I realized why." She looked at Gem again.

Shia was about to jump out of her skin. "Are you going to tell me?"

"She's the woman I asked about from the pictures."

The hair on the back of Shia's neck bristled again. "Is she some sort of stalker? Is that what you're saying?"

Mikayla rested a hand on her back. "What I'm saying is that I'm almost one hundred percent sure she's your mother."

Shia had to laugh. "She can't be. My mother died over fifteen years ago."

"I wouldn't even think about risking your emotional health over something I wasn't this sure about."

Something like a cloud of frozen air settled over Shia and made its way down her body. She knew Mikayla wouldn't approach something like this blithely. But somehow, she'd made a mistake. Shia's mother was gone. Dead. She was absolutely certain of it. "I don't think you're messing with me, but it's impossible. My mother died in prison. My grandmother told me. More than once. She always referred to her as dead."

"I don't know how to explain what your grandmother told you, but this woman looks exactly like you, Shia. She has the same shade of hair and the same eyes, but what got me was her smile. It's exactly the same, with the slightly higher left side, the same number of teeth showing, and that slight crease on the left cheek. Hers is more prominent, but she's what you'll look like sixteen years from now."

"She's…what do they call it? A doppelganger. They say we all have one."

"Honey. I looked her up. She goes by Sharon Henderson, but Sharon Turning also came up. She was born in Bonsall, raised in Oceanside, and still lives here. She's worked at North County Wild

Birds and Habitats Society for ten years. Her mother and father are Linda and Horace Turning."

Shia sat flipping through all the data in her mind for the evidence she needed to make this not true. It had been many years, and most of the memories had been driven deep into her unconscious. With or without evidence, she knew with certainty that her mother was dead. She had to be.

She would have come to get her if she was alive.

Wouldn't she?

CHAPTER EIGHTEEN

What was Shia doing?

The question floated through Rose's mind for what seemed the millionth time that night as she shared a bowl of grapes with Chad while they read the latest book from their favorite sapphic romance author. She always covered Chad's eyes during the steamy parts, but he loved the happy endings.

At the moment, though, Rose was having a hard time concentrating. Her mind kept going back to Shia and what she might be doing at that exact moment. She'd told Shia she wouldn't be home until late. However, dinner had been early because she'd brought her grandfather, who rarely stayed up past eight. Tonight had been no exception. He'd started to do long blinks right after, so she'd taken him home hours before she'd expected to.

Since then, she'd been trying to ignore the phone that was practically taunting her, begging her to text Shia. However, she was stronger than that. So what if this was the longest they'd stayed apart since they'd met? It didn't keep her from wondering what Shia was doing. Was she already asleep? Or was she watching television? Flipping through a magazine?

Her phone dinged on the bed, startling her from her thoughts. Chad barely budged when she rolled slightly to pick it up. He was snoring with a grape still clutched in his little pink hands. She didn't blame him. The two main characters in the book had jumped into bed too soon. Consequently, the author was having a hard time keeping the tension ramped up. Rose suspected something unrealistic was going to happen to save the story. She hated when that happened. Chad despised it.

Hey, whatcha doing? R you in a cuddle pile w/yr family watching TV?

Negatory on the cuddle pile unless you count Chad. I'm in my room in Oceana. Dinner was over early. She snapped a picture of Chad and his grape and sent it.

So cute! Disappointed about the human cuddle pile but cool about getting some rat love. I thought cuddling up to watch TV was a rule of family nights.

Says who?

Just every wholesome television show ever made.

LOL Not ours. Are you aware of how stinky 15yo boys are?

I never got too close to them. Still disappointed.

Rose wondered if she was feeling left out. *Does this mean you want to cuddle?* Anticipation leaped inside her chest.

Yes, came the immediate answer.

Do you want me to come over? You can come here if you want. She added the last part on impulse because she wanted Shia to know they had options, but she knew Shia wouldn't want to. It would put pressure on the casual thing. As soon as she sent it, she wished she hadn't.

Can you come here?

She knew it was coming. Still, it stung. Which she had no right to feel. She reminded herself she'd knowingly agreed to the arrangement. And given the choice, she'd still choose to continue what they were doing rather than not having time with Shia at all. Besides, it helped her remain focused on her own work, too. Having the boundaries made sure she didn't…

What? Not daydream at work? Not sneak away to spend time with Shia? Not become so preoccupied with what she said or did that she became distracted from whatever she was doing? She snort-laughed. All of that was a common phenomenon. She reminded herself that she'd even almost missed an appointment to show the units. No matter that her calendar was off one day, probably because she'd been distracted when she'd put it in there. Oh well. She'd try to be better.

Be there in a few.

She gave Chad some extra treats and tucked him into the hammock in his condo before she slipped her feet into her sandals and headed downstairs. She already knew Gem was at Mikayla's and would probably stay the night, so she popped her head into the living room to tell her grandfather she was leaving. His snores rumbled over the sound of the television that was tuned—very loudly—to one of the police dramas. As far as she knew, he never slept in his own room, preferring the recliner.

She quietly backed out of the room and left through the kitchen door, locking it as she closed it behind her. As Gem and her grandfather had told her many times, there was no reason to lock it since there had never been a single robbery in Oceana, but after years of living in Escondido, the habit was strong.

The walk to Shia's was quick and uneventful, her mind on the text exchange and Shia's comments about cuddles and families. Maybe it was that they were via text and not a face-to-face conversation, but something about it made Rose wonder if Shia was thinking about her own family, and again, she chided herself for speaking so cavalierly.

Shia was holding the screen door open for her when she arrived. As she walked past, Shia took her hand and pulled her into her arms, holding her tightly, burying her face in her neck. It was the first time she and Shia had embraced without it being overtly sexual. At first, Rose was confused, but very quickly, she molded her body to Shia's and held her until their heartbeats and breathing synced. A sensation of melancholy mixed with longing drifted through her, quickly followed by surprise and something like love all swirled together. They stood there swaying to the tempo of their heartbeats for several minutes. Rose would have stayed there all night, but Shia slowed the sway, cradled Rose's face, and gave her a tender kiss.

When she pulled back, Rose noticed Shia's eyes were sparkling with tears. She finally knew where the sadness was coming from, and while the longing, surprise, and love felt like they were inside her, she realized they weren't her emotions but Shia's. Memories, emotions, and some of the confusion she'd felt in the past sort of clicked, and some of what Gem had told her that afternoon seemed to make more sense. The emotions became more complex, and she knew what it meant when people said they had conflicting emotions because it felt like all of them were present, but some took a more prominent position.

Was she sensing Shia's essence? As soon as she thought it, the wisps of emotion she'd sifted out as being Shia's swirled away, leaving her with a question about whether she'd actually picked up on anything at all. Was it wishful thinking? Suggestions planted during her conversation with Gem?

"What's wrong?" she asked.

Shia's expression went through a succession of rapid, yet subtle changes before it stilled into one that almost looked relaxed, but a tangle of emotions seemed to seethe within her, and Rose knew at once that she had perfected that expression to mask her emotions.

Shia's mouth worked, but no words came out. Rose guessed she was trying to express what was going on inside her without revealing the extent of her turmoil. "Um." Shia covered her mouth with one hand and slid it over her chin, finally scratching the back of her neck. "I'm…I mean, I found, actually, I can't…hmm." Her struggle demonstrated her scattered thoughts.

"Hey, it's okay." Rose took her hand, led her to the sofa, and pulled her down. She settled into the cushions in the corner and snuggled Shia, who curled up against her. With Shia's head on her chest, she began to slowly run her fingers through her hair. "You don't have to talk about it if you don't want to. We can cuddle. If you feel like talking, I'm here." Rose took a few deep breaths and let them out slowly, the way she'd seen Gem do when her grandfather became impatient with a task he used to know how to do but that had been affected by his strokes. He would invariably copy her breathing and calm himself. She smiled when Shia matched her breaths, relaxing completely against her.

It was several minutes before Shia spoke. "I found out that my mother is still alive."

Rose tried not to have a reaction, but this explained the emotions Shia was struggling with. "How?"

Shia recounted a conversation she'd had with Mikayla.

"This sort of flips everything you thought you knew about your mother on its head, doesn't it?"

"Does it ever." Shia absently played with the string on Rose's sweatpants.

"Do you think there's a chance Mikayla could be wrong?"

"At first, I did. But when I came home, I did a few searches and saw exactly what she told me. It's the same person. My grandmother is listed online as her mother. She's my mom. I have no doubt. Plus, like Mikayla said, she looks exactly like me. Or I look exactly like her."

"How do you feel?" Rose knew how she felt. It was rolling off her in waves, a cacophony of insecurity, hurt, confusion, fear, anger, and resentment, but surprisingly, there was a big dose of anticipation and hope.

"Confused and angry, mostly."

"I think you have every right to those emotions and a whole lot more."

"I've been overreacting and shutting down and doing it all over again, over and over. It's exhausting."

"I'm not sure there's a limit to a reaction to news like this. What are you going to do?"

Shia sucked in a breath. "Nothing, probably."

"Are you curious?"

"Beyond curious but I'm not sure I want to go down that path. It feels dangerous. I like my life as it is."

"You don't even want to find out why she hasn't contacted you all this time?"

Shia didn't answer immediately, and Rose worried that the question had gone too far. "There are probably numerous reasons. All of them are probably valid, too. Her life was a mess when she went away." Shia paused, playing with the hem of Rose's shirt.

Rose took note of the amplified confusion within her, but as soon as she did, it faded. Like Gem had said, she had to use the corners of her eyes.

"But I'm not sure I want to know, to be honest. Especially since my grandmother said she'd died in prison, which she obviously didn't, so this doesn't make sense. I'm worried that I might be disappointed."

"I completely understand. Why'd she go to prison?"

"Drugs. That's all I was told, and that she died from an overdose soon after she went in. I was three, so I don't have any memories of her. All I remember was that it was me and Grandma Turning until she died, too. Grandma hardly ever talked about her except to warn me not to end up like her."

"So you don't know much about her?"

"Grandma showed me some pictures. She looked like me. She was only sixteen when she had me. Basically a kid herself. In my head, she's like her last school picture. She was nineteen when she died. Supposedly died, I mean. All I can think is, what else isn't true? When I looked her up, I found she's been living nearby for a long time, maybe always. I couldn't find any information about her going to prison, so was she really sent away?"

"I can't even imagine how you're dealing with this right now." Rose really couldn't. She sensed the tumult, but she had no idea what Shia was thinking or planning, only confusion being the dominant emotion, followed by hurt and anger. But knowing what Shia felt and that she was sensing it because of the gift and not guessing gave her a clarity of perception she'd never had before. It fascinated her. It was like Gem had said it would be. She felt like nothing had changed, but everything had. Now wasn't the time to think about it. Right now, she had to be there for Shia. "Is there anything I can do?"

Shia lifted her head, looking her in the eyes, and the sensation of something shifting into place fell over her, followed by the impression of falling and then floating. Rose couldn't separate what Shia was feeling from her own feelings, and it was disorienting until she remembered what Gem had told her about trying. As soon as she stopped, everything was clear again. It was as if she could actually see the emotions.

"You're doing it right now, being here with me." Shia looked away and then right back. "Normally, I'd keep to myself, you know, for something like this. I don't really know how to…"

The trembling of her chin made Rose's heart shatter. She held her tighter. "Oh, honey, you don't need to explain. I get it."

"All I wanted was to be with you."

Tears filled Rose's eyes. She cleared her throat to dislodge the lump. "Thank you. I wouldn't want you to be alone with this." She cradled her face, kissing her. It was a slow, tender kiss, one she hoped showed Shia how deeply her letting Rose in on the pain affected her.

Shia pulled back slightly. "Can you stay the night? I don't want to be alone."

Rose kissed her again. While the kiss was tender, there was a lot more communicated this time.

CHAPTER NINETEEN

Sometime during the night, they moved into the bedroom. Shia awoke before the sun rose with the delicious press of Rose's body against hers. They hadn't had sex. In fact, they were still dressed in the clothes they'd been in the night before, but in a way, the relaxed familiarity of waking together after an evening of sharing her pain was more intimate than any act they'd previously shared. As the sun rose and her consciousness awakened, anxiety replaced comfort. Watching her bedroom go from darkness to pale morning light, Shia fought a battle of whether to get up and go for her morning swim or remain in Rose's arms. It wasn't that the arms around her had lost their comfort. Exactly the opposite, and that was where the anxiety originated. She couldn't want this. It wasn't casual. It was against the rules.

Slowly, she turned to face Rose, ready to slide out of bed, hoping not to disturb her, but when she caught sight of Rose's face relaxed in sleep, a slight smile curling the corner of her mouth, she grew transfixed, pulled in by Rose's natural beauty. Her body relaxed as she watched. She must have dozed off because the next thing she knew, she was being gently awakened by a warm hand stroking her arm.

"Good morning, gorgeous." A series of light kisses trailed up her arm. The legs languidly entwined with hers moved, making Shia realize how sensitive her center was when Rose's thigh pressed into it very lightly. Her hips lightly rolled along it as Rose smoothed a hand along her back and leisurely into the back of her loose shorts. Shia rolled her hips again, this time applying pressure to the place she needed it, and a shot of pure desire flared through her. She buried her face in Rose's neck and pulled her close, tasting her sleep-warmed skin. Her earlier anxiety might have been a dream, and without the distractions and tensions of the day upon them yet, she focused on the desires of her body, the stirring of her physical need. Her focus centered solely on her corporeal responses, sharpening the awareness and reactions of her body.

The intensity transformed the sleepy motions of seconds ago into a ravenous exploration. When Shia reached into Rose's sweatpants and found her wet center, Rose slid her fingers into Shia. They began to move against each other with a rapt emotional intent beyond any they'd shared before. Within minutes, Shia came with her mouth open, gasping against Rose's throat. As soon as the explosion of sensation swept through her, she once again took up the thrusting she'd been unable to continue and resumed the tempo, guiding the slide of her fingers in and out of Rose's wet heat, bringing Rose to her own powerful orgasm seconds later, her muscles wrapping around Shia's hand, causing her own walls to pulse in time with the contractions happening inside Rose. While Shia didn't quite reach a second orgasm, the sympathetic fluttering inside her sent waves of additional pleasure through her body.

Bodies limp with release, they remained tangled together, breathing hard. Shia caught Rose's earlobe with her lips, relishing the soft warmth of it with her tongue as her body molded itself to Rose's once again. She didn't even mind the somewhat awkward way her arm was trapped between them, her fingers remaining buried in the hot hollow between Rose's legs, the waning ripples of pleasure against her hand erotic and intimate.

"I'm not sure if anyone has ever told you this before, but you're an amazing lover," Rose whispered before she ran her tongue along the column of Shia's throat. The sensation, hot and wet against her sensitive skin, made her vagina pulse around Rose's fingers. When Rose's muscles responded by contracting around Shia's fingers, both of them moaned, tilting their hips forward.

"I think it's a very mutual sentiment."

"I think you're right," Rose murmured against her neck. "We're pretty good at this sex thing, you and me."

Shia stretched her body along Rose's, enjoying her well-worked muscles. She molded against Rose when she relaxed, initiating a deep and satisfied sigh. "I love how it doesn't matter how many times you make me come, I feel like I could do it again. I can't get enough of you."

"Does that mean you'd like me to resume?"

While Shia hadn't initially had a motive for her comment, Rose's suggestion filled her with anticipation, initiating a renewed need for more closeness, more connection, more everything. "It means that I'm currently thinking about how badly I want your mouth on me right now." Shia shivered with the effort it was taking not to press against Rose's fingers. Still, a strong contraction rolled through her, followed by Rose's core tightening around her. She wanted to come in her mouth.

"That's good because I was thinking how much I wanted to put my mouth on you," Rose said as she began trailing kisses down Shia's body while her fingers continued to fill Shia's center. When Rose's tongue traced along the skin of Shia's inner thigh, Shia rose on her elbows to watch Rose slowly remove the shorts, helping to kick them off when they slid to her lower legs. Rose settled between her legs and dipped her head, sliding her tongue through Shia's slick folds. When Rose's tongue lightly brushed her clit, her hips rose, seeking a firmer touch. Rose seemed to know not to tease her. It wasn't long before Rose's talented lips and tongue had her arching in ultimate pleasure. When she caught her breath, she rolled her head to the side to look at Rose, who'd moved back up to curl around her.

Shia weakly grasped the hand Rose had rested in the space between her breasts. "I'm a spent woman, but give me a few minutes. It's your turn, sexy."

Rose cracked an amused smile. "That sounds like a threat."

"Threat, promise, it's all semantics, but you'll be seeing stars when I can get these hands on you." Shia flailed them above her.

Rose groaned, pinning her hands. "That's probably the creepiest pickup line I've ever received."

"But you're turned on, right?"

"Indescribably." Rose released her and sat up.

"Wait. Where are you going? I believe the feeling is coming back to my extremities."

Rose stood, dodging her. "I could do this all day long, but I have an early meeting with DJ. We're going to update the flooring in the common room."

Shia tugged her hand. "How early is your meeting?"

"Seven-thirty."

"That's more than an hour and a half from now."

"I don't want to overstay my…you know."

"This is weird for you, isn't it?" Shia asked.

Rose rocked her head from side to side with a shy smile. "A little."

"That's my fault."

"No. We have an agreement. It's okay. I'm a big girl. I can follow the rules."

"Maybe it's time to adjust them."

Rose sat on the bed next to her. "I'm not asking to."

"I know. Thank you for being patient with me. But I think things have been changing whether we were trying or not."

Rose seemed guarded. "What do you mean?"

Shia wasn't sure how to describe it. "I like spending time with you."

Rose glanced at the bed where the covers were in disarray. "I think the feeling is mutual."

Shia squeezed her hand. "I'm not talking about sex, although it's definitely part of it. I like spending time with you in other ways. I miss you when I don't get to see you."

"I miss you, too." A little of Rose's guard seemed to fade.

"Right? It's hard to know you're only a few houses away sometimes."

"What kind of adjustment are you suggesting?" Rose asked. The guard inched up a little.

"I'm not sure. I guess, I want to see where things might go."

Rose's brows scrunched up a little, causing Shia's concern to mount, but it was also cute. Still, she didn't know how this was landing with her. "I thought that's what we've been doing."

"It is, but I…I get the feeling that you wait for me to suggest when we get together." Shia didn't know she felt this way until she said it, but it was exactly how it seemed to be. As soon as she said it, she worried that by giving up this control she hadn't realized she had, she'd open up a bigger problem. Which was? That Rose would want to see her more often? She realized that was exactly what she wanted.

The brow furrow smoothed out, mostly. "It's true. But I'm good with it."

"I'm happy to keep taking the lead, but would you, maybe, like, want to do it sometimes? I mean, if we weren't trying to keep it casual?" Shia covered her eyes and laughed. "God. That sounds so…so…I don't know how it sounds." She dragged her hands down her face. "But I don't feel casual. I never really did. I've always felt a major connection with you. The opposite of casual."

Rose studied her for a moment. Shia worried that she was thinking about how inconsistent she was, shifting the rules.

Shia took her hands. "I like being around you. I think about you when I'm not around you. I wonder what you're doing. I wonder when I'll see you again. I miss you as soon as you leave." It was a relief to say it out loud, but it introduced a sense of anxiety, a worry that maybe Rose might think she was being too intense after she'd insisted on playing it loose for all this time. But it really hadn't been that long. A few weeks. Was she taking things too fast, even as she'd been so intent on keeping things casual?

Rose stepped close. The furrow was completely gone. Her clear blue eyes were open, welcoming, loving. "Hey. I see you overthinking this. Don't worry. We're on the same page. I've been into you since the day we met. If I'm honest, and why wouldn't I be? Actually, I can think of a few reasons why I shouldn't be, but fuck it. I'm an honest person. I was past casual the first time we were together. I like being with you, too, and I miss you when I don't see you. I'd love to hit you up to do things instead of waiting for you to initiate. You might even have to tell me to give you some space. And if that happens, I want you to tell me. I don't want to smother you. But to be clear, I'd consume you if I could. And I'm not at all sorry I said that, as scary as it sounds. It's the only metaphor I think that comes close to what I feel."

Shia felt giddy. This whole thing was unexpected but awesome. "I'm not sure you can smother me, and metaphor or not, I think I want you to consume me." She laughed. "But I get it. I want you to tell me, too. If you want to leave now, you can. I mean for work. Now that the gates are completely open, I will be devastated if you chose to leave this…thing we have."

Rose kissed both of Shia's hands. "Well, we both need a shower."

"You want to shower with me?"

"God, I've been thinking about it since that morning in the pool building."

Shia led Rose to her shower with a whole new perspective about what being with her meant. This time, it wasn't her body leading her. It was her heart. And while she could now admit that her heart had been involved for most of their time together, she didn't need to pretend it wasn't anymore. It opened up a whole new level of connection for them. More than anything, she wasn't alone anymore. It made her feel like she could handle almost anything. Even her dead mother turning out to be very much alive.

Chapter Twenty

It was a typical Saturday in July. The Canteen was busting out of its seams with locals, tourists, and Marines from the nearby military base who'd come down to the beach for the day. The glass doors that made up the entire front side of the building were wide open. Music was playing on the outdoor speakers, while inside, the music had been turned down so people could watch the surf competition going on up in Newport Beach.

Hop, a co-coordinator of the event, was at the beach along with Mikayla, who was there supporting Shia, who, of course, was competing. Before he'd left, Hop had told Gem she could use his reserved table to watch the event, which was why Rose, Alice, and a few others were there, gathered around the booth, eyes glued to the television in the corner. Shia was currently in mid-heat, shredding her second wave. The whole thing was being broadcast by ESPN on the television across from their table. They watched as Shia performed a couple of three-sixties on the face of the wave, followed by a snap, and then an aerial that she landed flawlessly. Rose only knew the names of the moves because the commentator said them. The flawless part was evident. Seeing Shia in her element was like witnessing an unrestrained dance. All the power, passion, and talent laid out before them; Rose could barely contain all the emotion that watching Shia inspired in her.

"She makes it look so easy, like she's dancing with the wave," Gem said, taking a drink of beer.

"Makes you want to get out there and do it yourself, doesn't it?" Rose said. She wished she didn't sound so breathless, but seeing Shia surf was almost a physical experience. But then again, everything related to Shia was a physical experience for her.

"Nope." Gem shook her head vigorously. "I'm not into being shark bait."

Rose laughed. "It kills me how you have this fear now. When we were kids, we spent entire summers playing in the waves, floating on our boogie boards out past the breakers. You were the bravest person I ever knew."

"I'm still brave, just smarter." Gem tapped her temple and winked.

Right before her heat, Shia had given an interview while among a group of several young women who had been vying for her attention. If Rose hadn't seen it happen in the two previous competitions, she might have gotten jealous, but she knew Shia better now and could see that it was part of the job. Because of that, she could smile at the earnestness of the young women in the presence of their hero. Proud of Shia, she thought about how every young person should have such a wonderful role model.

They all paused to watch Shia drop in on the third wave of her last heat. It had been a hard day of surfing for everyone. The waves were a decent size, but it had been a heavy shore break all day long, which meant the waves were breaking quickly, crashing into shallow water, and abruptly ending the rides. The surfers were doing everything they could to lengthen their rides, and that meant everyone, including Shia, had found themselves in the washing machine more than once.

Shia dropped into a quickly breaking barrel for a couple of seconds of gorgeous surfing before the wave collapsed, forcing her to kick out, shooting her into the air, and both she and her board fell behind the wave. Rose imagined how tired she must be, but she knew Shia was having a good time because they'd spoken on the phone during her last break. Rose felt the heat rise through her at the memory of Shia saying she missed her.

"You ever have a feeling that you'd be so good at something if you simply tried it?" Alice asked, pulling Rose from her daydreams. "You know, like it would come super easy the first try, and you'd naturally excel at it?"

"I think so. I took to sailing the first time I tried it," Gem said.

Even as Shia's face was all she could see in her mind, Rose tried to think of something she'd exceled at the first time. There were a lot of things she did well, but she couldn't think of anything she specifically exceled at. She considered herself a jack-of-all trades, master of none, a saying she'd picked up from her father. When he said it, he did so with a sort of ambivalent tone, as if he wished he were more of an expert at something, but she thought of it a little differently. She'd take being competent at many things over being an expert at one or two. It seemed like life was more interesting that way, at least to her.

Shia was different. Her entire focus was on surfing. She more than exceled at it.

Rose smiled at Alice, trying to imagine her on a surfboard. "Have you ever surfed?"

"I've tried it. I couldn't do it no matter how hard I tried. But gosh, can you imagine being able to stand up on a wave like that and slide over the surface while all that water curves over you?" She moved her hands like they were moving across a wave. Her eyes grew dreamy. "It must feel like you're in the presence of God."

Rose felt a tingle across her skin. Alice had described the feeling that washed over her every time Shia explained how she felt when she surfed and how she said that even her worst days of surfing were better than her best days not surfing.

When Rose glanced around, Gem was looking at her as if she knew exactly what Rose was thinking. And she probably was. In the last week, since Rose had become aware of her own gift, she'd had a hard time not being aware of it operating almost constantly. Her awareness of her family was a natural part of her, as she'd been around them her entire life. It was when she was out in public that it became more evident. Even now, she was sensing all the people around her. Some, like her new friends, were stronger than others, but even when Jake had dropped off their drinks earlier, she'd sensed a mix of his innermost feelings and intent. When she'd realized they aligned with the way she'd always thought of him, a sense of relief came over her, and that was how it had been with almost everyone she knew. She couldn't imagine discovering that someone she cared about was not the person she thought she knew, let alone secretly evil or something.

In fact, her biggest surprise so far was Alice. She'd only just met her recently, but she felt like she knew her better through some of the stories Shia had told about her. The woman Shia knew and loved was hiding something, but it was wrapped up good and tight. And Rose wasn't about to try to figure it out. It was Alice's business. Overall, she wasn't surprised that there were no major disparities between how she'd previously perceived people and how she saw them now with her gift. Because on some level, the gift had already been working for her. She just hadn't zeroed in on it yet. But now that she had, she was being flooded with additional nuances that gave her a lot more information.

It was almost overwhelming. Sometimes, she wished she had a way to turn it off or at least dim it.

"Rose? Did you hear what I said?"

Rose turned to Gem feeling a little disoriented. "I'm sorry. Can you repeat it?"

"I asked if you'd talked to Shia today."

"I did. She's enjoying herself, especially the change in surf conditions. But she's getting a little beat up."

"Looks like she's going to take third in this one," Gem said, looking at her phone, presumably checking the scores. As soon as she said it, the leaderboard was displayed on the TV screen.

"Lisa's in second. Maria Maruga is going to take first," Gem said.

"Maria is killing it this season," Alice said.

"I had no idea you followed the sport so closely," Gem said.

"I think I'd be a terrible friend if I didn't. It's Shia's entire life." Alice appeared shocked that Gem would think otherwise.

The comment gave Rose a shot of her own insight. While she knew without a doubt that she and Shia were beyond excellent in bed, it caused her to question what kind of friends they were outside of it. She didn't know much about Shia's career at all, except how passionate Shia was about it. As she was contemplating that, it occurred to her that in the week since Shia had found out that her mother was alive, they hadn't discussed that, either. She knew in her heart that they had more than sex in common, but she'd done very little to expand on that, mostly due to her worries about not pressuring Shia beyond their casual agreement, even in the week since they'd determined they weren't simply casual. They'd spent a lot of time in bed since then. After all, Shia had asked her to initiate more of their time together, which she'd been doing.

Alice's comment prompted her to make a new decision, though. She was going to learn what Shia was into outside of surfing.

"I'm going to grab a beer. Does anyone want one?" Gem asked, sliding out of the booth.

"I'll go with you," Rose said, sliding with her. Shia's heat was over, and she needed a little space.

"No, thanks. I think I'm going to go for a walk," Alice said, standing. "I've spent too many hours this week sitting." She waved and headed toward the door.

Gem had already made it to the bar and was leaning against it, chatting with Lincoln. Rose stood behind her, catching some of the highlights of the competition on one of the screens behind the bar. As she did, a woman slid off a seat a few stools down, and Rose had to take a second look because for a second, she could have sworn it was Shia. Taken aback, she knew it had to be her mother. She nudged Gem and subtly nodded toward the woman, who was pulling on a zippered hoodie. When she saw a look of recognition cross Gem's face, she knew she wasn't seeing things. She looked away, hoping the woman hadn't noticed her gaping.

"Shit. I'm sorry," a man said as he crossed behind Shia's mom. He'd splashed beer on the woman's jacket.

Rose took a handful of napkins from the bar and offered them to her. "Here you go."

"Thank you," the woman said, looking at her with eerily familiar eyes while dabbing at the spot. A wave of compassion hit Rose. She also detected a faint thread of sadness, but there was an overwhelming sense of strength and gratitude there, too. All of it was disorienting, but Rose maintained her cool.

"I'm sorry," the man who'd spilled said again. "I wasn't looking where I was going."

"It'll dry," the woman said with a smile, taking her jacket off. "It's probably karma getting back at me for all the times I've spilled on someone else." She patted the man's arm, smiled at him and Rose, and continued on her way. The man watched her for a few seconds before he walked to a nearby table.

Rose was stunned. "She looks exactly like…"

"Shia," she and Gem finished together.

"You saw it, too."

Gem nodded. "I've seen her at the last couple of competitions. Usually with sunglasses on. But yeah. Take the glasses off and she definitely looks like her."

Rose continued to watch as Shia's mom walked away and was surprised when Alice intercepted her near the door. They spoke as if they knew each other. Rose got Gem's attention again and subtly pointed toward them.

Gem's expression changed to surprise once again. "I wonder how Alice knows her."

"That's for sure her," Rose whispered. She didn't know why she whispered, but it seemed necessary.

Gem leaned back against the bar. "I suppose Shia told you Mikayla met her at a meeting with the people at the Wild Birds and Habitats Society last week," Gem said.

Rose nodded. "She was pretty upset about it, too. She hasn't brought it up since."

"Mikayla said neither of them mentioned Shia in the meeting, so she probably doesn't know that Mikayla and Shia know each other, let alone work together. Mikayla was startled by how much they resemble each other, so she did some research, and bam! God. It's so weird. It sort of feels like I'm hallucinating."

They watched for another minute. Part of Rose hoped the woman would catch them staring. Maybe it would force the issue one way or another. But it wasn't her business. She wondered if she should even tell Shia they'd seen her.

Gem sighed. "I'm glad Shia isn't here. Seeing her would be traumatizing."

Rose felt the same. "She had a hard enough time simply hearing she's alive and well. Seeing her would be even worse."

Gem crossed her arms. "I think there's a good chance Shia will run into her at some point, what with her hanging around the competitions, not to mention with the surf park project ramping up."

Rose considered this. "I think I should tell her we saw her. It will freak her out if she runs into her without warning."

Gem shrugged again and shook her head. "I think we wait and see? I'll tell Mikayla we saw her here and get a feel for it from her. Having met her already, she might have an idea."

Everything in Rose wanted to protect Shia from possibly running into her mother unexpectedly. Being prepared that it might happen could save her from a lot of trauma. She hoped Mikayla would have some good advice. Until then, as much as she didn't want to, she'd wait.

Chapter Twenty-one

The mid-July morning sun was already hot. It felt good on Shia's skin as she toweled off after a quick rinse at the always shockingly cold outdoor shower next to the nearly empty south jetty parking lot. It wouldn't remain empty for long, being prime tourist season. Soon, the parking lot and beach would be teeming with sunburned people, kids toting boogie boards, and locals complaining about all of them. She glanced at Mikayla, who'd already rinsed off and leaned against a nearby picnic table in her flowy beach tunic, staring over the water or maybe at the few people who were on the beach for an early walk.

Shia finished rinsing off, pulled on her shorts, and slid her damp feet into her flip-flops. Normally, she'd put on a hoodie, but she opted to leave it at her bathing suit top to try to even out her tan that, despite liberal use of sunscreen, was still quite deep. She rolled her wet suit in her changing mat, a waterproof yoga mat she used to keep the sand she took home to a minimum.

"You look as if you're contemplating something over here," Shia said.

Mikayla turned, and the look of concentration changed to a smile. "Ah, you know how it is. Mulling over the solution to world peace. As I do."

"That's all?" Shia deadpanned as they fell into step for their walk back to Oceana. She wondered how Rose was doing and if she'd seen the coffee Shia had made for her before she'd left for her swim. She hadn't had the heart to wake Rose an extra half hour before her alarm went off. They were both used to being tired in the morning but usually for other reasons. However, last night, they'd stayed up later than intended playing *Mario Kart* after Shia had discovered that it was Rose's favorite game, too. She could nap during the day, but Rose rarely had that luxury.

Mikayla studied the ground as they walked. "Actually, I was wondering how to tell you that Hop invited Sharon Henderson to the meeting this afternoon."

Shia's stomach lurched, but she refrained from stopping at the mention of her mother's name. "The meeting to go over the plans for the water park?" She already knew it had to be that since they didn't have anything else scheduled, but she had to respond somehow, and that was what came out.

"Yep." Mikayla glanced at her before going back to watching her feet. "Hop's inviting the conservation group to all the initial meetings for full transparency. I think it's a good idea. It'll prevent delays in the project if they're aware of all the plans, including the ones that don't even concern them. Over time, the group will relax as Hop demonstrates his commitment to protecting the environment. His invitation has already calmed a couple of the resistant members, as has Sharon Henderson. I guess she and Hop are old friends."

"Hop's a great businessman," Shia said through her distraction. "It's probably a good idea. Is this why you were concentrating so hard back there?"

Mikayla glanced at her again, nodding. "You haven't mentioned her since I told you I met her, and I wasn't about to bring it up during the competition this weekend. I know you said you didn't believe it. But how much of it are you churning in your mind? And your heart?"

Shia glanced at her and then away. She didn't know what to call what she felt. It was almost as if she had all of what she imagined were appropriate emotions going on inside her—hurt, anger, confusion—but it was wrapped in a blanket of cotton, muffling the effect. When the subject didn't get brought up, she didn't think about it. "I'm okay. I did the research after we talked. I believe it now. I'm sorry I doubted you. It's just so…" She shook her head. "I don't know what it is."

Mikayla stopped walking. Slightly startled, Shia stopped too and faced her.

"I don't want to invade your space, but I'm not sure how to proceed with the surf park stuff while keeping your privacy and protecting your feelings. I know you haven't asked me to do any of that, but I care about you. I don't want to see you hurt. And to be honest, you've always been open and forthcoming with me, but you haven't been lately, so even while this is not about me, I'm trying hard to figure out how to handle this with you." Mikayla said everything in a sort of rush, as if she was getting it off her chest.

Shia realized she'd been mostly oblivious to everything lately. Well, everything except surfing and Rose. She'd done well staying on track with her schedule and anything related to her work, but she'd been neglecting or avoiding everything else. She blew out a breath and shook her head. "I'm really sorry."

"You don't need to be sorry."

"Yes, I do."

Shia kicked a small stone. It hit the leg of a decorative cement bench placed along the path they were walking.

"Do you want to sit for a minute?" Mikayla took a seat without waiting for an answer.

Shia straddled the bench so she could look at her. "What's up, boss?"

Mikayla looked at her through narrowed eyes. "I'm not your boss." When Shia grinned, amused at the response her baiting had evoked, Mikayla pinched her cheeks. "If it weren't for this cute face." Her expression became serious again. She dropped her hand and patted Shia's arm. "This has got to be difficult for you. You've probably been thinking about it day and night."

"Actually, I have years of practice stuffing things away. I'd have been in a bad place mentally if I didn't know how. It's called disassociating. I'm a professional at it." She laughed, even though it wasn't funny.

Mikayla shifted, pulling her legs up to sit cross-legged. "I wonder if I'm the right person to talk to."

"You're the perfect person. I respect you as well as like you. You're probably the safest person I know next to Gem." She almost added Rose, but their situation automatically put her heart at risk, actually making Rose the most dangerous person she knew. "I know we haven't known each other long. What's it been? Four or five months since you and Brandi swapped houses?"

"I moved here at the beginning of March, so a little over four months."

"It feels like longer." It was true. So much had happened in the last few months that it gave that impression.

"It sure does. Brandi will be coming home from London in a

couple of months. I suppose I have to figure out a new living situation." From the expression that passed across her face, she hadn't done much in the way of planning.

"Dang. I didn't mean to bring up that stress."

"It's not such a terrible thing. But we were talking about you."

Shia sighed. "I guess we were. You said a few things back there." She tipped her head in the direction they'd come from. "One of them was that I haven't been forthcoming lately. That hasn't been on purpose. I've been preoccupied."

"Do you mean with a certain person?"

Shia looked at her through her lashes. "Yes, if you want to be specific."

"Only if you want to be specific."

"It's no secret that Rose and I have sort of, well, we've…"

"Become an item?"

"What does that mean?"

"I don't know. It's something my mom used to say when two people were dating."

Shia snorted. They'd jumped in hot and heavy and had skipped the dating part. "I'm not sure dating describes us, but yes, I guess we're an item. Hanging out and whatnot."

Mikayla poked Shia's shoulder. "Is that what the kids are calling it these days? Hanging out?"

Shia tilted her head to the side. "Well, when we aren't skipping off to playdates with our mommies."

"I didn't mean it that way, and you know it."

"I know." Shia laughed. "You're not much older than me, you know."

"Thirteen years."

"That's not that much, but I get what you're saying. I don't feel like I'm only twenty-two. I've been on my own for a long time."

"You've lived a lot of life."

Shia brushed grains of sand off the bench. "My mom was sixteen when she had me. She was a kid when she had a kid."

"I suppose she was."

Shia hadn't wanted to talk about her mom. She'd spent so many years justifying why her mother had gone to jail and how she'd died that she didn't have a clue how to feel about it all being a lie.

"I've never really known her. I don't have any memories of

her. I've always been able to keep an emotional distance from it all. Thinking she was just a kid and that she'd died young made it easy to feel sorry for her."

"And maybe forgive her?"

"Yeah, that, too." Shia traced a faint crack in the bench surface. "I looked her up that night after I left your house. I probably found more than you did because I know family names and all that. It wasn't that I didn't trust you. It was more like I wanted to keep everything the way it had been." She paused. "Because if I didn't, it meant that she'd deserted me. I'm sure my grandma had her reasons for saying she'd died. Maybe she even thought she had. It must be hard to lose your own kid." Shia lifted her head. "Everyone has their reasons, you know? I'm sure everyone was trying their best. But…but what about—" She stopped. She wouldn't be a victim.

"What about what, Shia?"

She couldn't say it. "Nothing."

Mikayla hummed a little as if she didn't believe her.

Shia picked at the hem of her shorts. "Okay. Whatever. I was going to say, 'what about me?'" She sat up and looked out over the beach. "But what does that do? Here I am. I'm happy. I have a good life. I'm living my dream. I'm going to help others have good lives, too."

Mikayla smiled. "Yes. Here you are being the best you."

"Right?"

"Right."

They were quiet for a minute.

"So?" Mikayla said.

"So what about the meeting today? I'm supposed to be there. That's what you mean, right?"

Mikayla nodded. "Yeah. You can skip it, you know."

"It's my work. This will not get in the way of it." She stared at the ocean again. "Have you told anyone that this Sharon person might be my mother?"

Mikayla shook her head vigorously. "Only Gem."

"I told Rose." Shia picked at a thread on her towel. "Sharon Henderson probably knows exactly who I am. If she doesn't, she's in for a shock, not me. Let's not make it a thing, then. I'll play stupid. I won't bring it up. She probably won't, either. We'll get this project done, and then me and this Sharon person go our separate ways. Besides, I won't be part of building the surf park. I probably won't even see her that much. Apparently, we've lived in the same city for all these years and never crossed paths. There's no reason we can't keep on steering clear of one another."

If only her stomach felt as confident as she was acting.

Chapter Twenty-two

Rose smiled at the message on her phone: *Wanna come by for lunch?*

Do I wanna? Yes. Do I have time? Unfortunately not. Rose balanced her chin on her fist and smiled. *Besides, I'm a little sore today.*

Sore? What kind of sore?

Different than usual.

Oh yeah?

Yeah. I think my thumbs are toast.

In the gaming world, we call those gamer thumbs. Maybe you need a massage.

I do. Is there such a thing as gamer boobs? I think I have that, too. But that brings us back to the time issue.

There was a short pause before the jumping ellipsis showed Shia typing her response: *Sorry. I glitched out a little. Can I give you a rain check on the massage and drop some lunch off wherever you are? If I promise you don't need to use your thumbs to eat it? Or your boobs?*

Rose laughed. *I would love that.*

Excellent. I'll be there in a few.

A cloud of butterflies took off in Rose's stomach, even though she didn't have the time to hang out with Shia on her lunch break. Something told her that normally super-independent Shia needed to touch base, and it made her feel awesome that Shia needed her. Even if she had a dozen complaints about insects invading residents' homes. Even if she needed to come up with a solution. Even if she'd been hung up on by the pest control Oceana had used for the past ten years.

It seemed that her grandfather had fired them earlier in the year without telling anyone. Now she was trying to find a service that only used environmentally safe chemicals and could come out immediately.

The problem was that North County was in a drought. Insects were getting into everyone's houses looking for water, so all the pest control services were busy, with the good ones booked out for months. In the meantime, she and DJ had been spraying the units themselves. On top of that, she'd been battling the yawns because she'd stayed up way too late playing games. Not that she was complaining.

Her email dinged. Another complaint. Another ding. Another complaint. Had the mobile home park been built on a giant ant farm? She looked up another service and dialed them. Fifteen minutes later, she'd heard four more no's and was in the process of getting another one as the person on the other end of the phone explained that they didn't have an opening big enough to accommodate Oceana until September. When the salesperson transferred her for the third time, she lost patience and slammed the phone down.

"Jackass." She glared at it, then picked it up to make sure she hadn't cracked the screen. Luckily, she hadn't.

"Remind me not to piss you off." Shia was leaning against the doorjamb holding a paper bag that promised to have something delicious in it based on the aroma.

Rose dropped her forehead into her hands, then looked back up. "This day started off so good. Now I just want to go back to bed."

Shia grinned and gave a sexy side-eye. "That can still be arranged. But what about that pesky time thing you were whining about?" She took a seat on the small couch to the side of the desk.

"I did not whine," Rose whined.

Shia rolled her eyes. "Okay, Whiney McNotWhinerson. What's causing you all this distress?"

Her email dinged right on cue. It was her turn to roll her eyes. "I've received about—" Her phone rang. It was one of the residents who had submitted a work order about the ants in her kitchen. "I have to get this," she whispered. "I have no idea why I'm whispering," she whispered again.

"Probably so you don't yell when you answer the call," Shia whispered back.

Even though it was true and not even remotely funny, Rose started to laugh. "Hello. This is Rose."

There was a harrumph over the line. A literal harumph. "Are you laughing at me, young lady?"

"Not at all, Mrs. Bosley. I hit my funny bone in my haste to answer your call." She grimaced at Shia, who gave her a thumbs-up.

"That's good. I wanted to tell you that my son came over and killed all the ants, so you can cancel the work ticket thing. He used both cans, so they shouldn't be back anytime soon."

"I'm sorry you had to call your son, Mrs. Bosley. I'll reimburse you for the spray."

"That's not necessary, but you're sweet for offering. I'll follow up on my note to your grandfather and Gem that you offered to reimburse me, though."

Rose lowered her head into her free hand. "You wrote them a note?"

"I called it a note, but it was an email. I wanted to let them know that the ants aren't your fault. It's hot. They're looking for moisture. Same with the spiders. Insects want water, too."

"You have spiders, too?"

"Not anymore. My boy Lawrence took care of them. He's next door helping Mae with her ants. I can't say that I've ever seen so many critters in all the seventeen years I've lived here. Mae was chattering on about plagues being a sign of the end-times, and while it's enticing to believe it, what with all the politics being what they are these days, I'm chalking it up to climate change. Insects will inherit the Earth. That's what the Good Book is talking about when it mentions the meek. The insects will get bigger than we are. That'll be the next age. Lord, I hope Lawrence got all the ants. I don't want any of them handing down stories about little old Ingrid Bosley in 782 and her part in the July eighteenth massacre."

Rose listened for a few more minutes, thanked Mrs. Bosley, and finally hung up. At least two of the work orders could be closed.

"You're dealing with an ant infestation? Is that it? What happened with the company that used to come? The one with the aardvark character in a breathing mask and the sprayer thing strapped to its back?"

"I guess my grandfather fired them and didn't tell anyone, but when I asked him about it, he didn't remember."

"Oh gosh. I wonder if it was because of the strokes. Can you explain and ask them to come back?"

Rose shook her head. "I tried. He was so verbally abusive, they don't want to deal with us again, but even if they did, their schedule was already full. I've called all the companies between San Diego and Los Angeles and as far east as Palm Springs, but everyone is slammed. The drought is driving insects indoors."

"Have you tried Deluca and Sons?"

Rose tried to remember. "I don't think so." She went back to her search. "They aren't listed when I look for exterminators."

Shia pulled up the Deluca and Sons website on her phone. "It comes up when I search their name."

"I'm not sure if it matters, but they call themselves pest control rather than exterminators, which is what I searched for."

"Do you mind if I call them? Saul and I went to school. We had chemistry together."

"Chemistry?"

"The class kind. Not the kind we have." Shia winked, setting off a series of physical responses that resulted in a near inability for Rose to respond coherently.

"Sure," she managed to squeak out.

Shia dialed her friend while Rose balanced her head on her propped-up hands, watching. Seeing Shia interact with others allowed Rose to see a side of her that she didn't get to see very often. Shia probably didn't realize she gave off a strong sense of relief and pride in herself for being able to help. Rose made a note to show her gratitude with a considerable amount of extra appreciation the next time they had their clothes off. When Shia lowered the phone and gave her the thumbs-up, she had to admit she was more than a little turned on. She didn't even know if Shia's call had been fruitful because she was so distracted.

"He said he'd personally come out today to give you a quote, even though he doesn't usually go on calls himself. They're as busy as everyone else."

"I love you for doing this." Her heart dropped into her stomach. What had she said? "I mean, I don't know what I would have done without you." Holy hell. Was that any better? "Um, did he tell you that you'd have to make it worth his while? You know, like promising him your firstborn or go out on a date with him?" God, she was making it worse every time she opened her mouth.

Shia slid to stand between her and the desk, leaning with her hands on the arms of the desk chair. She was close enough to kiss if Rose leaned forward. "I don't think his husband would appreciate what you just insinuated."

Rose hardly heard her because she was thinking about kissing her. "I can't wait to meet him."

"He'll be here in about thirty minutes for the estimate." Shia paused and raised an eyebrow. "I can't be here for it, but you should offer to give him an open-mouthed kiss from me."

"Okay, but I'm not gonna do that"—she shivered—"thing you do. That bottom lip nibble-suck-lick thing that makes my pants accidentally fall down."

"Fair enough. His loss but we want all the pants staying on, seeing how Oceana is a professional operation. Since I won't be here, I guess I should tell you now so you're not surprised that if you take it, he'll spray at night so it will have a chance to dry before people take their dogs out for their morning walks."

A weird sense of out-of-body dread came over Rose. "I'll need to do an automated call and email to let the residents know."

"I can help after my thing this afternoon."

She really did love Shia for being who she was. "No. It's really not that big a deal. I don't know why I stressed like that. You're my hero, you know."

Shia grinned. "It's all in a day's work." She reached into the bag she'd put on the desk, took out a wrapped sandwich, and placed the bag in front of Rose. The smell of meatballs wafted enticingly up at her.

"Delvecchio's. Not only are you my hero, you're a mind reader. I was craving one of these earlier this week."

"I'm not saying you talk in your sleep, but I'm saying you talk in your sleep."

"I do not. Do I?" Rose was a little embarrassed, but it was overridden by the little thrill that Shia knew this about her.

"You do. I was jealous about all the moaning and groaning you were doing until you thanked someone for the delicious meatball sandwich."

Rose tossed a packet of sticky notes at her. "I'm too tired and hungry to flirt back at you, so I'm going to save my energy for the actual eating of the real-life sandwich. You're a peach, Shia. I mean it."

"And with that, I will be on my way." She leaned over and gave her a kiss. Rose's pants somehow stayed on but only barely. She had to center herself to find her voice again. That was when she noticed what Shia was wearing.

"By the way, you look super sexy in that outfit. I have a pocket watch with a chain that would go great with that vest." She looked her up and down. "And those spiffy pants and your shoes are all shiny. God, if I wasn't swamped, they'd be in a pile getting all wrinkled right about now."

Shia usually would have offered to make the wrinkled pile happen, but she didn't, and Rose wondered what the meeting was for. "It's just a business meeting. Will I see you tonight?"

Rose enjoyed the tingle that ran along the edges of her skin. "I can't promise to stay awake past seven, but give me a text when you're done swimming with the fishes." When Shia left, Rose spent a minute wondering about the meeting but was soon answering more calls and getting ready for Saul Deluca's visit. Shia couldn't possibly know how much she'd helped her today.

CHAPTER TWENTY-THREE

Shia counted out the tempo of her heel beats against the cement from the only dress shoes she owned. One, two, three, four. One, two, three, four. The crunch of sand beneath them and against the concrete added a little top hat percussion. *Chish, chish, chish, chish. Chish, chish, chish, chish.*

If she was a poet, she would have composed a song in her mind to go with it. She let the rhythm of her body moving in time complete the music. If there was one thing she knew how to do, it was move in time with the rhythm of her surroundings, especially on water. It wasn't the big movements that made surfing the almost spiritual thing it was. It was the subtle movements that carried the board along the face of a wave, uniting the surfer with the board and the board with the ocean. Focusing on the movements of her body and the tempo her walk created allowed her to fall into a sort of meditation, where she could ignore where the walk was taking her and who would be at the end of her journey.

Mikayla walked beside her, headed to the Canteen for the meeting with Hop and Sharon Henderson. A group of kids ran out of the saltwater taffy shop a few doors down, bringing Shia back to the here and now. As soon as her meditation broke, everything she'd worked so hard to not think about rushed back. To top it off was her regret over the Philly cheesesteak she'd had for lunch. She imagined it sloshing around in her stomach with all the acid trying to bubble up into her throat. She'd do it again, though. Seeing Rose had definitely gotten her mind off how nervous she was about seeing her mother. She'd have crawled out of her skin waiting if she had been left to her own devices.

"Are you going to be okay?" Mikayla asked as they arrived at the door to the Canteen.

"Who, me?" She tried to smile. "I'm totally fine. As far as anyone knows, I've never met her."

Mikayla gave her a single nod before they entered. "I'll take your lead."

Hop was up at the bar talking to Lincoln and another man. When he saw them, Hop met them in the middle of the room, all smiles, ushering them to his table. Shia asked for a ginger ale while scanning the room for Sharon Henderson. She'd already decided she didn't want to call her Mom.

"I'll be right back with those drinks," Hop said amiably as she and Mikayla slid into the booth.

When he came back, he was with another man he introduced as his brother Gary, who was also his silent business partner. They chatted while Shia's anxiety heightened at the knowledge that Sharon Henderson would be there any minute. She was grateful for Mikayla, the master of light conversation due to all of her years entertaining clients with her ex-husband. Listening to the others talk, Shia was able to calm down.

Shia felt the air in the room change the moment Sharon Henderson walked into the bar.

"There she is," Hop said, shifting his glance. He and Gary got up while Shia tried to regulate her breathing. She was beginning to feel like the meeting was a mistake.

Thankfully, the others stopped at the bar and gave Shia a moment to pull herself together. Mikayla rested a hand on hers, but she barely felt it. She barely registered anything as the blood rushed in her ears, blocking it all out.

"Your hand is cold. Are you breathing?" Mikayla said, squeezing.

Shia simply stared at Mikayla, soaking in the warmth of her hand.

"I'm right here, Shia. Just breathe. I'll do all the talking if you need me to." Mikayla adjusted her gaze toward the bar.

Shia followed it. Even from across the room, she would have recognized her mother. She looked exactly like she had in her grandmother's photographs. More eerily, the face was basically the same one she saw in the mirror every day. She even wore her blond hair up in a loose updo, like Shia wore hers sometimes. Except for the clothing—Shia wore plain clothes compared to the diaphanous, flowy tunic with pink hibiscus flowers over white capri pants and sparkly sandals—they were more alike than not.

When her mother looked their way, Shia shifted her gaze and

studied the condensation on her glass, rethinking her plan. There was no way she was going to be able to pretend she didn't know who this was. She had to get out of there.

"I…I need to go to the bathroom," she said and slid out to hurry to the restroom. Mikayla said something, but she couldn't hear over the rushing of blood in her ears.

She barely made it to the toilet when the Philly cheesesteak came back up. Fortunately, her sickness was short-lived. After she splashed water on her face and dried it with the rough paper towels from the dispenser, she leaned against the counter, washed her mouth out, and tried to collect herself.

"It's her," she whispered. Despite having looked her up and linking all the details together, she still hadn't really believed it. But now there was no denying it. Her mother was fifteen feet away, and Shia was caught between wanting to stay and running away. In either case, she wasn't sure her legs would work.

"Are you okay?"

She hadn't heard the door open, but Mikayla's worried face appeared over her shoulder in the mirror. That steady composure comforted her, and she stood straighter. "I think I am."

"You looked like you were going to be sick." Mikayla rested a hand on her shoulder, grounding her even more.

She wished Rose was there. "I was. Note to self: No Philly cheesesteak on the day you see your dead mother." She laughed much louder than she intended.

Mikayla smiled and tilted her head. "Do you want to go? It's fine if you do. I'll go with you. I won't leave you alone."

"Part of me wants to. The other part is curious. Why the hell did I think this was a good idea?"

"It wasn't your idea. It was Hop's. It's a normal business meeting for him. He'll understand, but you don't need to tell him, either."

Shia blew out a stream of air. "It's tempting to leave, but now that I've seen her, there's no pretending she's still dead and gone."

"I guess not. But it doesn't mean you need to interact with her."

"True." Shia dropped her head and closed her eyes. Even if she could magically transport herself back to her own house, would she?

"Look. You don't need to decide anything. I'm going to go out there and tell them that you aren't feeling well and that I'm going to take you home." Mikayla turned to leave.

"Wait. I'm okay. Do I look okay?"

Mikayla smiled. "You look beautiful as always."

Shia felt herself blush. "Stop. I think I can go back. I'm not sure how much of a conversationalist I'll be, but I'm not going to run away."

"Are you sure?"

"Yep. I'm curious about this woman who gave birth to me and then abandoned me."

Mikayla studied her for a moment. "Maybe—"

Shia pushed away from the counter, grateful her legs didn't give out on her. "I'm not about to come out and say that. Or anything like it. I'm just shoring myself up."

When they approached the table, Shia got second thoughts about the whole thing, but she felt committed now, and she focused on sliding into the booth before looking at anyone, especially her mother, who was sitting directly opposite. This was going to be so uncomfortable.

"You ran out of here like you saw a ghost, kid," Hop said.

Shia cleared her throat. "I had something at lunch that didn't agree with me. I feel a lot better now."

"Jesus. You two could be sisters," Gary said, looking between Shia and her mother. Shia wanted to shrink into the leather-like material of the booth. "I know I just met you, Shia, but you two must be related, right? Sharon? I'd put money on it."

"Who? Shia and Sharon?" Hop squinted between them and shook his head. "It's the facial agnosia. I usually can't recognize faces unless they're really distinctive."

Shia heard him, but her awareness was on her mother, even if she couldn't bring herself to look at her. In fact, she looked anywhere but until she matched her gaze to Mikayla's and could see concern and curiosity jockeying for control.

"Hello, Shia," Sharon said, almost as if she was talking to herself.

"Do you know each other?" Gary asked.

"Um, well, Shia's my…my daughter." Sharon tapped her fingers against the table on either side of her glass.

Hop slapped the table with his beefy hand. "No kidding? How come I didn't know this? I mean…" He ran his fingers along his chin.

Shia had been open about her background in interviews since the beginning. After four years surfing in the competitions he organized, Hop was probably familiar with it, so she guessed what he was thinking.

"I'm out of my element here. Can't control my stupid mouth," he said, taking a long drink of the amber liquid in his glass.

Gary looked like he was trying to piece things together along with the discomfort around the table. Finally, he placed both elbows on the table, interlaced his fingers, and dropped his chin onto them. "Shit. I'm gonna say it because that's the kind of person I am. This is better than a reality show. Sharon, we've known each other how long? A decade? Maybe longer? You never mentioned you had a daughter."

Sharon seemed as surprised as Shia and dropped her hands into her lap before resting them on the table again. Shia only saw this in her periphery because she couldn't bring herself to look. A weird wooden feeling was firmly in place inside her. If she looked directly at her mother, let alone made eye contact, she was afraid she'd lose it. Maybe even vomit again because her stomach was a caldera of acid. God, she regretted that damn sandwich so much.

Sharon breathed out heavily. "It's a long story, Gary."

Shia sensed more than saw Sharon reach partly across the table. Finally, she looked. Thankfully, the wooden sensation held, became even more rigid.

"Shia. This was never supposed to happen. I'm sorry."

Shia believed her. There was no way this woman would have ever tried to see her, let alone meet her. She was a stranger. It was weird because they shared DNA, but other than that, Sharon obviously had no interest in knowing her. She'd made that clear for over nineteen years.

Shia cleared her throat and lifted her ginger ale, hoping her smile made it to her eyes. "It's okay. I was surprised. I had to let the pieces fall into place. I'm good now." She wasn't even close to good. But she wasn't about to admit it, even if it was no doubt displayed like a billboard across her forehead.

Sharon's brow creased, but other than that, her expression remained the same. Shia felt like she was being studied. Curiosity, probably. That was all it was.

She took a sip and hoped she'd be able to swallow around the knot in her throat. Thankfully, it went down. She set her glass back on the table with only the slightest shaking. "We're here to talk about the park?" she said.

Hop rubbed his chin. "I think we should reschedule. This is, um, just a walk-through of the plans so everyone could get an idea of what we intend to do. Sharon, you've received all the environmental impact reports and our responses. The rest is to make sure we have"—he paused to sip—"open dialogue. That way, we can all feel more comfortable bringing up any issues or concerns. We're all going to be involved in it for various reasons, so...well, I'm babbling now. How about we reschedule?" He looked around. Everyone nodded. Shia had no way of knowing what any of them were thinking, but she knew it had to do with her, and she hated it.

"I better get back to the office. I have a stack of work to sort through. It's never-ending, you know." Sharon made to stand, but since she was blocked on one side by Hop and Gary, with Mikayla and Shia on the other, she could only sit forward with her bag pulled onto her shoulder and her hands flat on the table.

Hop scrambled to get up. "I'll get back to you, Sharon," he said as she passed him.

She turned and waved, looking uncertain as Shia and Mikayla slid out of the booth. "Just shoot me another email. Tuesdays are best for me. It was nice meeting you, Mikayla and, uh, Shia. See you all soon." And with that, she left. Soon after, Hop and Gary made their excuses and promises for the follow-up meeting as they disappeared into the back room.

Mikayla pulled the straps of her bag over her arm and sighed. "That was…I don't know what that was, but do you want to get coffee or something?"

Shia rubbed her stomach; the acid was still burning uncomfortably. "I'm not sure I can manage anything right now. I think I want to be alone. I'm going to hit the water a little early today if that's okay."

"Sure. I have a few phone calls I need to return anyway. I think I'll swing by Seaside Café. I mean, unless you need to talk or something. I can also walk back with you and make the calls when I get home. Whatever sounds good to you."

"I'm fine. It was a little weird at first, but it wasn't as…" She searched for the right word. "Impactful as I thought it might be. I'm just going to hit the waves and let it all sink in. I'm okay, though. Promise." And she was, aside from the acid burning its way through her stomach walls.

Hitting the waves sounded like the most appropriate thing to do. Surfing had always centered her. And afterward, she'd ask Rose to come over. Once she processed everything, she'd be fine. She'd gone through way worse. Probably.

Chapter Twenty-four

Rose stifled a yawn as she listened to Saul Deluca talk to his crew about the game plan. She'd gotten a natural boost of energy while walking through the park, showing Saul the layout, but that had worn off soon after they'd signed the work contract and agreed on a plan of action.

The short-notice overnight eradication efforts would cost extra money, but Gem had already signed off on it and had even praised Rose for how quickly she'd taken care of the mess her grandfather had caused. A tiny part of her was ashamed about how much she craved Gem's praise, but she'd long ago come to terms with her hero worship of her aunt, who one hundred percent deserved it. And right now, Shia was right up there with Gem on the hero list for being the one to save the day by calling her friend Saul. It was sobering to think that Rose had very nearly allowed herself to become overwhelmed by the insect issue simply because she hadn't asked for help. She wondered how long she would have let it go on if Shia hadn't come by.

Her phone vibrated: *Hey beautiful. Are you still up for tonight? I was thinking Chinese delivery and binging something on Netflix.*

A familiar tingle ran through Rose as she read the text. *Sounds perfect. I'll probably fall asleep watching whatever you decide on, though. I'm a tired unit.*

The ellipsis kept appearing and disappearing. Rose wondered if she'd said something wrong.

Are you sure you want to come over?

The uncertainty of Shia's response caused a wave of tenderness to cascade through her. Shia had displayed small cracks in her usual capable and confident armor in the last week. Rose wondered if the thing about her mother was bothering her more than she let on. She'd tried not to pry because it was obvious that Shia didn't want to talk about it, but she wondered if she should at least check in with her. In the meantime, all she wanted to do was reassure her. *I've been dreaming about snuggling with you all day.*

Me too. Can you stay the night?

This was the first time Shia had asked her to stay over before she was already there. Rose liked how it felt. *I'd love to. I'll give Chad some extra snacks as a guilt offering for neglecting him.*

Bring him with you.

This was new, too. Shia hadn't seemed very keen about Chad. *Are you sure? I have a travel case for him, but you didn't sound very enthused when I told you about him.*

I haven't been around rats before. I'd love to meet him. He's your family.

The last part made Rose's heart swell. *Cool. I'll be there as soon as Saul has his plan in place.* She giggled and then added, *BTW the kiss went better than expected.*

I just threw up a little.

She was smiling about the last text when Saul approached with his notes. Before he said anything, she knew things were going to work out. His whole being projected confidence and genuine goodwill. The somewhat guilty feeling she'd started to get when she accidentally picked up on a person's essence wafted through her again. She wondered what people would do if they knew she was doing it. But she wasn't *doing* it. It was passive, if anything. All her life, she'd thought she would love to have her grandfather's and Gem's gift. And for the most part, she did. She just never thought it would come with mixed emotions like this.

❖

Rose arrived and, true to her word, fell asleep almost immediately after they ate. Shia sat against the headboard of her bed, holding Chad while Rose slept curled up beside her. Chad's white fur seemed to glow in the dim light of the Netflix home page behind him. She'd turned off the show they'd started watching during dinner because the inside of her head was too noisy to concentrate. Besides, eating dinner in bed, playing with Chad, and having Rose so close to her was enough to occupy her mind and body. It all made seeing her mother earlier that day a background thought.

She'd hoped to talk to Rose about it, but Rose was wiped out when she'd showed up. Shia didn't want to add to the stress of her day. It was consolation enough to be near her, but when Rose fell asleep, the whole situation came back to Shia in vivid detail, bringing with it the embarrassment of leaving to be sick and the disappointment that she couldn't force herself to remain unconnected to the event of her mother being very much alive. More than anything, though, a suffocating sense of grief threaded its way through her. It was probably the worst part of the whole day. She hated that she felt that way. How could she grieve something she'd never really had?

Chad seemed to sense what was going on, and although she'd never handled a rat, she let him climb onto her shoulder, where he nuzzled her ear before he moved back to Rose to burrow into the space between her neck and shoulder. She could see how this was probably a frequent thing, as Rose's dark hair acted as a sort of blanket for him. She chuckled quietly when Chad shut his eyes and nuzzled against her with a tiny groan. Shia's heart couldn't stand the cuteness. She took a couple of pictures to show Rose when she woke up.

Tired but restless, Shia eased out of bed to collect their dishes and take them out to the kitchen. While there, she cleaned up the boxes the food had come in, wiped down the counters, and poured a glass of water. While she drank it, she stared at the third-place trophy on her counter that she'd won at her last competition. She appreciated it as much as she did the first-place trophy she'd won in Oceanside a few weeks ago. Maria had won the event handily, with Lisa barely beating out Shia for second place. She wasn't even mad. She was proud of herself. Maria and Lisa were, by far, better surfers, but she was rapidly gaining on them.

After draining the glass, she continued to stand at the counter, thinking about her life. It wasn't something she chose to do often, but when she did, it was more of a shuffle through events to find a specific memory rather than a walk down memory lane. Spending time in her past was never pleasant. Bad memories outnumbered the good ones at least ten to one, so even thinking about a good time ultimately segued into darkness. It was best to visit her past in quick, in and right back out segments. Still, some things were simply too painful to think about. She'd tucked those securely away, and that was the way she wanted them to stay.

Permanently. When Shia went through those memories, it was usually against her will and only for information, a way to help her solve a problem. She didn't spend time dwelling. One of those moments was bothering her now. She'd tucked it away so well, she couldn't access it. She wasn't even sure she wanted to. She suspected it had something to do with her mother but couldn't pinpoint it, and no matter how she tried, she couldn't sweep it away. What did her mother's reappearance in her life mean?

Actually, it wasn't a reappearance. It was an intrusion. Her mother had left a long time ago. Shia had only been three, but her mother had been gone even before then. Her grandmother had said that by the time her mom went to prison, she was spending more time away chasing drugs and parties than she was spending at home. Because of that, Shia didn't owe her anything.

With that in mind, she realized that the hard part had been done. She had come face-to-face with the woman who had deserted her. And she was still standing. Not only standing, thriving. There was nothing her mother could do to affect her more than she already had. Was that what her memory was trying to tell her?

A light knock on the door pulled her from her thoughts. With Rose sleeping in the next room, she wondered who it could be. Alice was probably asleep. Maybe it was Mikayla checking in on her.

She was not prepared to see her mother standing on her doorstep, illuminated by the porch light, looking unsure and wary.

Neither of them said anything for a couple of moments that felt like an hour. Finally, Shia couldn't stand it. "How do you know where I live?"

Her mother had the grace to look uncomfortable. "This is awkward."

Shia agreed, but she didn't answer. Words were the last thing on her mind. Her mother was uninvited, and her arm itched to slam the door in her face.

"Um." Sharon pushed a strand of her hair behind her ear. "I haven't stopped thinking about the meeting today. I could see that you were shocked. I worried that you might not be doing well. I know I'm not doing well with it. I needed to see how you were, even though I'm probably the last person who can make you feel better. Jesus. I'm not making any sense. I honestly don't know why I'm here. I…After all these years of thinking I would never be able to talk to you, I couldn't leave it like that, with you in shock. I simply…couldn't do it."

Shia tracked each word but had no idea what they meant. She'd been too preoccupied with the chaotic thoughts that had been in her mind all day, and now they'd abruptly gone absolutely silent. The absence of their noise was painfully deafening. Her innermost vault had closed, and she was stuck in a middle place of unfamiliar pathways. Would she find her way back?

"Can I come in?" her mother asked. Without thinking about it, Shia pushed the screen door open and stood to the side.

And Sharon walked in. Shia's mother was in her house.

Her mother looked around as if taking it in, finally sitting on the edge of the couch, clutching her bag, looking very much like she wasn't sure she should be there at all. Shia balanced on the edge of wishing like hell her mother was not there and some other feeling that consisted of curiosity and longing, uninvited emotions she absolutely didn't want to explore. She followed her mother into the living room, sitting on the other side of the couch. "I…I didn't come here with a goal in mind or anything. I don't know what to say, really," her mother said.

"Grandma used to tell me to keep my eye on the goal," Shia said, almost to herself. She didn't know why. It was the only thing she could see in her mind's eye.

"She used to tell me the same thing."

"I played soccer for a couple of years. She was trying to relate." She felt Sharon turn toward her.

"She was talking about not becoming me."

"What do you mean?" But she knew.

"She was talking about sticking to your goals, not giving up. She was telling you not to be me."

"Why would she do that?" Again, Shia knew why but didn't want to sound like a jerk.

"She wanted me to set goals and stick to them. Maybe because she got pregnant young and never finished high school. I don't know. She never told me."

Maybe it was abandoning that baby? Or choosing drugs? "I get it," Shia said, but she didn't mean it. Not for her mother, anyway.

"People change."

Shia nodded. "Yeah. People change."

Her mother fiddled with a bracelet and abruptly shifted to face her. "I didn't know you were going to be there today. I thought I was meeting Gary." She laid her palm on her forehead just like her grandmother used to, and the familiar gesture brought up a flash of grief. A grief she hadn't felt in many years.

In an instant, she was twelve, barely able to keep upright, bright sunshine making her sweat despite the ocean breeze, and the seat of a plastic chair pressed into the back of her legs the only thing holding her up. Her grandmother was supposedly in the shiny coffin being held over a hole by some kind of brass elevator thing, and she knew she wasn't ever going to see the worn green chair Grandma had sat in reading her books or smell the musty, under-the-sink smell in the kitchen or the warm misty scent of the green bath bombs Grandma used to buy for her, or…

Her mother's voice cut through the gooey film of sorrow she was suffocating in. "And I had no idea you were involved with the surf park. No clue at all. I would never have agreed to work with them. I'm going to turn the project over to one of my colleagues. You don't have to worry about—"

Shia swallowed the thing in her throat that threatened to choke her. "Grandma said you were dead. She said you died in prison." She sensed rather than saw her mother's shocked reaction. Her internal vision was still in the past, staring at the thin band of darkness which was the void that would swallow her grandmother between the edge of the grass and the brass structure holding up the coffin.

"I never went to prison. I never even got in trouble with the police. Lord knows I should have, but I didn't."

"If you didn't go to prison, what kept you…away?" Shia asked, even as she wasn't in her body. She felt nothing. Or maybe it was everything. So much emotion, she couldn't feel anything.

"There isn't a day I don't ask myself the same thing." Sharon leaned forward, hugging herself, rocking a little. Shia slowly moved out of the past. This was important. "I got pregnant at fifteen and had a baby at sixteen. That's what happened. We weren't old enough to drive yet. I didn't know I was pregnant until I felt you kick. Kirk went out with his buddies and got drunk the night I told him. He was so sure his dad would beat his ass. His dad never had the chance. Pauly was screwing around near Ponto Beach. The pickup ended up on its roof in the lagoon. All of them made it out, but Kirk took in too much water trying to swim out. He dry-drowned while the cops were trying to figure out what happened. One minute, he was fine. And then he collapsed. Pauly said they all thought it was the alcohol. But he never woke up."

The mention of Ponto Beach brought Shia out of the haze of

memories. She'd surfed there a few times. "Grandma said you didn't know who my father was and that you died of an overdose in prison."

Her mother expelled a sharp breath. "I knew Kirk since we were little kids. She fed him more meals than his own mother did. She was part of the people who teased us all the time that we were boyfriend and girlfriend. But we weren't. I loved him like a brother more than anything else. But people joked. We denied it, but it didn't stop them."

Shia must have missed something. "But you said he was..."

Her mother stared at her hands. "We messed around a couple of times. But we didn't love each other like that. All it takes is once when the time is right, it turns out."

She paused. Shia wondered why she was telling her all of this. She didn't really know any of the people. Except that she did. At least some of them. This person Kirk was her father, but he wasn't on her birth certificate. She never knew he had a name. Well, of course he did. But no one had told her what it was. It was as if she'd fallen into quicksand, physically and emotionally, slowly being sucked into the couch while listening to someone else's conversation. At some point, her mother started talking again.

"Your grandma and Kirk's mom used to be best friends, so we grew up together. When Kirk's older brother Pauly ended up having a problem with drugs, it all changed. Your grandma forbade me from hanging out with either of them. She started talking bad about Kirk's mom, like it was her fault or something. Her forbidding me to hang out with them only made me want to hang out with them even more, and that added to Kirk and me messing around. My brother and Pauly were the bad kids. Ironically, Kirk and I were pretty straitlaced. I mean, even though we snuck around to see each other, we mostly met up at a frozen yogurt place a block and a half down the street. Pauly getting busted for drugs kept Kirk from going near them. I think the night when...when he died might have been the first time he ever drank."

She paused again. Shia didn't feel solid, like maybe she was floating outside of her body. All this time, she'd thought of her mother as a delinquent the way her grandmother had described her.

"Everything changed after that. I was over five months pregnant when Kirk died. I felt responsible for it, so I went into a major depression. I stopped going to school. My mom still didn't know I was pregnant. She didn't figure it out until I was well into my seventh month. All she knew was that I spent most days in bed crying, and she thought I was overreacting to Kirk's death. She was always yelling at me to get my act together. It only got worse when she figured out that I was knocked up. Before I went to the hospital to have you, I hadn't taken a step out of the house in two months. I hardly left my bedroom."

She'd been sitting forward as if she'd been ready to leave any second, and now sat heavily back against the couch cushions. "When you were born, I was still depressed and blaming myself for Kirk's death. Your grandma went from yelling at me all the time to helping me get a GED, telling me I needed to get it together to raise a kid. I got my GED, but I had no idea how to take care of a kid when I was still a kid myself, so she took care of you. I felt useless, so I took advantage of her help and started hanging out with Pauly, who felt as guilty for Kirk's death as I did. He introduced me to drugs. I needed something to get out of my head. By nineteen, my mom had become your primary caretaker, and I was strung out on anything that would stop me from thinking."

Something clicked for Shia. She remembered sitting on someone's lap, looking at her grandmother across a table in a big room. She didn't remember why they were there or who they were there to see, but she guessed her grandma had taken her to see her mother in rehab, and she was sitting in her mother's lap. "You went to rehab instead of prison? How long were you in?"

Her mother sighed. "It took me almost a year to finally kick all the shit I was taking. Tell me you don't do drugs."

"I don't." Prideful arrogance swept through her at the thought that she was better than her mother.

"Good. You have addicts on both sides of your family. Mine with my dad, who took off when I was five and died of liver failure a few years after that and of course, me. Then there's your dad's brother, Pauly. I have no idea where he is or if he's even alive."

"Uncle Ricky, too." Memories of the time she'd lived with her mother's brother and his wife Junie were normally vague but came back to her in technicolor right then: the comforter she'd had at Grandma's house spread over musty bedding on a lumpy bed in a dusty room that was half occupied by storage boxes; the closet she preferred to hide in when Uncle Ricky and Aunt Junie had friends over, which was all the time; her beloved pink poodle she'd left in the park that Aunt Junie wouldn't go back for; the cigarette-smoke-filled house; the cinnamon whiskey scent of her uncle's breath; getting punished for sneaking food into her room and having to spend the night in the backyard; the night they took her away from Uncle Ricky's house when she wouldn't respond to her social worker's questions about bruises and scabs; and more. Much more.

"Yeah. Ricky had a lot of problems." Her mother's voice sounded distant and disappointed. "I've been clean for almost eighteen years, but the hardest thing I ever did was give it up to my higher power. Not God, though. Love. I'm not talking badly about God, mind you, but religion has never been my thing like it was for your grandma. Love is my higher power."

Shia wanted to laugh in her face. Love? Yeah, right. "Why didn't you come back?" Maybe she was lucky her mother hadn't come back, even with how hard it had been to live with Uncle Ricky.

"I did, but you ran away from me. You cried when I tried to talk to you. She disowned me. You chose her. You were only three. It still broke my heart, but please don't hate me." She waved her hands and shook her head dismissively. "No. I don't have a right to ask anything of you." She fidgeted with the bracelet before dropping her head back with her eyes squeezed shut. Finally, she blew out her breath. "Part of me was relieved you didn't want anything to do with me. It allowed me the freedom to create a life for myself."

She was relieved? A life for herself? "I was three. You left me."

"You were doing so well. We'd never bonded, whether it was the depression or the drugs. You were safe and happy with your grandma. She wanted to raise you. She said she couldn't do it if I kept coming back and confusing you."

Her mother looked at her intently, as if she was willing Shia to confirm it, looking for a specific response. Shia was in no mood to give one to her. She felt the emptiness of the space in her head that she retreated to when she was overwhelmed but still needed to be aware of her surroundings. She hadn't needed to go there in a long time, but now that she was there, nothing could really affect her. It was the strength she received from her Oceana family that made her feel like she belonged. It was the comfort of Rose sleeping in the other room that made her feel wanted. The woman she called her mother was only her mother in the sense that she'd given birth to her. The heavy weight of expectations never manifested that had clung to her from her past seemed to slough away. In a way, she was free.

Now she wanted answers. Not that they would give her any sort of closure or comfort, but so she would know why she'd ended up with no family. "What about when she died? Why not then?"

"I didn't find out she'd died until nearly a year later."

"No one told you?"

Sharon shook her head. "My mom had disowned me. My brother took her side. They didn't know how to contact me. By the time I found out, you were already at my brother's house."

Shia wanted to tell her that being at Uncle Ricky's house was... She didn't want to go there, even to try to hurt her mother. Every element of her life was being called into this discussion. She'd been avoiding the topic for so long, had stuffed down and locked away things too painful to think about until she'd thought she'd lost the ability to access them. But they were parading through her mind now, stirred up like ancient sediment containing poisonous outcomes if she got too close to them. She felt more numb than she'd ever felt.

"What about when they took me from Uncle Ricky's and put me in a group home?"

Her mother stared at her, moving her mouth with nothing coming out before she dropped her gaze to her lap.

Silence descended. Shia couldn't find words. She was struggling when her mother pointed.

"Who's your little friend?"

Shia looked across the living room. Chad stood on his back legs, watching them. "That's Chad. He's not mine, he's—"

The toilet flushed in the bedroom bathroom. Her mother put a hand on her forehead, once again reminding Shia of her grandma. "God. It didn't occur to me that there might be someone else here. I hope I haven't kept him up." She bent toward Chad, who'd moved next to the couch at her feet. When she put out her hand, he crawled right into it. "He's so cute. Chad is the perfect name."

The simple gesture caused Shia to lose her struggle with getting back to her numb place, and a tsunami of emotions rose in her: huge, ugly, vicious emotions that threatened to come out in terrible ways. She was on the verge of screaming just to let the pain out when Rose came into the room rubbing her eyes, but as soon as she saw Shia's mother, she stopped and whipped her head toward Shia, at which point, her sleepy expression shifted to concern.

❖

Shia was having a breakdown. Rose had seen it as soon as she looked at her. She'd felt it from the bedroom before she'd even seen her. It had woken her up, sent her to the bathroom, where she thought she might have to vomit, but when nothing happened, a strong sensation of feelings she couldn't identify remained. She went back to the bedroom where she noticed Shia was missing. She decided to try the living room, but Sharon was there, too.

That was nothing to her once she saw Shia in what she could only describe as an emotional collapse.

"It's okay, baby. I have you. I'm here. You're okay." The words flowed from her mouth, but more importantly, they flowed from her heart. Something inside her knew Shia was connecting to that flow more than anything else. Rose held her, and her rigid body began to relax. The trembling calmed a little, and Rose continued to hold on, helping her through whatever had taken control of her.

Shia continued to relax in her arms until the paralysis loosened enough that she began to sob. Sobbing would have usually caused major concern to Rose, especially from Shia, who had never displayed this level of emotion. Maybe some tears the night she'd found out that her mother was alive. That was nothing compared to what was going on now.

Something major must have happened or been said. It could have been simply the presence of her mother, but Rose knew it was more than that, that something had been said or done to rip the careful emotional barriers away. "You're safe, baby. I've got you. Do you want to lie down?"

Shia nodded, moving toward the bedroom, indicating she was done with whatever had occurred in the living room. She pulled Rose's hand.

"Can you let yourself out?" Rose asked over her shoulder.

Sharon, who looked shell-shocked, held up Chad.

Rose let go of Shia's hand for a moment to take him and then hurried into the bedroom. The sound of the front door opening and closing told her that Sharon had left. She took Shia to bed and held her until she fell asleep. Rose didn't bother to ask what had happened or why Sharon was there. She'd find out soon enough. The thing she did know was that Shia had accessed some very old memories and was dealing with them now. All she needed in the moment was to know that she mattered to someone. And she did matter to Rose. More than she knew.

CHAPTER TWENTY-FIVE

Rose lay next to Shia, watching her in the early dawn light, marveling at the perfect way Shia's lips curved, how her defined jawline relaxed in sleep. Up close, she could make out each of the fine blond hairs on her cheeks and every one of the long lashes lining her closed eyes. As she watched, a sense of pure love filled her body. She slowly traced the lines of Shia's face and smiled when she sighed and turned her head into it before relaxing into the pillow. Reluctantly, Rose pulled her hand back and tucked it under her own cheek, not wanting to wake her, but she continued to watch for a minute more. And then another.

Eventually, with a sigh, she slid out of bed to get her phone so she could text Mikayla and tell her that Shia wasn't feeling well and wouldn't be able to swim that morning. No use pretending they were just friends. Finally, she wrote a note saying she was going to the Seaside Café to get them breakfast and that she'd be back soon.

She slipped into her shoes, taking in the salty air and gentle breeze with all the thoughts she had about Shia floating in her head. The main one being the magnitude of grief Shia had been feeling the night before. It had been so big, Rose had felt like vomiting. She couldn't imagine how much more intense it had to have been for Shia. She hadn't even tried to get her to talk because the emotions flowing into her were more detailed and told a clearer story. From the core emotions of a tiny child feeling confused, forgotten, and so much more, to an adult feeling all of that plus anger, resentment, and shame, Rose could imagine the emotional chaos Shia was experiencing and trying to forget. It was as if the fight to get rid of the feelings and memories was a life-or-death struggle.

When Shia had fallen asleep, she'd clung to Rose as if she was a raft in a raging current. Rose had tried to send loving feelings back to her that seemed to help as Shia relaxed into more peaceful sleep.

Curiosity plagued Rose about why Shia's mother had been at the house. Confident Shia would tell her, she also sensed that Shia was so used to holding difficult things close to her chest that it might be difficult for her to talk about it. Rose wanted to be there for her. A barrier had been removed last night that was both frightening and exciting at the same time.

With her mind thoroughly preoccupied, Rose barely acknowledged her surroundings as she ordered and sat on the bench near the pickup counter to wait. Thoughts swirled in her mind when she became aware of a presence, and when she looked up, Sharon was at the register.

An irrational urge to flee hit Rose at the same time Sharon turned, making eye contact. A brief pang of panic Rose wasn't sure was hers or Sharon's flashed through her before Sharon gave a small smile and approached. "Hello. I figured last night was a little awkward for introductions. It would be rude to leave a second time without exchanging names. Shia may have already told you, but my name is Sharon, and I'm…getting a cup of coffee before a meeting."

This wasn't at all the woman Rose had expected, although she hadn't imagined anything aside from generalizations. Most of her assumptions were about what Sharon *wasn't*. Things like kind, caring, warm, friendly, nurturing, etc. What Rose sensed from her right now, however, told her she would have to reassess those.

Part of her wished she'd paid attention to Sharon's essence the night before. "I'm Rose. I'm sorry for asking you to leave so abruptly. I had to take care of Shia," she said, pausing when she didn't know what to call herself in relation to why she'd been at Shia's house. Sharon could assume whatever she wanted.

"Is she okay?" She appeared truly concerned as she sat next to Rose on the bench.

"She's still sleeping."

Sharon played with her bracelet. "I shouldn't have come over. I don't know what compelled me to do it."

"I wondered about that."

Sharon placed a hand on her forehead the same way Shia did when she was trying to figure out something difficult. "It was selfish. We met unexpectedly yesterday. If she felt anything like me, she wasn't okay. I couldn't leave it like that."

Rose didn't feel comfortable talking like this, especially with Sharon. "Someone told her you were in the area. Her grandmother said you were dead." Sharon grimaced. Rose reached to touch her, then pulled her hand back, uncertain. "I'm sorry. That was blunt. It's a weird situation." Why was she trying to be gentle with her?

She knew why. She had a clear idea of what she could only describe as Sharon's heart. Being able to read people was becoming easier, leaving no doubt for Rose that Sharon was operating from a place of love. There was also fear, reservation, regret, embarrassment, and a myriad of other emotions, but more than anything, there was love. The idea that Sharon didn't seem to have a secret agenda was a relief, even as it occurred to Rose that there was still a big risk that Shia and Sharon were at cross-purposes that could still end up with someone getting hurt. Even if they were both good people.

In that moment, Rose understood that the gift she and her grandfather and Gem shared was so much more than feeling someone's emotions. It was an unspoken language. The concept staggered her. However, as much as she wanted to contemplate it, now was not the right time.

Sharon looked at her with an intense gaze that reminded her of Shia. "I don't know the right thing to do. I don't deserve it, even if she were open to it, and I doubt she is, but if there's a chance, I'd like to get to know my daughter."

It wasn't Rose's place to get in the middle, but something inside her said that both Shia and Sharon wanted the same thing. But ultimately, it was up to Shia. "It might be a good idea to give her some space right now. Let her decide the next step."

Sharon nodded. "She can get my number from Mikayla."

"I'll let her know." Rose's name was called to pick up her order. Before she left, she paused and turned to Sharon. "Why was she told you were dead?"

"It would be easy to say I was young and stupid, among many other things. Depression, guilt, what I saw as my mother's complete hatred of me, drugs. But ultimately, a bad decision started a downward spiral in a family so fragile, almost anything could have toppled it. When I ran away, I left a note telling my mother she should raise Shia and consider me dead because I figured I would be soon enough.

"Somehow, I beat those odds. I wonder every day what the cost of it was, though." She stared into space for a moment while Rose took it all in: the emotions, the words, the indelible scars that had affected so many lives. It was so foreign to her. "I'd change it all if I had the power," Sharon finally said.

"Even if it meant never having Shia?"

She paused while Rose wondered what had compelled her to ask such a personal question. Yet she already knew the answer.

"I'm sorry, I shouldn't have—"

"There was a time I wished I'd never gotten pregnant. It was easy to think like that when I was so removed from her life. When I found her again, though, I couldn't imagine it."

"You mean yesterday? When you unexpectedly met?" It wasn't a graceful question, but Rose wanted to know how long Shia's mother had known Shia's whereabouts. The emotions she could sense from Sharon were far more complex than those the shock of a sudden reunion could summon. The answer to this would provide a better view into Sharon's intentions.

Sharon moved to the café's wide counter to get her coffee. "Having no legal right to her, I struggled to keep track of her over the years, but I tried. It got easier when she turned eighteen. I found her on the internet in a high school graduation announcement. I checked them, not expecting to ever see anything, but one day, there she was. Just a name in a list, but I was sure it was her. When I went to the ceremony, I knew it was her at first glance."

Rose could only describe the emotion as adoration, a feeling she had felt a few times herself when meeting her younger siblings for the first time or her baby cousins. Although what she'd felt wasn't nearly as strong as what was pouring out of Sharon. "You've known she's lived in Oceanside all this time?"

Sharon shook her head again. "The graduation announcement didn't give any other information about her, so I lost track of her again until I saw a scholarship awards list for UCSM. After that, she started getting mentioned a lot in the sports stats for surfing, first on the university team and then in other competitions."

"You've been following her career."

Sharon smiled brightly for the first time since they'd met. "Compulsively. She inherited her father's skill. He wasn't professional or anything, but he was good at it."

An alert sounded on Rose's phone. A new work order. When she glanced at the screen, she realized what time it was. Shia was probably up by now. She needed to check in and had work to get to. Not to mention deal with some of the emotional fractals inundating her.

"That means I need to get to work." Such a jarring way to end things, especially when she had no idea what to do with it all. She'd always felt the obligation to fix things, manage things, assess and organize, but it wasn't her job this time.

Sharon seemed to pull herself together. "Yes. Yes. I'm sorry. I can't believe I laid all that on you. I've never had access to anyone who…except Alice, and she made it clear our arrangement was one-way only, but I was greedy with you and…" She shook her head as if to clear it and tentatively smiled. "Anyway. I don't know if I'll get to see you again, Rose, but you seem like a beautiful person in so many ways. I'm so happy Shia has you in her life."

Those last words caused an almost physical shift in Rose, and an amazing sensation of certainty filled her. She didn't believe in destiny, but she did believe that the connections generated when the right things happened to the right people at the right time forged powerful unions. She and Shia were meant to be together, whether it was only for now or maybe forever. It didn't matter which, but she hoped it was the forever option. "It was nice to meet you," she managed as her thoughts and emotions tumbled within her.

The expression on Sharon's face revealed her uncertainty. "I hope we get to talk again."

They parted ways, Rose turning toward Oceana, Sharon walking in the opposite direction, and Rose wondered if Shia would be upset that they'd talked. It wasn't as if Rose had initiated anything. And it wasn't as if they'd talked about anything Rose wouldn't tell Shia, either. It might be a good way to bring up her new experiences with the gift, something she hadn't had the opportunity to bring up with everything going on.

CHAPTER TWENTY-SIX

A knock on the door stole Shia's concentration from the book she was reading. It had to be Alice, who had called to tell her, not ask, what time to expect her for a coffee date.

Shia was looking forward to catching up with her. When she opened the door, she was met first by the sight of a big plate of chocolate chip cookies, second by Alice's friendly smile, and third by a blast of heat from the early afternoon sun. She opened the door and ushered Alice in quickly before all the air-conditioning rushed out of her place.

"Dang. It's hot as the devil out there today." She shut the door as Alice breezed past her.

"My grandad used to say, 'It's hotter than Satan's toenails.'"

"What does that even mean?"

"I honestly don't know." Alice pursed her lips as she seemed to ponder. "Maybe it's because his feet are on the burning ground of hell."

"Or maybe Satan gets their nails done. Hot means they're sexy as f—"

Alice held up a hand. "Me bringing up H-E-L-L doesn't mean you have to start using foul language."

Shia laughed. She had no intention of actually cursing, but she liked to keep Alice on her toes. It was nice to have a break from the whole thing with her mom. "I was gonna say sexy as false eyelashes."

"Well, then. I'd have to agree with you. They are quite attractive on the right people." She studied Shia. "You could pull them off, I think, although your natural lashes are already quite long and lustrous. I, on the other hand, would look quite the clown."

"Don't sell yourself short, Alice. I think you'd look great in anything." Shia meant it. Alice might be more comfortable in the below-the-knee skirts and button-up blouses, but she'd also look great in whatever. "It's all about the confidence. I bet you'd look fabulous walking a red carpet in a little sequined number."

"Well, I'm confident I wouldn't feel confident in an evening gown, let alone false eyelashes."

"I think the next bonfire needs to be a formal affair."

"That would be lovely. I can add a brooch to my suit jacket and a pair of dark pantyhose." Alice did a hysterical impression of Betty Boop, complete with a finger on her lips and a cocking of the leg to show off her ankle and calf. Shia couldn't believe Alice was wearing low-heeled leather shoes on such a blazing hot day. Her legs were shapely, though.

"I'll start planning it." She relieved Alice of the cookies and went into the kitchen. "But first, we eat cookies, and you tell me all the gossip you haven't filled me in on in, what? Has it been three weeks?"

Alice leaned on her elbows at the kitchen counter. "I believe it's been four, but who's counting?"

"Four weeks? Really?"

"Almost five, now that I think about it. You've been busy."

"I'm never too busy for you."

Alice gave the side-eye. "I guess only you would know between all the recent noon and evening rendezvous."

Shia was shocked. Partly because Alice rarely made sexual references but mostly at the idea that she and Rose had not been as discreet as she'd thought. These days, there was no sneaking around, though. Both Rose and Chad were regular overnight guests.

"Does your silence indicate that your calendar might indeed be too full to fit in a coffee date with your matronly neighbor?"

"Sorry. No, it does not. I will always make time for you. Besides, you are not matronly."

"I am forty-seven and a half. More than twice your age. I think that is the definition of matronly."

"Do you feel matronly?" Shia brought everything to the dining table where she and Alice sat, Alice with her coffee and Shia with iced tea.

"Not really. I honestly don't think forty-seven is remotely matronly, nor is fifty-seven or even sixty-seven. It's all in the mind." She tapped her temple. "In my head, I'm the same person at forty-seven as I was when I left Topeka at eighteen, only a little smarter.

I'm probably in better shape now, too, thanks to online yoga and my power walks."

That was news to Shia. "Yoga? Since when?"

Alice flapped her hand. "I don't know. Twenty years ago or so."

"How come I didn't know this?"

"Because you don't peep into people's houses, I suppose. The back room of my place is my studio. Recently, I've added freestyle Pilates."

"Good to know in case I decide to start peeping."

"What comes around goes around. Remember that." The side-eye was back.

"You're naughty."

"Not as naughty as the couple in unit 312."

Shia knew that unit and wasn't sure she wanted to hear about how naughty they were. "Are you talking about Deb and Diane?"

"Yes, I am. Do you know what a pineapple represents?"

Shia knew. But in case Alice was talking about something else, she decided not to disclose that. "Good food? Fancy fruity drink garnishes? Major pizza debates?"

Alice leaned closer. "Swingers. You know, partner swapping?"

"Really?" Shia pretended to be surprised.

Alice nodded. "Apparently, Deb and Diane are swingers now."

"How'd you find out?" Shia had known for a long time. It didn't bother her at all. To each their own.

"Harper noticed they have a pineapple on their welcome mat."

"Maybe they don't know what it means."

Alice pursed her lips. "I never thought of that. Do you think I should tell them?"

Shia held back a laugh, imagining anyone answering a knock on the door from prim and proper Alice, telling them that they might be unknowingly advertising that they were swingers. "I think they're okay figuring it out themselves."

"What if swingers come by and proposition them?"

"They'll be able to handle it." Shia coughed to hide her laughter at the idea of anyone approaching Deb and Diane, who appeared to be almost as prim and proper as Alice.

"I'll trust you." Alice picked at a piece of cookie. "There's something else. I saw it myself."

Shia loved hearing reports about the community. She rarely

dished on them herself, but Alice's came with a large portion of genuine concern rather than malice. She always saw the good in people. "Oh yeah?"

"I saw a woman come here late Wednesday night. Because you've been seeing Rose, I was pretty sure it wasn't a romantic visit. But by the time I retrieved my glasses, she was gone."

Remembering her mother, Shia felt the statement like a physical blow. "Definitely not romantic. It was late. Past your normal bedtime."

"I was up later than normal, having gotten a little too engrossed in social media. I was signing off and closing my blinds when I happened to see her walk up." She looked more than just casually interested in who the visitor was.

While Shia was still trying to process all that had transpired during her mother's visit, she also knew that Alice's main source of entertainment outside of the mission was the goings-on at Oceana. And because Alice was her friend, Shia thought she should let her know. "That particular person was my long-lost mother."

Alice seemed almost as shocked as Shia had been. "I thought your mother was deceased?"

"I did, too. But we ran into each other at a business meeting earlier this week. She found out where I lived and came over."

Alice appeared to mull the information over, probably in an effort to not cause more distress. She rested a hand on Shia's forearm. "This must be a huge deal for you. How are you doing, dear?"

Shia traced a scratch in the varnish of her dining table. "I don't know, actually. You know me, I've always been able to tuck difficult events behind a barrier that at least takes the emotion out of them while I deal, you know? But this one is right there, trying to make me focus on it."

"What would happen if you did?"

"I honestly don't know. I don't think it would be good, though." She was relieved that Alice didn't ask for details. It had been hard enough to tell Rose what she and her mother had talked about. They hadn't spoken about it since, although she suspected Rose wanted to. But that would mean admitting that she couldn't stop thinking about how her mother had abandoned her and let her fall into the foster system with no family, no one to tell her that she mattered, no one to protect her from the bad people in the world. Basically, how blame and resentment were forefront on her mind. It wasn't who she wanted to be.

Alice rubbed her arm. "Sometimes, it just takes some time to settle. You'll be able to find a way to handle this new thing."

Shia shrugged and even managed a small smile. Alice was a glass-half-full person. While Shia couldn't always see the positive of a situation, she needed the encouraging energy Alice brought to the world.

CHAPTER TWENTY-SEVEN

Ding. Ding.

Rose checked her phone and saw two new work orders sitting in the queue. This was in addition to the two dozen that day. They kept flowing in. She couldn't seem to get ahead. The deflated feeling of slowly sliding backward gave her little energy to even try.

The worst part was that the constant juggling of the work didn't let her do any of the creative solutioning she really enjoyed. It was a temporary situation because most of the work orders were different issues stemming from one general cause: The window air-conditioning units were getting a little old, making them ineffective against the current heat wave. After the ant infestation that had been completely remediated, thanks to Saul Deluca, Gem had even warned her that midsummer heat waves were one of the hardest things to deal with because of the work they brought with them.

The minutes until quitting time couldn't move quickly enough.

Her phone dinged again, almost causing her to drop her head onto her arms before she realized it was a text. Shia's name on the screen managed to bring a little joy to her overwhelmed heart:

Whatcha doing, sexy?

Rose grinned. *Trying not to drown in work orders. What about you?*

Hoping you'll say yes to "lunch" today.

Rose wished she could. It had been a few days since they'd had "lunch," and Shia had been feeling down since her mother's visit. Rose hadn't even been able to find the right time to tell her about talking to her mother at the Seaside Café, which was starting to get uncomfortable the longer it went unmentioned.

Rose had been happy to snuggle during the night, but the idea of "lunch" gave her a buzz of arousal she wished she had time to take care of. *There is nothing more I'd rather do. Nothing. But I can't.* She watched the dancing ellipsis until she got the feeling that Shia was about to tease her. Her heart couldn't take it. She needed to head it off. *Don't even think about telling me that you'll take care of it yourself.*

The dancing ellipsis disappeared. Rose could almost see Shia erasing the message before the ellipsis started again.

You wield dangerous magic with your mind reading. Well then, how about meeting me at the Canteen after work? Gary asked me and Mikayla to come by for a drink.

Sounds good. Maybe I'll have made a dent in the number of work orders. But even if I don't, I won't have the energy to deal with them anymore. 5:15?

Perfect. And I'll save my appetite for "dinner."

The short exchange along with the upswing in Shia's mood gave Rose the energy to continue with her day while she counted the minutes until five fifteen.

❖

Coming up behind Shia at the bar, Rose wrapped her arms around her, and Shia leaned into her before slipping off the barstool and giving her a proper hug and a kiss. Being able to hug and kiss her in public was sublimely wonderful.

"Did you make a dent in the work orders?" Shia asked before she gave her another quick kiss.

"I was able to take it back down to what I started with this morning, which isn't great but better than starting tomorrow with even more than I did today."

"We'll call it a win, then. Do you want a glass of wine or a beer to celebrate?"

While a beer sounded good, she couldn't. "I'm on call tonight. What are you having?"

"I'm going hard-core tonight. Virgin strawberry daiquiri."

"Ooh, sounds like trouble. I'll take a double."

"You got it." Shia turned back toward the bar, pointing at her drink. "Gary, can I get another of these?"

"Is that Hop's brother?" Rose asked close to Shia's ear. "I don't think we've met."

Shia glanced at her and smiled, a twinkle in her eyes that reached into Rose's heart. "No? It feels like you've always been here."

"I hope that's a good thing," Rose said.

Shia squeezed her hand. "It's a very good thing."

"Here you go, Shia. Is it for your friend?" Gary said, sliding the drink across the bar and nodding at Rose.

"It's for my…" Shia glanced at him and turned back to Rose with the same smile and the same twinkle. "Girlfriend?" she finished as if it was a question.

A wave of warmth rushed through Rose, settling in the center of her chest. She reached past Shia for the drink. In the same movement, she pressed against her, whispering in her ear, "Yes, please." Rose pried her eyes away, counting the minutes until they could slip away for "dinner." "Nice to meet you, Gary. I'm Rose."

"You look like you could be Gem's sister. Am I right?"

"Close. I'm her niece. You look like you could be Hop's brother. Am I right?" She felt Shia's arm slide around her waist and pressed in, enjoying the casual affection.

Gary gave a small bow. "You are correct. His younger, handsomer brother."

"Where is Hop?" Mikayla asked after taking a sip of wine.

"He's up in Newport, coordinating some sort of event." He leaned over the bar on his elbows, glancing between Shia and Mikayla. "I figured I owed…" He moved his gaze to a point behind them and stood up straight. "Well, there she is. The gang's all here."

When Rose turned, she saw a very uncomfortable Sharon standing a step or two inside the doorway, looking startled to see them.

Gary waved her over. "Come on over. What do you want to drink?"

Sharon hesitated but seemed to regain her composure as she walked toward them. "You seem to have your hands full. I could come back."

"I'm guessing a Diet Coke with lime?" Gary said, filling a glass with ice and starting to pour the Coke before she could answer.

Her eyes scanned the group but rested on Shia a little longer, and Rose sensed waves of uncertainty. Gary pushed the drink toward her and leaned back over the bar. "I was about to tell these ladies that I invited you all here to apologize for how the meeting went last week. I figured a little time has passed, and the shock has maybe worn off a little. It's none of my business, but I felt like I should try to, you know, balance the energy somehow. What's a better way to do that than over a drink?" He scratched the back of his neck. "I guess we can see how this goes."

Sharon reached across the bar and patted his arm. "I know you mean well, but you don't need to balance anything with us. That's why you waited for Hop to go out of town, isn't it? He told you to stay out of it."

Gary scratched the back of his neck again. "I couldn't leave it like that. I had no idea—"

Sharon leaned closer. "Gary, we can manage ourselves, but I appreciate your concern. You're a kind, kind man."

Rose watched the exchange and felt his adoration of Sharon, as if he was a puppy trying to please his owner. Her feelings for him were like a loving sister. He gave her a meek look and made an excuse to go into the back room.

Sharon turned. "Hello, Shia. Hello, Rose. May I speak to you, Shia? Just for a moment?"

"Um, sure," Shia said, dropping her arm from around Rose's waist and stepping back. Rose sensed her muted emotions, signifying her defenses engaging. They walked a few steps away. Rose slid onto the barstool next to Mikayla.

"I guess it has to get awkward to get better, but it's hard to watch, isn't it?" Mikayla said, using a napkin to wipe a ring of water from the bar.

"So hard," Rose said. She drew lines in the condensation of her glass. The sweet frozen concoction, even without alcohol, was a mistake after skipping lunch. The few sips she'd taken sat like a mild acid ball in her stomach as she sensed Shia's chaotic emotions swirling in a cloud all around them.

Mikayla wadded up the napkin. "Tell me about your day. Shia said you've been working a lot just to tread water."

"I've been swamped about inefficient air-conditioning over the last week. It's an issue the park has had for the last several years. Some of it is that many of the units are getting old, including the AC equipment, but it's also about uninsulated windows on the older homes and the rolling power usage restrictions. I feel like I'm playing Whac-A-Mole trying to keep up with them."

"Have you considered going solar at Oceana?"

Rose had been considering it, but mainly because of the cost of the power bill that was a third higher than last year. "I've been meaning to look into it, but I'm not sure what that will do to help with the aging units and insulation."

Mikayla nodded. "Part of the surf park plan is to renovate a nearby hotel. Sharon was telling me about a solar refit program the state is offering for multi-family housing situations. It covers things like replacing uninsulated windows, energy assessments, upgrading heating and cooling units. You should talk to her about it."

Rose had one of those moments that reminded her once again that she didn't have to handle everything all by herself, that leaning on the people around her, even if it was only to bounce ideas or vent, was often met with solutions. And it didn't mean she was failing. "Have you talked to Gem about this?"

"Not yet. She's been preoccupied by her license renewal. Do you want me to?"

"No. Feel free to tell her about it if it comes up, but let her know that I've got it covered. I'll fill her in when I get all the details." She rested a hand on Mikayla's shoulder. "You've helped more than you know."

Mikayla beamed. "That's all I ever want to do. I'm glad it helped."

An unexpected surge of gratitude came from Mikayla, along with a shot of satisfaction. Rose suspected that she'd witnessed what her grandfather sometimes referred to as a person's core essence. Mikayla, so put together and capable, was driven by being useful. Rose guessed that she gained most of her self-worth from being a positive force in another's life.

For the first time, Rose was aware of using her gift without it turning off as soon as she noticed. Gem had been right about it becoming second nature. She couldn't wait to talk to Shia about it.

Shia's gentle presence enveloped her. She and Sharon were back. Rose searched Shia's eyes to see how her talk with Sharon had gone and sensed she was trying not to think about it. The tamped-down emotional stream did little to mute Shia's sexual energy, though. The blast of desire was still blazing hot and sent a jolt to a specific place in Rose's lower body.

Shia's eyes grew a little darker. A sly smile crooked her lips as she pushed a strand of hair off Rose's forehead and rested a hand on Rose's collarbone. It conveyed intimacy and comfort at the same time. "You can put away the concern in your beautiful eyes. I'm okay. She wanted to apologize for coming over without arranging it first the other night. That was mostly it."

"I'm happy you're okay. I'm always here for you if that changes, you know."

Shia smiled. "I know."

Mikayla leaned toward them. "Hey, Shia, I need to meet with a Realtor tomorrow during our regular meeting time. Can I borrow you for a minute to fill you in on some things while we're here? Otherwise, we can meet later in the day if you like."

"Now's fine," Shia said to Mikayla and then turned to Rose. "What's with all these women wanting me all of a sudden? I'd rather head back home for 'dinner' with the one woman I want," she whispered as she backed toward the other side of Mikayla.

Rose's pulse sped up. Smiling, she drew lines in the condensation while she thought about going home with Shia. Movement beside her roused her from her daydream when Sharon slid onto the barstool next to her.

"It's good to see you again, Rose."

"Hi." It took a second to switch gears from fantasies about Shia. She shifted in her seat, remembering what Mikayla had suggested about the solar options. "Hey. Oceana needs an energy upgrade. Mikayla said you know something about a solar program?"

Sharon became animated, and Rose felt a wave of relief come from her. "I have an excellent consultant I can set you up with."

Rose couldn't believe how things were falling into place while she excitedly explained what she was thinking about. Several minutes later, she heard the ding of the consultant's contact information being delivered to her phone, and a strange feeling came over her. Looking over her shoulder, she found Shia standing behind her with an expression Rose could only describe as controlled.

"Hey, I'm going to head home," Shia said.

It was abrupt, and something seemed off. Shia was closed completely off. Rose couldn't sense anything from her. Nothing. "Let me just—"

"Go ahead and continue whatever you were talking about." Shia's eyes dropped to the bar as if she was impatient. "I'll talk to you later."

Rose was stunned. It felt like she had somehow missed a scene transition while watching a television show. Everything was as it had been just seconds before: the drone of conversation, background music, and the steady low roar of the ocean coming in through the open front of the bar, but everything Rose had been anticipating had been shifted.

What happened?

Chapter Twenty-eight

A trickle of sweat made its way down the center of Shia's back, under her tank top and into the waistband of her shorts. It was less than a half a mile round-trip from her house to the grocery store, but the heat of the day that late morning was already teasing its way into triple digits. Shia couldn't remember the last time the temperature had been so high this close to the water. Normally, the breeze kept it comfortable. Looking out over the water, Shia understood why locals and tourists were bobbing shoulder to shoulder in the churning waves.

All the tourists made her afternoon surfing sessions almost impossible, which was just as well because she needed to focus on smoothing things over with Rose. The night before at the bar had started off good, then had gone weird when her mother had showed up. She'd been nervous, but even their conversation had turned out okay after her mother had apologized for dropping in on her. Well, as okay as the situation allowed it to be.

She didn't trust her mother. Trust her about what, she didn't know. Basically everything, she supposed. So she'd put her guard up. It was what she'd always done. With everyone. Except for Rose. She'd already gotten used to not having her guard up around Rose. It felt safe, but more importantly, she felt like she finally mattered. The electric charge that flowed between them had become almost physical.

But last night, though…last night, something had happened at the bar when she'd seen Rose and her mother talking. Her mother being all relaxed and charming, as if she had every right to be part of Shia's life, had filled her with a corrosive rage that had scared her. It was almost violent. It wasn't Rose's fault, but Rose, by virtue of simply talking to her mother, was now in the blast zone. She'd needed to get out of there so the terrible rage she felt didn't pull Rose into it. When Rose had texted about it minutes after Shia had left, she'd been understandably worried. But there'd been no way for Shia to access her normal, easygoing self. She claimed to be tired, which was true. She said that running into her mother had made it worse. Also true. What she didn't say was that she'd actually gotten mad at Rose for getting to be with her charming mother when Shia only got the fucked-up version. It wasn't rational. So she'd left.

While their texts had been somewhat normal, Shia knew Rose was confused about how they'd gone from all flirty and wanting to tear each other's clothes off to each of them going home to their own beds.

She had to make it up to her.

She transferred her full grocery bag from one hand to the other, continuing her walk back home. In the bag was a simple meal her grandma used to grill on hot evenings so she didn't heat the house: a small filet that she would cube, along with chunks of pineapple, whole mushrooms, sliced bell peppers, and red onion to make into kabobs. She'd also picked up some plain rice bowls she could heat up in the microwave, a bottle of wine, and a Sara Lee chocolate layer cake. She hadn't had any alcohol since the sangria at Gem's house, but a small glass of wine sounded good. She didn't have a nice porch, but she did have a camp table and chairs she could set up on the small pad of decorative bricks in front of her house. She envisioned watching the sunset with Rose to make up for her behavior. Despite a little nervousness, a pleasant tickle of anticipation ran down her spine.

❖

Shia caught sight of Rose walking over. She opened the door, pulled Rose in, and offered her the small bouquet of flowers she'd picked up in the grocery store. "I'm sorry about last night. I was a jerk," she said in answer to Rose's questioning expression.

"You weren't. You didn't anticipate seeing your mother at the bar. I sort of figured she said something. You aren't required to talk to me about it. I suspect that you don't even have words for it most of the time."

Shia stared. "You are eerily dead-on. I didn't expect her to be there, I don't know how I feel about what she said to me, and I don't have words for it to explain it, but it's not cool for me to shut you out like that."

Rose's shoulders dropped a bit, and the electrical emotional channel between them opened up a little. "I didn't like that part. But you know, people can't bundle up their messy feelings in a neat little box simply because it's not nice to leave others in the dark. Sometimes, we need time to let things marinate. This thing with your mom is going to take a lot of time to figure out."

"I don't know how you get me, but you do." Shia watched Rose's expression shift through a few emotions. "I'd like to tell you more about why I was such a jerk. Not to excuse it but to give you context. Are you up for it?"

Rose pulled on the collar of her polo. "Sure. But can we do it in the bedroom? It's cooler in there with the dark curtains drawn and the fan going."

"Awesome idea." Things were going smoother than Shia'd hoped. After she put the flowers with their cute little vase on the dining table, they went into the bedroom, where it was at least ten degrees cooler. They crawled onto the bed, moved the pillows around, and sat with their backs against the headboard. It occurred to Shia that it was the first time they'd gone into her bedroom without sex or sleep on their minds.

A bubble of anticipation floated in her stomach at the thought that their relationship seemed to be growing. She took Rose's hand. "After my mother apologized for coming over the way she did, she said that if I was open to us getting to know each other, she would try to go into it with no expectations and the idea that it would be a work in progress. She pretty much left it up to me, and I was okay with that."

"It seems like a good plan. So what changed?" asked Rose.

"You mean, why did I go from being cool to a jerk minutes later?"

Rose rubbed a hand down Shia's leg. "Can we agree that jerk is not the right word?"

"I guess." Shia played with Rose's fingers. "I got irrationally irritated that you and she were having a conversation like it was the most normal thing in the world."

"That was it?"

"Yeah. I saw you two down the bar like old friends. Something seemed to break open in me. All of these crazy emotions: jealousy, resentment, things like that. I tried to make them go away, but I couldn't. I started thinking about how she seemed like this decent person. But she isn't. She cared more about herself than her baby. She walked away and never turned back. Then, when we meet by accident, she wants to act like nothing happened? She has no idea what happened to me. She hasn't even asked. And I hated her for it."

"Did you hate me? Even a little bit? Because I was talking to her?"

Shia dropped her chin to her chest, breathing out heavily. "Hate is a strong word. Maybe guilty by association."

"Would it help you to know that it wasn't a random conversation? And that I was asking her about a solar program for Oceana?"

Shia considered. "Not really. That you were talking to her as if it was the most natural thing in the world was enough." She felt stupid saying it, but it was the truth.

"Do you still feel that way?"

Shia didn't hesitate. "No. Not at you, anyway." It was true. She'd been angry the night before, but she wasn't anymore. She didn't want her mother's reappearance in her life to poison the good things that were already there, and Rose was the best thing by far.

"But still angry."

How did Rose see her so clearly? Was it the weird energy between them? Shia hated to admit the anger was still there, but she could defeat it. She had to. "I hate that she gets to do whatever she wants, live her life, walk right into mine, and I…ugh. Never mind. It's irrational."

"And you what?"

Shia's resentment was immense, even if, thankfully, Rose wasn't the target. It wasn't fair to drag her into all of this mess. "And I…I… I've had to battle my way to where I am. I'll always be a foster kid. I'll always know that I was cast away so a selfish woman could live her best life." She barely recognized the bitterness tinging her words as her own voice.

"But she wasn't a woman. She was a child, right? And she left you with family."

"She left me. That's the thing."

Rose kissed her hand, grounding her. It was the exact right thing to do. She loved Rose for her ability to give her peace. Everything she'd been feeling was still there, but the chaotic spinning of it all settled within her. Blessedly, her thoughts became manageable.

"All of what you're feeling right now is valid. Some of what you've gone through has been horrible, but your past doesn't define you," Rose said, her words buoying Shia like swells on the calmest ocean. "Our past teaches us, and if we listen to it, we learn how to be better people. Do you believe that? Do you see how much you've accomplished?"

Shia shifted so they were facing each other. "I do. So many people have helped me along the way, too. The social worker who watched over me and took me from bad situations. The mission that supported me. My friends here at Oceana who took a chance at letting a teenager with nothing to her name live here." As hokey as the thought felt, gratitude filled her.

"And…" Rose paused as if considering her words carefully. "I guess that's the same for all of us, right? Even your mother?"

The last bit carried a discordant edge. "I don't know about that. How could she have learned anything from having left her baby?"

"I don't know. No one can see inside a person…to understand what compels them." Shia wondered what made her pause. "It's possible she isn't aware of what she's learned. She isn't the same kid who took what appears to be the easy way out of a very messed-up situation. She's a person who has grown roots in her community and who cares for it. From what I can see, she regrets how her decisions affected you. She seems like a kind person."

Shia wasn't sure how much she heard because the idea that Rose seemed to be defending her mother cut her to the bone. She stood and started pacing next to the bed while Rose hugged a pillow. "You can't possibly be excusing what she did. Are you?" She pushed her hair back. The irrational anger of last night surged within her again. "That can't be what you're saying."

"I'm…I'm not defending or excusing or justifying anything. I'm saying people make mistakes. They learn. I think your mother made a mistake. That's all."

Shia pulled away when Rose tried to touch her again. Shame flared within her but it was no match for her hurt feelings. "How can you possibly know that?"

Rose looked startled. "It's just a feeling I have from talking with her."

"You've decided that she regrets what she did to me based on one conversation? About solar panels?"

"You've met people who give off a vibe that they're good people, haven't you?"

The more Rose reached for justification for her thoughts, the more out of control Shia felt. "Not if they've done shitty things to people I care about."

Rose looked stunned. How could she have decided that the person who had hurt Shia more than anyone else in the world was a kind person? "Listen. You need to know something about me. I can tell if people are kind. I can tell if they regret things they've done. Your mother is a genuinely kind person. She may not have been back then. Or more likely, she was battling demons that caused her to do things she might not have done if she hadn't been under that kind of stress. But I'm not telling you this to make you like her. You get to decide that. I'm telling you so you can make an informed decision. And maybe if you give her a chance, you can mend some of the places that have been hurt inside you. I don't know. I think—"

"Stop! Just stop." Shia threw her hands up. Thoughts and feelings tumbled inside her head and heart. The numb space she'd receded into was narrowing in on her, suffocating her. "Have you been talking to her about me?"

"It's not like that."

"I don't get how you think you can tell what kind of person she is, then."

Rose paused and pursed her lips as if thinking. "It's a thing my grandfather calls the gift. I can sense other people's emotions. I'm still trying—"

"Whoa. Whoa. Whoa. I know about Mr. Helmstaad's gift. Everyone does. You're saying you can see what people are thinking, too? Or their essence or something?"

Rose looked relieved. "That's basically it. It's still kind of—"

Shia had only half believed the lore surrounding Mr. Helmstaad's superpower and the idea that Oceana possessed a special energy for helping people when they needed it. Over time, she'd come to accept that something seemed to imbue Mr. Helmstaad and the park with a special feeling, but she'd thought it was more about the idea of it being a special place rather than a real power or anything. "How come you never told me?"

"I wasn't aware I had it until recently. Sometimes, I wondered how I knew certain things about people, and it kind of freaked me out a little. I always dismissed it. But when I moved to Oceana, it seemed to get stronger."

"So you can read my mind?" Shia knew she sounded judgy and critical, like she was trying to cause a fight. And maybe she was. She was tired of holding back everything to maintain the peace.

"Not your mind. It's more about emotions and intentions."

"You know all that about me?" Shia was both cynical and affronted by the idea that Rose could read her mind. She knew she was playing both sides of a very questionable subject, but either way, she was angry because Rose was minimizing her feelings.

"I wouldn't say it was all-encompassing, and it's not definitive. But I can tell if someone is lying or nervous and that kind of thing."

"How am I feeling now?"

"You're angry. Confused. Hurt. Apprehensive. But it's all kind of muted, like you're trying to hide it not only from me but from yourself. But always, there's a—"

The hiding thing was scary because it was true. It was all true, and that terrified her. "Stop. Stop. It's enough. I…that's too much. I can't. I just can't."

Rose seemed scared, worried. "Can't what? What can I do to help?"

Shia collapsed further into her walled-off place. Her words and feelings felt wooden. "I don't want your help. I don't want anyone's help. I've done fine taking care of myself, and now, there are too many people wanting to help me."

"Did I do something?"

Shia gaped at her, amazed that she couldn't see how awful it was that anyone could see her private thoughts. It was the most appalling breach of privacy. It was as if Rose had thumbed through the most secret and embarrassing parts of Shia and shown them to the world. "You just…I can't." She left the room.

Rose followed her to the living room. The sunset through the window was beautiful, reminding Shia that the meal she'd prepared for them was sitting in the kitchen, ready to grill. The idea that tonight was supposed to be a special night pierced her heart. "I need to…I don't know. But could you please go?"

The confusion and hurt on Rose's face as she left without a word sliced right through Shia's heart, but she couldn't help but resent that, too.

CHAPTER TWENTY-NINE

The heat wave had finally broken, drawing Rose outside to enjoy the cooler weather. She and Chad sat in one of the metal garden chairs in the shade of the giant magnolia in the backyard. She was going through the three different bids she'd received for the solar work. Chad slept on her shoulder with his head tucked under his arm, grunting occasionally when he adjusted his position. The idyllic scene would have been wonderful if it wasn't for her broken heart.

Shia hadn't spoken to her since she'd asked her to leave. Rose didn't know what to do with herself. The temptation to confront Shia or to beg her to talk to her, depending on where her swinging emotions were at any given moment, was constant. The right thing to do was to respect Shia's boundaries and wait, but it had been three days, longer than they'd ever gone without seeing each other. What if Shia never called? A sharp pain stabbed through her heart, an event that occurred numerous times a day.

"Rose? Are you okay?"

She roused herself from her thoughts to see Gem standing on the other side of the table. "Yeah. Why?" She sighed, tired of everyone checking in on her.

"I said hello twice, and when I didn't get an answer, I jumped up and down and waved my arms around. No response."

"I didn't hear you come up," she said with a smile that felt fake. Was fake. Could in no way be mistaken as not fake. She knew it didn't reach her eyes, her swollen, red from crying eyes. The ones that had greeted her in the bathroom mirror after yet another night of no sleep. She was the definition of pathetic, and what people could actually see was nothing even close to how she felt inside.

"It didn't look like you were thinking of anything pleasant." Gem pulled out a chair and sat. "What's going on? You've been walking around like a zombie the last few days, and all you say is 'fine' when I ask how you are. I'm not asking this time. I'm ordering you to tell me what's going on with you."

To her humiliation, a sob ripped from her throat. She slumped, dropping her head into her hands. Chad pressed his little body into her neck, something he'd done many times in the last few days. Normally, his cute display of empathy distracted her from her troubles. This time, it did the opposite. She derided herself for being so stupid, for not keeping her interest in Shia casual. She would have minded her own business, wouldn't have tried to get Shia to give her mother a chance, and there would have been no confrontation. But she hadn't kept it casual. She'd interfered, had tried to get her and her mother back together. Now, she was paying the price.

Hands, presumably Gem's, rubbed her back, and when Rose looked up, she saw that Gem had moved around the table to the chair next to her. "What's wrong, kid? Did you and Shia have a fight?"

Rose couldn't make a sound through the lump in her throat, so she nodded.

Gem watched her for a few seconds, love and compassion flowing from her like a river. Rose soaked it up. She'd never felt this kind of pain before. She didn't even mind that Gem had called her kid, a thing that would have usually set her off.

"I'll give you a few minutes before I start to interrogate you. In the meantime, what are these?" Gem picked up a brochure from one of the solar companies.

Switching to a more neutral subject, Rose cleared her throat. "I'm researching solar options for Oceana." Talking about stupid solar options distracted her enough to keep the tears at bay. At least for now. "There are a few programs where we can roll in new AC units, window replacements, and insulation upgrades where they're needed. And the good news is, we wouldn't have to do the labor."

"Was this precipitated by the annual influx of air-conditioning 'emergencies'?"

Rose would have bristled at it if it weren't for the sympathy she sensed. Not to mention, she lacked any emotional energy after using it all up, and then some, on… No. She was in the middle of being distracted from that. "You don't think they're acting entitled, or whatever the air quotes were supposed to indicate, for wanting the air-conditioning to work. Why did you try to imply it?"

"Do you think they're acting entitled?" Gem asked, scanning the brochure.

"Not at all. In fact, a few residents have reported their units not operating correctly or in some cases, at all, but have said they were just letting me know and would understand if it took a while to address so we could focus on keeping the elderly or compromised residents comfortable."

Gem's eyes twinkled with pleasure. "You don't need to get approval from me or Grandpa for this. You've proven your ability to make decisions, but more than that, you have the community in mind when you do. All you need to do is let us know what you decide."

Rose settled back in her chair. Chad heaved his little body into a sitting position. "Was that whole emergency comment some sort of test?"

Gem reached over and picked Chad up, giving his little cheek a kiss before snuggling him to her chest. "Not so much a test. I just wanted to know what was motivating you."

"What do you mean? There are a lot of things motivating me."

"But you put the residents over everything else. That's the most important thing. I knew you already leaned that way, but it was cool to see it in action on such a big project." She stroked Chad's haunches, something he loved more than food, which was saying something. "It's perfectly fine if you were trying to cut costs or even if you wanted to impress us. People like to get acknowledgment for their work. But you were putting the residents above any of that. You're a Helmstaad. I wouldn't have expected otherwise." She winked.

"You got all of that out of a brochure and maybe four sentences?"

Gem's eyes shifted to the side and back to her. "I think you know that's not the case."

Rose knew exactly what she meant. "Has anyone ever had a bad reaction to your gift?"

Gem appeared to think about it, but Rose was aware of her swift shift to a more cautious vibe. "Only when they knew about it, if that's what you mean. I think people sense that I have a deeper awareness, thinking it's a heightened sense of empathy most of the time. But I've had a few people not like that I can perceive things in a more…specific manner. I don't blame them. I hated, I mean *hated*, that Grandpa knew what I was feeling even before I did when I was younger. I felt almost violated that I didn't have privacy. I built a wall between him and me so he couldn't read me as easily. I regret it now."

"Is that why you hide it?"

"It's why I used to. I'm trying to be more open about it. At least with the people I love. Mikayla helps." Gem seemed to recede into her own thoughts for a moment, and Rose felt a sparkly kaleidoscope of sensation coming from her. "She thinks of it as an evolved level of communication." She leaned forward, her face alive. It was more than excitement. It was the pure engagement and acceptance of a new concept that filled her with passion. "You know how some people are just so easy to be around? It's almost like they fill you with energy."

"Yeah. Like you do."

Gem sat back. "Really?"

"Absolutely."

"That makes me feel good." Gem seemed to attempt to collect herself. "Um, well, I..." She reached across the table and rested a hand on Rose's. "Seriously, that means so much to me."

Rose placed her other hand atop Gem's. "Same. You're the big sister I never had and my favorite aunt. I think I got the best deal."

Gem sat back again. "I think you're going to truly understand this, then. There are those people who seem to bring the best out in you. It's because they're really good communicators. Not only with their words. It's a very layered thing. What they say and do is exactly how they think and feel. No pretenses. No holding back. That's you, by the way."

"Me? Really? I guess I try."

"The less you try and the more you just be, the closer to it you'll come."

"That makes total sense."

"That's why most people want to be around people like you. There's no hidden agenda, mixed signals, any of that."

"Do you think it has anything to do with the gift?"

"For me, it does. In a huge way," Gem said, nodding. "When I realized my gift was a good thing and not something to be ashamed of, it enhanced my ability to communicate."

"What about the people who saw it as a violation?"

Gem studied her. "The last time we spoke, you said you didn't think you had it. Has that changed?" Rose nodded. "I was wondering. Something seemed tuned in. It makes you understand your emotions better, doesn't it?"

"Yeah. They don't feel different, but I'm not wary of them anymore. I guess that's how to describe it." She didn't say that she was beginning to believe it was making her feel things more vividly, more deeply, than she'd ever felt them before. A painful thing to be happening at a time when her heart was being annihilated.

"Uh-huh." Gem bobbed her head. "Exactly. I'm not sure if you've experienced it yet, but when that wariness fades, the openness that comes with it, well, some people can feel it. It sort of enhances your connection with them, almost creating a two-way connection. Mikayla was the one who told me that. She says it's like an emotional hug. When I asked my dad about it, he said he had it with my mom."

"I don't know. When I started to become aware of it, it made some of my memories make more sense because I guess I've been using it without knowing. As far as I know, it's always been a one-way kind of deal, from them to me. I haven't tuned into directing it outward. At least, no one has said they've felt me in that way."

"I'll bet they do. You have a way with people. But if not, maybe in time," Gem said. "Have you talked to Shia about it yet?"

The ache in her throat came back in full stereo. "She freaked out. I could feel how violated she felt. Even worse, I felt her shame. It was awful feeling it from another person, that bleak desire to not be seen, to not exist. I've never sensed anything from her that would cause shame, though. She's beautiful inside and out. Literally." A sob ripped from her. "Sorry. She hasn't talked to me since Wednesday when I told her about it." Rose couldn't hold back her tears.

Gem sighed, rubbing her back again. "I had a feeling that might happen. I hoped that it would actually help her heal from her past, but with her mother showing up and all the changes going on, I suspected that it could go either way."

"What do you mean?"

"She's had a tough life. One that taught her to be careful about showing her real emotions. She's a very kind person, so she doesn't come off as cold or aloof, but most people with her experiences can be emotionally walled-off. It's a protective mechanism. She might feel exceptionally vulnerable thinking that someone has access to what she feels, especially if she's been hurt for expressing those feelings in the past." Gem leaned forward. "I'm just guessing here. She and I have never discussed this, but I've known her for four years. I'd be surprised if this wasn't the case."

Rose felt like she had lost part of herself. "I don't know what to do. All I want to do is talk to her about it. But I'm afraid she'll shut me out even more."

"I wish I had better advice, but you're going to have to follow your heart and hope it leads you in the right direction."

It wasn't the response she was hoping for, but it wasn't unexpected, either. She'd hoped Gem would know the perfect way to win Shia back, but love was rarely that easy. While her heart ached from having caused Shia pain and their separation, Rose chose to hope that she'd find a way to fix it. The hardest part was having to wait until she had an opportunity. If one ever came up.

CHAPTER THIRTY

It had been a few weeks since Shia had visited the Oceana hot tub. With the weather so warm, it hadn't been on her mind. However, she'd been training more than usual to keep her mind off things, and after her swim on Monday, the thought of warm jets against her shoulders drew her down to the pool.

As soon as she got there, though, a glance at the shower building made her miss Rose. As she peeled off her clothes down to her bathing suit, her eyes stung with tears. And as usual, she stuffed down her grief. At first, her anger at Rose had been a good defense against the pain that threatened to pierce her heart every time she thought about her, which was excruciatingly frequent. But in less than a day, her anger had faded, replaced by a kind of missing Rose that was more painful than any physical or emotional pain she'd ever experienced. And that was saying a lot. As a consequence, Shia had been spending a lot of time sending all those feelings into the walled-off bunker where she kept her most painful memories. Her self-preservation was on autopilot.

Having rinsed off the sand from her ocean swim, she stepped into the warm hot tub and cranked the jets to full throttle, settling back in the hope that they and the hot water would help loosen the tight muscles of her neck and shoulders.

"Mind if I join you, young lady?"

Shia opened her eyes to see someone who looked like Alice standing near the edge of the hot tub in a long velour robe and flip-flops. It was definitely Alice, but with her hair down and her wire glasses in hand, she appeared years younger. "Hop in."

"I'll use the stairs, if that's okay," Alice said, taking off her robe and tucking her glasses into the pocket before hanging it over the back of a nearby chair. "Knowing me, I'd break a leg." She slid into the water, dunked completely under, and when she popped back up, chose a seat directly across from Shia, who was trying not to gawk at the woman who looked so different from the one she'd known for several years.

From her long dark hair, shapely form, and the unexpectedly red toenails, this Alice seemed like a completely different person. Her one-piece swimsuit was nothing in comparison to the string bikinis many women wore to the beach, including the one Shia wore, but on Alice, it was almost sexy. It suggested that her body might be used in ways that weren't limited to filling out shapeless blouses, boxy knee-length skirts, and comfortable shoes, not that Shia pictured her in anything other than her uniform of conservative clothing. It was simply unexpected.

"Do I have a boogie?" Alice asked, wiping her nose.

Shia averted her eyes, realizing she'd been staring. "I've just never seen your hair down," she said. It wasn't a lie. She could never lie to Alice.

Alice pulled her hair into a bunch behind her head and draped it over her shoulder. "It's so long that I get impatient for it to dry after a bath, so I always put it up."

"It's very pretty." Alice blushed bright red but didn't say anything. "I've also never seen you use the pool area."

"I burn so quickly in the sun. But Pilates is kicking my booty… literally. It feels like it's been kicked by a team of mules. I figured if the squirty things in my bathtub felt good, the ones out here in the Jacuzzi would be even better." She sighed as she leaned back against the jets. "And, oh my beloved Lord in Heaven, I was right."

Shia almost laughed at the use of the old-school word Jacuzzi, but when Alice sighed, it sounded almost sensual. Thinking of Alice in that context almost seemed irreverent. Sexy and sensual were not words she ever expected to apply to her. She cleared her throat. "This is a therapeutic hot tub. It's almost like physical therapy." Falling back to something sports medicine-y gave her a little buffer from her previous thoughts.

"Better, I'd say."

Shia tried to relax again. "That's why I come here. My shoulders get tight from swimming."

Alice waved a dripping finger at her. "Yoga would help."

With that, the usual Alice was with her. Shia was relieved. She didn't like feeling uncomfortable with her friend.

"I haven't seen Rose visiting lately. Is she doing okay?"

The prescient question took Shia aback. She didn't even think to figure out an ambiguous response. "We had a fight." Saying it out loud was like a poke to her very bruised heart.

"Oh dear. I can't imagine her fighting. Not that I can imagine you fighting, either, but Rose is a little more soft-spoken."

A blanket of shame settled over Shia. It wasn't the first time, either. She'd felt it each time she recalled their last words to each other. Rose had been calm and steady, whereas she had been volatile. So much so that she hadn't let Rose talk. She wasn't sure that Rose could have said anything to have made the situation better, but she wasn't proud of herself for shutting Rose down. "It wasn't that kind of fight."

"Do you want to talk about it? Knowing you, you've been holding it all inside because that's what you do. But either way, I can tell you're not happy. Your lights have been on late into the night. You're not leaving your house much, either. No food delivery. It's hard to see you like this after seeing you so happy these last several weeks."

Shia loved that Alice kept track of her. It had always made her feel cared for. But now she wasn't sure she liked that Alice could see this side of her. She preferred to appear capable. About to say she didn't want to talk about it, to her surprise, part of her did. The comment about having been happy the last several weeks really got to her.

"Do you want to talk about it?"

Shia pushed her wet hair back with both hands and, to her horror, started crying.

"Oh dear." Alice tipped her head to the side with a compassionate expression that made Shia cry harder.

She slipped underwater to hide. When she came back up, she took a couple of deep breaths, feeling a little better. "Sorry. Just a lot on my mind."

"I would think so. Your career is taking off, you have a new girlfriend, and then your mother shows up out of the blue. That's a lot to deal with, even if most of it's good."

Shia appreciated Alice's ability to always divine the primary thread of things, especially how events affected people's ability to be happy. Her natural role in life seemed to be to help people find happiness. The rumor that she'd once been a nun wasn't hard to believe. "It really is. And so much of it's tangled together."

"What do you mean?"

"My mother is involved with the surf park Hop's building."

"Oh dear," Alice said again. "What an unexpected situation. That does complicate things, doesn't it?"

Shia sighed long and loudly. "I'm not sure complicated is enough to describe what it is."

"How is your mother involved with it?"

"She's the head of the bird conservation group Hop's working with to maintain the habitat."

"That's great."

"Yeah. It's great, but if I'm going to be the spokesperson for the surf park, it makes it hard to not be around her."

"I had no idea any of this was going on."

Shia wondered why Alice seemed surprised. "Why would you know? I mean, except that you always know everything going on around here."

"I do like to keep my finger on the pulse," Alice said, as if her ability to keep track of everything was a simple thing.

"To add to it, Rose said I should give my mother a chance." Shia held her breath, waiting to see if Alice agreed or not. It wasn't that her opinion mattered more than Rose's, but Alice had the benefit of knowing Shia longer and of having gleaned more information about her family history.

Alice appeared to think it over. "If Rose is like her aunt and grandfather, she has a knack for telling if a person is good or not. If she says you should give someone a chance, it's probably with good reason."

The casual acknowledgement of Rose's psychic abilities absolutely struck her. "How do you know that?"

"It's part of the gift that family has. They can sort of read people and tell if they're right for the community or not. By community, I mean Oceana, but I suppose it goes beyond that, even though I haven't really thought about it like that. But it makes sense."

Shia gaped at Alice, who'd leaned back against the jets with her eyes closed, seemingly relaxed and unconcerned. "You really think so? It doesn't bother you?"

"Bother me that they can read a person and know that they're good? Heavens no. I wish I had that. It would make life easier, especially as a woman. I'd know who to steer clear of." Alice smiled, never moving away from the jets.

"But doesn't it bother you that they know what you're thinking?"

"It isn't like that. Tripp explained it to me as being able to see through a false front. He can pick up on emotions, but there's also an aspect that picks up on a person's core quality and not only their motivation at the moment. Because we all have moments where we let less prominent parts of us lead. For instance, I'm not one for coveting, but there's a man who lives on the other side of the park who walks his English bulldog every day. I make sure that my power walk crosses his path as often as possible. Joe is so handsome and sweet. And oh my goodness, so very affectionate. I've gotten so many stains from rolling in the grass with him."

Shia couldn't believe what she was hearing. Alice coveting some man? Rolling in the grass? "Coveting means desiring someone else's property, right? Is this man married?"

Alice shrugged. "Married or living together. Another man joins them on the walk sometimes. I chat them both up, just to get more time with Joe." She sighed like a teenager staring at a concert poster for her favorite band.

Shia tried to think if she knew of a male couple with an English bulldog in Oceana. She'd seen two men walking bulldogs. One wore a ball cap all the time. The other had a beard. "Does Joe wear a Padres ball cap most of the time?"

Alice cracked open one eye. "No, but it would be cute if he did."

"Ah. Then he must have a beard."

Alice scrunched her nose and shook her head. "Beard?"

"It's a big bushy beard, not the short scruffy kind." She held her hand a few inches below her chin.

"I think you have your breeds mixed up. Bulldogs don't have long hair."

Shia laughed. "My mistake. I was talking about Joe."

It was Alice's turn to laugh. "I was, too."

Shia didn't get it for a minute, then: "You covet Joe, the bulldog!"

Alice looked appalled. "You didn't think I was coveting some random man, did you?"

Honestly, Shia had never thought of Alice coveting anyone. "Definitely not."

"Anyway, my point is, at any given moment, I could covet or resent or despise or be feeling any number of things, but Tripp can see past that to what he calls a person's core essence. He says mine is kindness through helping people."

Shia knew that and didn't claim to be psychic. She didn't doubt

Mr. Helmstaad's abilities. He'd casually demonstrated them to her on several occasions, and there was no doubt that he really did have a knack for choosing residents for Oceana. But as far as she knew, Gem had never claimed to possess the skill.

And Rose?

Shia had basically accused her of being a psychic peeping Tom. What was she afraid of? "I knew about Mr. Helmstaad. But I didn't know about Gem. And I certainly didn't know about Rose." She wasn't sure what to think. The way Alice explained it, it sounded as if it was a talent for picking up on a person's general disposition, rather than a paranormal thing like reading minds. It wasn't any different than what she'd felt when she and Rose were making love, when there was this unspoken knowledge between them that they were open and connected on a different level. She loved it then. Thinking about it made her miss Rose with a searing ache.

"Was that what the fight was about? You thought she was secretly reading your mind?"

"You make it sound silly. But yes. Also, I didn't like her getting to talk to my mother like she was like any other person, and I couldn't." God, that sounded even sillier.

"Was it jealousy?"

"Partly. Another part of it was that I had no one to rely on for a huge part of my life, ever since I lost my grandmother, and it turned out I couldn't even rely on her because she lied to me about my mother being dead. I also had this sickening idea that Rose might casually share things about me that my mother has no right to know. She hasn't earned the privilege to know. She gave me up and left me to take care of myself. I mean, I had no one. I was a kid. I had *no* one." The tears started again. She didn't try to hide them this time. "Not until you, Alice. You and the mission. I know you've been working with them to help me get to a place where I can support myself. You've had my back. Not my mother. And now my mother is ruining what I have with Rose."

Alice slid around the hot tub to sit next to her. Shia was grateful for the hand on her shoulder. "Sweet girl. I'm going to tell you something. I swore I would never tell anyone this, but when holding a promise threatens to destroy a heart, I think it's the Lord's will to break the trust. Ironically, breaking the trust is both a literal and a figurative concept in this case."

Shia wiped her eyes. "I'm not sure I understand."

Alice took a deep breath as if deciding whether to elaborate.

"About five years ago, a lawyer approached me on behalf of an anonymous person. They asked me if, as the assistant to the executive director of the mission, I could help administer a trust set up for one of the children who lived at the group home affiliated with the mission. Initially, I didn't think it was appropriate that I become involved. I had no connection to the child or the anonymous person. The lawyer explained that was the reason they had selected me. They'd investigated me and believed that my background and affiliation with the mission made me the perfect person to manage the trust. I was still reluctant until they told me the situation."

Shia suspected she knew where this was going. Weirdly, she felt numb about it. "The kid was me, wasn't it? That's why the mission supported me all this time. It wasn't just a scholarship. There was a benefactor. Was it my grandmother?"

Alice smiled. "It was your mother."

"What?" It didn't make sense. It felt like information that wasn't attached to anything. Her mother wasn't dead. Her grandmother had lied to her. Her mother had never come to get her even when she was put into foster care. And the two entities that had helped her, the mission and Alice, weren't what she thought they were but merely shells to her mother's bidding? Even Alice?

Who else had betrayed her trust? How was Rose involved? She began to think that the anger she'd felt the night at the bar was justified. She felt it starting to rise again. "You've known about this all along?"

"I only knew that someone cared about you enough to want to help you. The only person I knew involved with the trust was the lawyer. Between what he told me and what I learned from your mother when I met her later, your mother has tried very hard to keep up with your life and to do her best to support you in the ways that she could."

Shia rolled her eyes. "You sound like Rose. As long as she got to live the life she wanted, right? I mean, I appreciate her help with rent and stuff, I really do. But I refuse to feel indebted to a woman who did as little as she could to justify her guilt. I deserved more." Shia's own guilt tried to tell her she was being petty, but Alice didn't know what she'd gone through. No one did except the court. And all of that was sealed.

Alice paused. "I know for a fact that your mother doesn't want you to feel indebted to her. It's her trust I'm breaking right now by telling you this. She doesn't want you to know any of this. We both knew it might come up someday. We talked it through, she told me I could make the call about whether the information or her anonymity was more important. She never intended to complicate your life." Alice seemed to study her with her kind eyes.

Try as she might, Shia couldn't find it in herself to be angry at her. Rose either. Her mother was a different story.

"There's more if you want to hear it."

Shia was torn. She wanted to refuse to learn another thing about her mother, but she didn't want to be surprised by anything about her ever again, either. There was also a huge amount of curiosity. How could a mother abandon a kid, then go to the trouble of creating a trust for her? "I might as well. I know she was married. I know she didn't have any other kids, at least that Google knows about."

"Yes, she was married. He passed away a few years ago. They founded North County Wild Birds and Habitats Society together. When she met him, she was doing community service for a land conservation organization. She'd also just gotten out of rehab for the second time, but she didn't tell him that. He assumed she was a volunteer like him, and she told him that she'd lost her mother to cancer and had no other family. Lying was still easy for her back then, or so she says. At the time, it wasn't that much of a stretch. She regretted it later when they fell in love. After that, she never found the courage to tell him about her earlier drug issues, rehab, or the daughter she'd let her mother adopt. She was afraid he'd leave her if he knew what a horrible person she was. Not my words, hers. They weren't wealthy, but they were well-off, and when she finally had some money, she sent it to your grandmother via the same lawyer she eventually set the trust up with. But your grandmother sent it back to her unopened."

"Yeah. Sounds like my grandma." Shia wondered if she could ever forgive her grandmother for lying to her about her mother being dead. That loss was one of the most painful revelations of this whole thing.

"I try not to judge. People do interesting things out of interesting belief systems."

Shia noticed how Alice avoided saying religion. She knew that was what she meant, though. To Shia, it was obvious that Alice, who talked about God and her faith all the time, was deeply conflicted about religion. Shia had always wanted to talk with her about it because her grandmother had been a bit of a zealot. Now wasn't the time, but she made another mental note to get back to it sometime soon.

"She put the money away, hoping that someday, she'd be able to give it to you. However, somewhere along the line, your grandmother passed away. Soon after, she lost track of you."

"That's what she told me."

"It was a terrible time in her life. She was finally doing better. She saw a chance to make everything up to you, be part of your life again. When she found out about your grandmother's death and that you had been sent to her brother's house, she panicked and tried to figure out how she could get you back, even if it meant upsetting her husband."

Alice's sympathetic nature flamed the anger in Shia again. But… if both Alice and Rose could see a kindness Shia could not, was it her own blindness getting in the way? Also, why had her mother panicked about her being at her uncle's house? The look in Alice's eyes said that Alice knew. That her mother had told her. Shame rushed over Shia that anyone knew her secret trauma, the abuse her uncle had subjected her to, the memories she never revisited. Ever. Fresh anger filled her about being put in that situation all those years ago. "My mother told you why she panicked, didn't she?"

Alice looked down. "Her brother had abused her as a child. She worried that he was doing the same to you. She called CPS anonymously, they investigated it, validating her fears, inflicting guilt, causing her to have a relapse in her sobriety. The relapse strained her marriage when her husband found out she'd never told him about her past issues with drugs. She knew then that he would leave her if he found out she had a daughter. The relapse also proved to her that she couldn't take care of you, even if she had the courage to tell her husband."

Shia had to agree with her mother's logic. She still thought her mother was a coward, but something kind of softened in her as she absorbed what Alice said. She and her mother weren't so different. Apparently, neither of them thought they were good enough to love or to be counted on. It seemed Shia had been on the verge of proving herself otherwise with Rose, but her mother hadn't been so lucky. Now Shia wondered if she'd blown her chance to break what seemed to be a family cycle.

Tears threatened at the thought of losing Rose. Fortunately, Alice kept talking and didn't seem to notice. "It took her a while to find you at the group home because she had no right to be advised about your status, having given you up. When she did find you, she made anonymous donations to the home to make sure you had what you needed. Things like a laptop for school, new clothes, and trips to local events like surf camps. She had something to do with the first surfboard your friend in the group home gave to you."

This bit of news hit in a big way, but Shia wasn't ready to explore it.

"Of course, the only way she could do that was to make sure the other kids got the same things. She still does it. She told me it was the least she could do. When her husband died five years ago, she created a trust with all the money she'd saved for you, plus much of the money she and her husband saved over the years."

"I can't believe it's not the mission." Shia was getting emotionally exhausted from all the swinging from emotion to emotion.

Alice cocked her head from side to side. "Technically, it is from the mission because she named it the Mission Trust. But that was only to give the impression that the mission was somehow involved if you ever decided to investigate. It's where your tax statements come from. But, no, the mission as you know it has nothing to do with the support you've received. Although, if you needed it, they would help you because I would make it so." She seemed pleased with herself for having the authority to influence how the mission provided assistance.

Despite Shia's initial irritation that Alice had been acting on her mother's behalf without her knowledge for so many years, she was grateful that the situation had brought her and Alice together. Plus, Alice didn't have an unkind bone in her body. "I feel like I should be mad at you for keeping this from me all this time. If it was anyone else, I would be. Why did they pick you?"

Alice's eyes glimmered. "You don't know how much I wanted to tell you." She cleared her throat. "They were simply looking for someone trustworthy who was affiliated in a believable way with the mission that could manage the trust. When I found out what it was for and that I wouldn't have to lie or do anything that would compromise my morals, I agreed. I also get a small stipend for being the trustee, which I donate to the group home."

"How does Brandi factor into this?"

Alice looked at her with a curious look. "She doesn't."

"My caseworker told me Brandi was the person who'd told her about Oceana. Was it really you?"

"Oh no, dear. That's an interesting story. I didn't have anything to do with getting you here. It might have been a conflict of interest if I had. I just manage the trust and pay the bills. It's all automated. Your caseworker knows Brandi, who told her about Oceana. It was serendipity that not only did I live here but that you became my neighbor. This was the strongest proof in all the twenty-five years I've lived here that Oceana is indeed a special place. I call it blessed. Either way, there is a higher force operating here."

Tingles went through Shia's limbs while goose bumps rose along her skin…at least the skin that hadn't begun to prune. They'd been in the hot tub for a long time. The jets had timed out a while ago. She had one more question, though. "When did you meet my mother?"

"Not until three years ago. Before that, I did a little research before I agreed to manage the trust. I wasn't about to do anything illegal. For all I knew, the lawyer could have been some sort of cartel or mob boss. I found your mother's name and connected her to you. I also made sure she wasn't a danger to you. I have a file of what I found that I'll be happy to share if you're interested."

Shia wasn't sure she'd ever want to look at it if Alice could answer one more question. This would be the last, she swore to herself. "Even if you knew my mother's name after investigating her, how did you end up meeting her?"

"I saw her at one of your competitions about three years ago. She stayed on the fringes, but I noticed her noticing you. At first, I thought you had your first stalker, but when I recognized her from my research, I decided to let her know who I was and that I had helped with the trust and getting you a place to live. I also told her that I considered you part of my family and that I wouldn't stand for her endangering you physically, mentally, or emotionally."

Tears sprang to Shia's eyes again, but this time, they were good tears. Seriously. How could she be mad at Alice? The thought made her think about how she'd reacted to Rose. The heat of shame infused her already warmed skin. She could probably blame her behavior on how overwhelmed she'd felt, but no. She wasn't going to take the easy way out. She'd made a big mistake. She had to fix it. Hopefully, Rose hadn't given up on her.

Chapter Thirty-one

In an attempt to drown out the constant wail of heartbreak, Rose worked through the weekend to decide which solar company to go with. Once she made a decision, she spent most of the following week meeting with the company's project management team to draw up the contract and settle on an installation plan.

Rose couldn't believe how quickly everything had come together. She couldn't wait to tell her grandpa and Gem that the project would start in a little over a week. She leaned back in her desk chair, stretching her arms over her head, glad to have closed the deal, her first major effort to make a real difference at Oceana. The process went so smoothly, she was almost disappointed when it was all planned out, and her part of it was finished. It also meant that she had time to think about how much she missed Shia.

The mere thought of Shia sent an ache directly to her heart. Her stretch became a quiet groan that morphed into a depressed slouch. It had been over a week since they'd last talked. Instead of the heartbreak starting to get better, it was getting worse. She'd never felt this kind of emotional pain before. It was like a piece of her was dying. If it wasn't for her responsibilities at Oceana, she wasn't sure where her mental state might have devolved to…might still devolve to if the worsening of her misery continued.

She'd decided to give Shia space, but now she was starting to think that decision was backfiring. What if space made it easier for Shia to leave for good? Maybe they should have continued to at least pretend they were casual. Maybe then she wouldn't have started thinking that they might have had a chance.

The prospect made her stomach clench. Shia had all the power, and all Rose could do was wait to see what she did. But Shia's way of taking care of herself had often entailed erecting walls. It was unbearable to think Rose had found herself on the outside of Shia's fortress.

Maybe she needed someone else to take care of her this time. This idea opened up a whole different perspective. Maybe Shia needed proof that Rose cared enough to fight for their relationship. What if all this time, Shia had been waiting for her to give an indication that she'd be there for her, that she wouldn't desert her? As they'd gotten to know each other on this rocket-ship romance, Rose had taken comfort in the knowledge that they were feeling a lot of the same things. She knew now that her gift had been working even before she was aware of it.

Shia had no such tool. She had only her experience to help her. And look how that had turned out.

A sort of panic took hold of Rose, filling her chest with a sense of dread. Was it too late? Had Shia written her off for being afraid and weak and lacking devotion? All things she'd always prided herself for actually being?

She stood and closed her laptop. This was ridiculous. She was driving herself crazy with doubt when what she needed to do was prove that she wasn't going anywhere. Not unless Shia told her to leave. And even then, she didn't plan to go without a fight. Shia was worth fighting for.

She barely registered the walk to Shia's place. Her heart was in her throat as she sifted through words to piece together a speech that would help make Shia see how sorry she was and how committed she was to making it up to her. Above all, she wanted Shia to know that she wasn't operating out of fear or doing this for herself. She was doing it for them. She was doing it for love.

Yes, love.

It wasn't the first time she'd realized she loved Shia, but it was the first time she knew it was more than that. It was their essences combined in a shimmering bond surrounded by love. It was the love she wanted to fight for until the end.

She just prayed that it was a happy ending.

With her heart beating out of her chest, she walked up the steps to Shia's door, the familiar steps that had always promised to lead her to the woman who excited her, delighted her, and gave her giddy sparks of excitement any time she thought of her. This time, she was also afraid. Because if Shia sent her away, she wasn't sure she'd ever be okay again. And she still didn't know what to say. Terror rose in her belly as she knocked. She'd figure it out. She had to.

A minute passed without an answer. Rose knew every sound the house made after two months. She would have heard the floor shift if Shia had approached and peeked through the peephole. She would have seen the curtains move. Moreover, she would have felt Shia's presence. Even so, she knocked again. Another minute passed. Two minutes. Three.

Shia wasn't home.

Rose went back the way she'd come. The sunshine seemed dimmer, the wind coming off the ocean less refreshing. She'd have to try again later. If Shia wasn't home then, she would call her. She'd get her chance. She had to.

In the meantime, she diverted to Mikayla's house. Gem usually worked late on Tuesdays, so she didn't worry about interrupting any alone time. But at the bottom of the steps, she heard Mikayla talking, and the tone sounded serious. She started to turn away, but Shia's voice responded.

Rose froze. She didn't want to interrupt, but she also didn't want to let another moment pass with Shia not knowing how she felt, how their essences were bonded. Before she knew it, she was at Mikayla's door with nothing but the screen between her and Shia.

Shia opened it. That was a good sign.

Rose barely registered that Mikayla said something in greeting. All she could see was Shia. All she wanted was Shia. All she could *feel* was Shia.

She could feel her!

And Shia was happy to see her. She'd never sensed a stronger emotion. Her heart rejoiced. The anger, fear, and betrayal she had felt the last time were gone. Hope replaced her own fear. Most of it, anyway. She couldn't help but worry that Shia might pull away again. It was an issue they'd have to address soon, but for now, Rose was elated.

Paper crinkling drew her eyes to Mikayla. "Are you moving?"

Mikayla paused, seemingly unsurprised. "Not for another six months. Brandi extended her contract in London until February." She placed a bubble-wrapped object into an open box on the floor.

"Why are you packing?" Rose didn't know why she asked. She was more interested in the magnetic waves of relief mixed with desire Shia was emitting. It was all she could do to stand there and not...do what? She didn't know.

"My worst nightmare came true. Brandi told me she finds my London house sterile and inhospitable."

"Not true," Shia said, her eyes still on Rose, who felt her intent gaze like a laser.

Mikayla shrugged. "Okay. She said she was a little homesick and wanted to add a few things from home to the decor."

Rose laughed because it was funny, but her heart wasn't in it. The only thing she cared about was Shia microwaving her with her eyes. But she didn't want to react and remind Shia of their fight. She tried to tuck her own feelings back so she could figure out how to tell Shia she was there to fight for them this time.

Mikayla sealed the box with shipping tape and straightened, stretching her arms over her head. "My shoulders are killing me. I'm going to soak in the tub. Shia, do you mind dropping a few shrimp snacks into the tank?" She disappeared into a back room before either of them could say good night.

Shia went into the kitchen, retrieved something from the freezer, and came back into the living room while Rose watched from the doorway. Shia captured her gaze and waited for a few beats before she spoke. "You can come in, you know. Do you want to give them their snacks?"

Rose went in, stopping a foot away. Shia's hands were trembling. So were hers. She shook her head. "I like to watch."

The corners of Shia's mouth rose before she went to the tank and dropped the cubes in. Several seahorses swam up from their perches and congregated to gulp the treat up as soon it defrosted and floated into the open water. Rose would have been fascinated if she wasn't trying to think of something to say.

They were both facing the tank, watching each other's reflections. Shia turned to her. Rose did the same, meeting that unwavering gaze. The moment became charged, and ignoring her fear, Rose dropped all caution and imagined herself as a transmitter, sending nothing but her love, trying to convey how she'd fight for them, how she'd never let Shia be alone again. With everything inside her, she willed Shia to sense her essence.

Shia's gaze flickered for a breath and then settled like a flame set to a welder's torch, the leap of brilliance followed by a steady bright light. "You can feel that, right? I'm not imagining it?"

Rose's stomach clenched as if she was about to be sucked into a cyclone and flung into open air. "I do."

"Does it feel like a bolt of energy wrapping around you?"

Rose nodded.

Shia smiled. "I didn't know how much I felt from you until it was gone."

"You felt me before?"

She nodded emphatically. "I always felt you. I just didn't know what it was. God, I'm so sorry. I missed you so much."

Rose took her hands. Their connection flowed through their arms, their entire beings. "I missed you, too."

Shia glanced at her arms as if she sensed it, too. "I felt you outside before you came up the steps. I was trying to explain it to Mikayla. She knew exactly what I was talking about. She described how, when she was close to Gem, she could send, like, these emotional feelers out by picturing them in her mind and adding her heart to it. I'm not describing it well, but she explained what I felt with you. I'm not sure I understand it, but it's there."

She sounded thunderstruck, compelling Rose to trace the back of Shia's hand with her fingertips and brush them up her arm, feeling the tiny hairs stand up. She finally rested her hand on the side of Shia's neck. Using her thumb, she skimmed the red skin of Shia's lips, remembering their taste. She drew Shia slowly toward her, sighing when their bodies touched, breathing in the scent of fresh green tea and honey before she kissed her.

❖

"Get a room."

Without breaking their kiss, Shia opened her eyes to see Mikayla standing in the hall in a robe and wet hair, holding a cup of tea and wearing an amused expression. Shia loosened her embrace and gently pulled away. "Guess we're not welcome here."

"You are always welcome here. I just want to save us all some embarrassment in case you forget where you are, and hands start going places, and clothes start to accidentally fall off."

"Fine, we're out of here. See you in the morning," Shia said, taking Rose by the hand. Before she turned toward the door, she saw Mikayla place a hand over her heart and sigh with a smile.

"I didn't realize how many people were invested in our relationship," Shia said as they walked into the street in front of Mikayla's place. The breeze from the ocean was refreshing in the early evening. Shia's heart swelled when Rose pushed her hair away from her face in the distracted way she often did. Just hours earlier, Shia had thought she might never see her do it again. "I love it when you push your hair back like that, with your fingers running across the top of your head. You look like you're in a shampoo commercial."

Rose smiled and looked away. "Stop."

Shia stopped walking and faced her, admiring the golden light of the sunset bathing her beautiful face. "I won't. You need to know how you affect me. I know you can feel it, but I want you to hear it in my words, too. And in the things I do. You probably already know that I love you because you can read my emotions." Rose's lips parted. "You probably knew it before I did. But I do. I love you. I wanted you to hear me say it."

Rose nodded slowly. "I felt it, but I wasn't sure if it was wishful thinking. Loving you made me aware that I inherited the family gift. I just thought I was a little more perceptive. Turns out, I have a superpower." Rose rolled her eyes comically before her face grew serious again. "By the way, I love you, too."

Despite the almost dismissive way Rose talked about her ability, she appeared proud of it. She felt proud of it. Shia could almost feel how pleased she was. And why wouldn't she be? Of all the superpowers, knowing the true heart of a person was near the top of the list. Shia hadn't anticipated how relieved she'd be at the thought. What if Rose had started to resent her gift because of Shia's reaction? "Hey."

"Hey what?"

"I want you to know that I think your gift is pretty cool. I was a little surprised when you told me, but it was never about that."

"I know."

"How could…Wait." Shia laughed. "I see what you did there. You…" She pointed a finger back and forth between them. Rose smiled and nodded. "I suppose you know what it was, then."

"Not specifically. I suspected that you were confused. You see your mother now: capable, dependable, and kind. Someone you could count on, maybe even be friends with. But years ago, she deserted you, setting you up for a difficult life. You probably find yourself wanting to trust her but are afraid she'll let you down again, as so many people in your life have. Meanwhile, the people around you only see the woman she is now, and it's probably frustrating. You can't let your guard down. Am I right?"

"Eerily."

"Most of that is based on what I know about you, not the feelings

I sense. It's when I put them all together that I start to see the whole picture."

"I think I get it now."

"But I can't sense what you want to do about her."

"I don't know yet. I need to give it time."

"I think that's probably a great idea." Rose had caught her gaze while they were talking and hadn't let it go. Now she was watching her intently.

An all-encompassing warmth that Shia could only describe as sparkly seemed to capture her as she returned Rose's scrutiny. "What am I feeling right now?" Shia asked.

"A lot of things. Happy. Excited. Loved. Safe."

"Safe?"

Rose shrugged. "Yep. That's my favorite."

"Why?"

"Safe means you know I won't leave. That I'll fight for us. I came here to tell you that, but you already knew. This is the first time I've sensed that particular emotion from you."

"I've been putting off that I feel unsafe before now?"

Rose shook her head and cradled her face. "More like the absence of feeling safe. You've spent your life feeling that way. I want to spend the rest of mine changing that for you."

Shia cocked an eyebrow. "What are your plans for tonight?"

"You mean besides telling you I love you over and over?" Rose glanced around. "Besides soaking you in with every fiber of my being?"

"Yeah. Besides those unimportant things. Do you think you might want to come back to my place?" She didn't know why the question made her nervous.

Rose's eyes grew soft as Shia watched her face in the golden light. "I do. But I want to be clear about something."

"I can feel it."

"What?"

Shia closed her eyes to concentrate. "Love." She squeezed Rose's hand. "Desire." Another squeeze. "Hmm…anticipation." She opened her eyes to see an amused smile on Rose's face. The next moment, Rose's expression grew serious. A sense of something pending settled in Shia's stomach. "Protective of me. Of us."

"All of that is true. But there's something else. When we met, it was supposed to be a one-time thing. At least for you. I wanted to see how it went. Then we decided to be casual. Again, that was you. I already knew I was falling for you."

"You did?"

Rose nodded. "After that first time. Then we decided to stay casual but accepted that there was something a little more than that going on and decided to make some boundaries that we never got around to making." Rose cleared her throat, and Shia sensed her nervousness. "If I go home with you tonight, it's with the expectation that we're building a life together. That's what I want. I love you. I will support your surfing career with all my heart because I know it's important to you. But I want you to love me more than your career. Because your career is important, but someday, it won't be. But I will always love you. I will always fight for us. I'm not going away." By the time she was finished, she had tears running down her face.

Shia wanted nothing more than to kiss them away. But she had something to say. She felt her eyes well, too. "I know. Me too. I've found my sweet spot in you, and I'm never letting you go."

The kiss that followed was tender with the promise of a future Shia had never envisioned for herself. Everything she felt, everything she was, she poured into it, knowing Rose was returning it with just as much feeling and intent.

Unimpeded, their tears flowed together. When their lips finally parted, it was if Shia had caught the sweetest spot on the mother of all waves.

Roses eyes gleamed in the last of the evening light. "I want you to show me this sweet spot you keep talking about."

Shia put her arm up with her hand curved forward. "The sweet spot is somewhere in here, if my arm were a wave—"

Rose grabbed her hand. "Shut up. Let's go start our forever, my love."

Shia followed her toward the house. "My love. I like the sound of that."

"I do, too." Rose stopped and kissed her in the salty, jasmine-scented breeze while the beginning of their forever together surrounded them in an effervescent tapestry of shared emotion. There was no sweeter spot than that.

About the Author

Kimberly Cooper Griffin is a software engineer by day and a romance novelist by night. Born in San Diego, California, Kimberly joined the Air Force, traveled the world, and eventually settled down in Denver, Colorado, where she lives with her wife, the youngest of her three daughters, and a menagerie of dogs and cats. When Kimberly isn't working or writing, she enjoys a variety of interests, but at the core of it all she has an insatiable desire to connect with people and experience life to its fullest. Every moment is collected and archived into memory, a candidate for being woven into the fabric of the tales she tells. Her novels explore the complexities of building relationships and finding balance when life has a tendency of getting in the way.

Books Available From Bold Strokes Books

A Calculated Risk by Cari Hunter. Detective Jo Shaw doesn't need complications, but the stabbing of a young woman brings plenty of those, and Jo will have to risk everything if she's going to make it through the case alive. (978-1-63679-477-8)

An Independent Woman by Kit Meredith. Alex and Rebecca's attraction won't stop smoldering, despite their reluctance to act on it and incompatible poly relationship styles. (978-1-63679-553-9)

Cherish by Kris Bryant. Josie and Olivia cherish the time spent together, but when the summer ends and their temporary romance melts into the real deal, reality gets complicated. (978-1-63679-567-6)

Cold Case Heat by Mary P. Burns. Sydney Hansen receives a threat in a very cold murder case that sends her to the police for help, where she finds more than justice with Detective Gale Sterling. (978-1-63679-374-0)

Proximity by Jordan Meadows. Joan really likes Ellie, but being alone with her could turn deadly unless she can keep her dangerous powers under control. (978-1-63679-476-1)

Sweet Spot by Kimberly Cooper Griffin. Pro surfer Shia Turning will have to take a chance if she wants to find the sweet spot. (978-1-63679-418-1)

The Haunting of Oak Springs by Crin Claxton. Ghosts and the past haunt the supernatural detective in a race to save the lesbians of Oak Springs farm. (978-1-63679-432-7)

Transitory by J.M. Redmann. The cops blow it off as a customer surprised by what was under the dress, but PI Micky Knight knows they're wrong—she either makes it her case or lets a murderer go free to kill again. (978-1-63679-251-4)

Unexpectedly Yours by Toni Logan. A private resort on a tropical island, a feisty old chief, and a kleptomaniac pet pig bring Suzanne and Allie together for unexpected love. (978-1-63679-160-9)

Crush by Ana Hartnett Reichardt. Josie Sanchez worked for years for the opportunity to create her own wine label, and nothing will stand in her way. Not even Mac, the owner's annoyingly beautiful niece Josie's forced to hire as her harvest intern. (978-1-63679-330-6)

Decadence by Ronica Black, Renee Roman & Piper Jordan. You are cordially invited to Decadence, Las Vegas's most talked about invitation-only Masquerade Ball. Come for the entertainment and stay for the erotic indulgence. We guarantee it'll be a party that lives up to its name. (978-1-63679-361-0)

Gimmicks and Glamour by Lauren Melissa Ellzey. Ashly has learned to hide her Sight, but as she speeds toward high school graduation she must protect the classmates she claims to hate from an evil that no one else sees. (978-1-63679-401-3)

Heart of Stone by Sam Ledel. Princess Keeva Glantor meets Maeve, a gorgon forced to live alone thanks to a decades-old lie, and together the two women battle forces they formerly thought to be good in the hopes of leading lives they can finally call their own. (978-1-63679-407-5)

Peaches and Cream by Georgia Beers. Adley Purcell is living her dreams owning Get the Scoop ice cream shop until national dessert chain Sweet Heaven opens less than two blocks away and Adley has to compete with the far too heavenly Sabrina James. (978-1-63679-412-9)

The Only Fish in the Sea by Angie Williams. Will love overcome years of bitter rivalry for the daughters of two crab fishing families in this queer modern-day spin on Romeo and Juliet? (978-1-63679-444-0)

Wildflower by Cathleen Collins. When a plane crash leaves eleven-year-old Lily Andrews stranded in the vast wilderness of Arkansas, will she be able to overcome the odds and make it back to civilization and the one person who holds the key to her future? (978-1-63679-621-5)

Witch Finder by Sheri Lewis Wohl. Tasmin, the Keeper of the Book of Darkness, is in terrible danger, and as a Witch Finder, Morrigan must protect her and the secrets she guards even if it costs Morrigan her life. (978-1-63679-335-1)

Digging for Heaven by Jenna Jarvis. Litz lives for dragons. Kella lives to kill them. The last thing they expect is to find each other attractive. (978-1-63679-453-2)

Forever's Promise by Missouri Vaun. Wesley Holden migrated west disguised as a man for the hope of a better life and with no designs to take a wife, but Charlotte Rose has other ideas. (978-1-63679-221-7)

Here For You by D. Jackson Leigh. A horse trainer must make a difficult business decision that could save her father's ranch from foreclosure but destroy her chance to win the heart of a feisty barrel racer vying for a spot in the National Rodeo Finals. (978-1-63679-299-6)

I Do, I Don't by Joy Argento. Creator of the romance algorithm, Nicole Hart doesn't expect to be starring in her own reality TV dating show, and falling for the show's executive producer Annie Jackson could ruin everything. (978-1-63679-420-4)

It's All in the Details by Dena Blake. Makeup artist Lane Donnelly and wedding planner Helen Trent can't stand each other, but they must set aside their differences to ensure Darcy gets the wedding of her dreams, and make a few of their own dreams come true. (978-1-63679-430-3)

Marigold by Melissa Brayden. Marigold Lavender vows to take down Alexis Wakefield, the harsh food critic who blasts her younger sister's restaurant. If only she wasn't as sexy as she is mean. (978-1-63679-436-5)

A Second Chance at Life by Genevieve McCluer. Vampires Dinah and Rachel reconnect, but a string of vampire killings begin and evidence seems to be pointing at Dinah. They must prove her innocence while finding out if the two of them are still compatible after all these years. (978-1-63679-459-4)

The Town That Built Us by Jesse J. Thoma. When her father dies, Grace Cook returns to her hometown and tries to avoid Bonnie Whitlock, the woman who pulverized her heart, only to discover her father's estate has been left to them jointly. (978-1-63679-439-6)